DRAMA
With a Capital D

a novel by

DENISE COLEMAN

This is a work of fiction. All of the characters, organizations, and events portrayed in this novel are either products of the author's imagination or are used fictitiously.

www.melodramapublishing.com

Library of Congress Control Number: 2010926185
ISBN-13: 978-1934157329
ISBN-10: 1934157325
First Edition: September 2010
10 9 8 7 6 5 4 3 2 1

Editors: Melissa Forbes, Brian Sandy, Candace K. Cottrell
Interior and Cover Design: Candace K. Cottrell
Cover photo: Frank Antonio

Dedication

This book is dedicated to my parents, Norris & Leslie Coleman, and to my children, Anthony, Candace, Jeff, and Erik. What a strong and powerful force you've been in my life. I love you all.

Especially to my sister Angela Coleman: thank you so much for all of your support and encouragement.

This piece is also dedicated to my friends, without whom I would not be such a happy chick. Inez, Ricky, Wanda, Marianne, Donna, Jabbar, Kay, Latarsha, Monica, Tjien, Melinda, and Anichelle.

Thank you for your love, laughter, wisdom and strength. Because of you I am a better me.

Chapter 1

Where the hell is he going? I asked myself when I saw my man's car going in the opposite direction of his job. I knew damned well that nigga told me he was going straight to work. Obviously that was a lie so I chose to follow his black ass. After just a few minutes of me trailing him, John stopped at a little house on the corner of whatever the hell street it was. This bitch had the nerve to be messing with someone who lived just a few blocks from us. I was breathing fire now.

I threw the Maxima into park and went up to the front door. I knocked and waited. I couldn't believe my eyes when this mystery person came to the door. She was honestly one of the most unattractive women I had ever seen, and judging by the fact that she had the nerve to continually call another woman's house for her man, she didn't have much class either. We couldn't have been more different on the outside. She wore a jacked-up homemade weave, her face was marred with old scratches, and one of her front teeth was missing. Now myself, not being the least bit vain, stands at five feet nine inches tall, with smooth caramel-colored skin and almond-shaped hazel eyes. I was wearing my hair straight down my back then. Shit, I had to keep a perm in this head. I didn't care whether or not I looked the part of a beauty, but I was certainly a far cry better looking than that chick. How could a man be attracted to two women who were so very different? What the hell was his type? Let me answer that myself. Free sex was his type.

"Can I help you?" she asked.

"Tell that muthafucka to come out here now!" I yelled.

"Who the hell are you?"

"Bitch, you know exactly who I am. You've been calling my house and hanging up for weeks. Now tell that punk John to get his ass out here now!"

Johnny came to the door to see what the commotion was. "Lonnie, what are you doing here?"

"Busting your ass. What? You didn't think I was going to find out about this shit?"

He grabbed my arm. "Look, baby, I was going to tell you what was up as soon as I made a decision."

I snatched my arm away from him. "Made a decision? You mean to tell me you don't know if you want me? She can't be that important to you."

At that moment, sister girl chose to speak up. "Hell, yeah, I'm important, bitch! And I'm pregnant with his baby!"

I damn near dropped dead on the spot. This man done got this bitch pregnant! What the hell had my life come to? Drama with a capital D!

My head was spinning. This situation was so much worse than I had imagined. I trusted this man with everything. Not only had he cheated on me, but he got this outside hood rat pregnant too.

I began to cry hysterically. "How could you do this to me?" I yelled.

I could no longer hear anything. I could no longer see anything but red. Before I could begin to control the rage that came over me, I kicked the shit out of that man. While he was doubled over in pain, I grabbed ol' girl by her hair and punched her in the face so hard, she fell backward into the house.

Just as I was about to start kicking the shit out of her too, Johnny grabbed me from behind. With the back of my foot, I kicked him in the shin.

When he let go of me, I turned around and started pummeling his face until I lost all strength. Finally, I backed away slowly. Looking at him, I couldn't believe my life had come to this.

Johnny gathered himself and walked toward me. For a split second I was afraid of what he might try to do to me. Then I noticed the look on his face, and somehow it put me at ease. He looked as if he regretted what he had done. Or maybe he was afraid I'd kick his ass again. Who knew?

I also realized at that moment that the chick didn't try to attack me. She could have hurt me out there since I had my back turned to her, but she didn't. When I turned to look in her direction, she had the strangest look on her face. Instead of displaying anger, she wore a smirk on her face.

"Lonnie, I'm so sorry this had to happen," Johnny said.

"Sorry for what exactly, John? Sorry for cheating, or sorry you got caught?"

The ho interjected. "Why are you apologizing to her?"

"Shut up, Cherie!" he yelled at her. He turned back to me. "I didn't mean for any of this to happen." "But it did. Why did you feel the need to be with someone else?"

"I don't know, baby. I guess I just got scared. I don't know. I really don't have an answer for you."

"You might as well take your ass back where you came from!" The chick, who I gathered was named Cherie, yelled. "He's mine, and I'm having his baby. You're done!"

"You really got this whore pregnant?"

John just stared at me as if it were the end of the world. His silence was all the proof I needed to know that Cherie was indeed carrying his child. Feeling defeated, I could do no more than get in my car and leave this scene behind.

During the short drive home, I prayed that what had just transpired wasn't true, that by some bizarre occurrence in the universe it had all been a dream. No such luck. I went back home, packed John's things, and put them out front. It surely wasn't as easy as it sounds.

Johnny began calling shortly after I finished getting rid of his things, blowing up the house phone and my cell phone nonstop for the next three hours. I couldn't even consider talking to him. The pain from his betrayal was the worst thing I had ever felt in my life. I had to call my older sister, Lena. Lena, our little brother Jerry, who everyone called Tank, and I were pretty tight. Because she was the oldest, Lena always felt the need to be the protector. There wasn't a kid in our neighborhood, boy or girl, who could get away with even looking at me or Tank sideways. She took our parents' guidance to look out for her little brother and sister to a whole other level. And as an adult she would still kick ass on our behalf in a heartbeat.

Tank, acquired that nickname because of his size—six feet four and two hundred seventy five pounds. He spent his childhood trying to keep up with Lena. Being the only male child and the youngest, Tank would go extra hard at everything, trying to prove that he could keep the girls safe.

That night I needed some familial support. Lena heard the sadness in my voice as soon as I said hello.

"What's wrong Lon? You sound like shit" Lena said with so much concern in her voice. I proceeded to tell her what had gone down and as was her usual way, Lena was ready to do battle.

"Oh it's like that? Just let me call our peoples so we can go show that bitch what it is."

"No Lena, we can't do that."

"Why the fuck not?!"

"Because I told you, she's pregnant."

"So what?"

"Come on now Lele, as much as I want to hurt that girl, we can't risk catching charges. I need my job and my freedom and so do you. This ain't worth no real jail time, but, for sure, after she has that baby it's going to be on."

"I know that's right. So do you need me to come over there?'

"Nah, I'm cool. For now."

After talking to Lena, I was pissed off even more than before because I knew I couldn't do anything to Cherie in her condition.

I didn't know how to release or contain the rage I felt, so I called my girl Sandy, who would, without question, be there for me in my time of need. Before I could get the entire story out, Sandy told me, "Sit tight. I'm on my way."

I felt a little better already, knowing I wouldn't be alone with my pain.

"Hey, *chica*! Are you all right?" Sandy asked before she had even cleared the threshold.

"I'm better than I was when I called you. At least now I don't want to vomit," I said with a half-smile.

"You don't have to try to be strong with me, *mami*. Just go with whatever it is you feel."

That was just what I needed to hear. I didn't think I should fall apart over this situation, but sometimes that was all a person could do to recover. Without any unnecessary coaxing from

Sandy, I began to cry hysterically. I could no longer hold it in. The sounds coming from me were animalistic and unfamiliar to my own ears. I felt as if someone was ripping my soul from my body.

Sandy simply held me and rubbed my back, which meant everything in the world to me at that moment. I was so very grateful for her patience and understanding. There was no way I could have gotten through that first evening without her.

Chapter 2

After my confrontation with John and Cherie, I thought I might be able to get some rest. I simply wanted to sleep through the pain. That didn't happen.

Sometime around midnight Johnny came knocking on my door. Thankfully, Sandy was still with me. From the sofa I had camped out on, I could hear Sandy out on the front porch talking to him. Actually, what I heard was a lot of cussing and fussing.

"How dare you bring your black ass around here after what you've done to my girl?"

"Listen, Sandy, I didn't come here for this shit. I need to see Lonnie, so I can explain to her how this thing happened."

"'This thing'? What the hell do you mean, this thing? What you did was foul, yo. You intentionally stuck your piece inside another woman and you weren't even responsible enough not to get her pregnant, you fucking *pendejo!*"

"I really don't need this shit. I came to speak to Lonnie, not you. Now let me in to see her."

"Hell, no! And if you don't get away from here now, I'll call the police and have your trifling ass locked up!"

By now I had made my way to the front door, and just as Sandy turned to come back into the house, I stepped out.

Sandy asked me, "You sure you want to do this?"

No matter how much I was hurting, I knew I had to face this man. I had to know why this affair of his happened. "Yes," I said. "I need to get this over with as soon as possible."

"OK, just yell if you need me to come back out here, *mami.*" Sandy went back inside the house.

I was shocked to see that John had a black eye and a busted lip. I barely remembered hitting him in the face. Nevertheless, I could do no more than stare at the person who, in just a matter of months, had become a stranger to me. Besides, I had come to listen, not speak. This fool was the one with a story to tell.

After a few moments of staring, Johnny finally said, "Lonnie, I am very sorry for what I've done. Whether you can believe it or not, hurting you wasn't something I set out to do."

"Keep it real, John. When you were with that woman, you weren't thinking about me at all. You weren't concerned with whether I would get hurt. Just explain this one thing to me. Why did this happen at all?"

"I'm not sure. I didn't go looking to get involved with someone else. It was just a bad time for me when I met her. You and I were not as close as we used to be, and I had become so restless and bored with our life."

He could have knocked me over with a feather when I heard those words. This man was telling me that I bored him—that I couldn't keep him interested in me. Johnny must have read the look on my face.

"I don't mean I was bored with you specifically, but with the situation as it was. It was like we'd become an old married couple. We stopped going out like we used to. We stopped talking and laughing.

Don't you remember we would talk about everything under the sun? And laughter and passion was a constant in our life together. Then it was gone without warning."

I just continued to stare at him standing there, trying to give him an answer to what had happened to change us so much. I came up short. There was no defining moment, from what I could gather. But he was right. We were different with each other and started taking each other for granted.

"Johnny, even if what you say about us as a couple is true, it still doesn't explain why you went to another woman. I have been just as bored with us as you, but I've certainly never felt the need to go screw someone else."

He started to say something, but I raised my hand to stop him.

"I'm not finished. I can concede that you're right about what's been going on between us, but why wouldn't you talk to me about it? Just like you said, we could talk about anything, but you didn't bother to try and work things out with me."

At this point I couldn't stop the tears from flowing. The last thing I wanted was for this man to see me cry, but I simply couldn't control it.

He tried to put his arms around me, but I pushed him away. "Please don't touch me. There's nothing you can say or do that would make this situation better right now."

He backed off. "Please, Lonnie . . . I need you to understand that I never intended to start this affair, and I certainly didn't intend to continue with it."

I wiped my eyes with the back of my hand. "That's pretty much irrelevant at this point. The fact is, you did it, and now you're stuck with it for the rest of your life. How could you be so stupid as to get this girl pregnant?"

"I don't know how this happened. I swear I used protection every time I went near her."

This was too much for me to deal with at that moment. I wasn't going to get whatever answers I thought I needed, so I asked him to leave.

Johnny looked as if he had just lost his best friend. Maybe he had, but so what? That was his problem. I had to deal with my own personal fallout from this crap. I had no more words for him, but, as I turned to go in the house, John said, "One more thing before you go in. I had your brother arrested." I turned back and looked at John like he had lost his ever loving mind.

"What the hell are you talking about?"

"Don't you see my face? That nigga made it a point to come and find me and we got into it. Now I can understand him defending you, but fuck that, Lonnie. I wasn't going to let that shit go."

"How the hell did he know what happened? Never mind, don't even answer that. I already know."

"Listen Lonnie, I know I fucked up, but I wasn't just going to let your brother get his shit off and get away with it."

"So you called the cops on him? That's not how we handle shit in the hood! Where is he now?"

"I guess he's in the county. As a matter of fact, Lena and that faggot-ass Reggie were with him. They probably followed him."

"You punk-ass bitch! You had my brother arrested over a fist fight? Get the fuck off my porch and don't come back!"

Without another word, I went back into the house and slammed the door in his face. Once inside I leaned on the door and began to hyperventilate, and Sandy came over and helped me to the sofa.

First he cheats on me, and then he gets my brother arrested? I wondered if I ever really knew who that man was.

I truly believed that John and I would spend the rest of our lives together. In fact, not more than a month earlier, we'd been talking a lot about marriage and what kind of future we saw for ourselves. A person's life can change drastically from one day to the next, and although I didn't realize it then, this was a useful lesson for me to learn. Never take anything for granted. It would have served me better to pay closer attention to our relationship and to speak up about anything that didn't feel right.

Finally I calmed down and just as I started to doze off, I heard another knock at the door and Sandy saying, "*¡Ay Dios mío!*. What is this, Grand Central Station or something?"

Then I heard Lena, Reggie, and Tank's voices. I was so relieved that my brother hadn't been held. Lucky for John. I was also relieved when Sandy told them to keep it down because I was finally asleep. As much as I loved my people and wanted details of what had gone down, I was exhausted and didn't have the energy to help plan a terrorist-type attack on John and Cherie. Instead, I slept..

The next day didn't begin any better than the day before had ended. I awoke with the weight of the world on my chest. For the first time in my life I was experiencing true heartbreak. I knew for sure that this wasn't something I was strong enough to handle. I was the tough talker. Lena and Tank were the true ass kickers. I tried to keep up with them, but honestly, my heart was fragile. I hurt easily. I'd spent my entire life listening to friends talk about their bad relationships, and then watching them go back to these sorry-ass men who had caused the pain. I'd always said to myself that I would never let a man hurt me so badly, and by no means would I go back to him. I didn't think I could handle taking a second chance with my heart.

I guess I didn't know myself as well as I thought I did, because, less than twenty-four hours later, all I could think about was him not being there with me. I thought I might actually be crazy for feeling this way. How on earth could I be missing and wanting that asshole, when he was the one who cheated on me? Obviously, my fragile-ass heart was the one in control.

Sandy was still at my house, but I couldn't share any of this with her. She would just tell me to forget about him and try to get me to focus on something else. I didn't want that right then. I wanted her to understand, but I wasn't sure she would.

Only women are able to rationalize giving a man a break in these situations. We have a way of making his actions "not so bad," even though we're suffering because of him. The people around these women, however, don't want to hear that bull.

But, honestly, how could I expect Sandy to understand my need to see him when I didn't understand it myself? It was just a few hours earlier that I was closing the door in his face, determined not to give a damn about any of it.

Chapter 3

A week passed without a word from John. It's amazing the different changes one can go through when a relationship ends. I went from confusion, to feeling betrayed, to hating him, and then on to missing him, all within the first twenty-four hours of the breakup. Now I simply hated his guts.

There was no way in hell I could talk to him again. But, as usual, I'd spoken too soon. The moment I sat down at my desk at work, my phone rang.

"Hi, Lonnie."

"Johnny, what do you want?"

"I want to talk to you, baby."

" 'Baby'? I am not your baby anymore. Cherie is your baby, and she's carrying your baby."

"Please, don't be that way. I miss you so much. I don't know what to do with myself."

"Well, brotha, you should have thought about how much you'd be missing me before you cheated on me."

"Lonnie, you know it wasn't that simple. It was a mistake."

Right then I didn't want to hear another word from that man's mouth. Hatred was still in full effect. I banged on his ass and sat there daring that punk to call back.

Those two minutes of conversation stirred up all the anger I was trying to keep a lid on. I was boiling mad. I was so pissed off, I couldn't concentrate on anything. Johnny had effectively ruined my entire day.

I called Sandy to see what she was up to. I needed a distraction in a major way. We decided to skip work in the afternoon and go out together.

Lunch with my girl and a stop at the nail salon for a manicure did the trick.

By the time I got home that evening, I was feeling better, and Johnny was forgotten again. Until my phone started ringing.

I checked the caller ID, saw it was him, turned off the ringer, and kept it moving.

I decided to do some chores I had been ignoring for the last couple of days. I was hoping that getting busy would help me to release some of the anger that hearing from Johnny had brought back in me.

It did help a little. At least it helped enough to get me through the evening without plotting murderous revenge on him and Cherie.

When I went downstairs the next morning, I saw on the caller ID that that fool had called twelve times. Each time he left a message. I couldn't believe he didn't get the message to leave me the hell alone.

I wasn't impressed by his persistence. In fact, I looked at his behavior as an act of desperation, which was a turn-off. I decided to erase his messages without listening to them. I believed that if I continued to ignore him, he would eventually leave me be.

For the next week, Johnny was calling so much, I had to stop answering my phone at work as well as at home. But, to tell the truth, he was beginning to wear me down. Erasing his messages was no longer helping me. In fact, he stayed on my mind because he continued to call me. I couldn't get a break from thinking about him.

Before I knew it, my anger began to subside, and I began to start missing him all over again. I wish I had an explanation for these feelings, but I didn't then, and I don't have one now.

I was lying in bed thinking about how and why my man had turned away from me. Was it something I had done, or was he simply going through some things that I hadn't noticed? I thought maybe he needed me and I wasn't there for him. It could have also been the fact that I had a serious temper and didn't bother to hide it from him. I grew up sandwiched in between two hotheaded nuts. Lena and Tank knew just how push my buttons, and I would take the bait every time. My temper was a major part of me, as was my sentimental side. The two were in constant battle.

Therefore, by the time the phone rang that night I had convinced myself that some of the blame was mine, and I felt nothing but regret for blowing it. Hearing his voice pretty much did me in. I blamed myself. What I heard or thought I heard in his voice when he spoke to me was sadness, which touched something deep inside me. I felt exactly what I believed he felt.

"Hi, Lonnie. Please don't hang up on me," he said.

I didn't respond. I couldn't respond. I just listened.

"I know I hurt you, and I know you're angry, but please try to understand that what I did wasn't about you. It was about me and what I was going through."

I realized in that moment that I couldn't have this conversation over the phone. I needed to look into his eyes and see what he was feeling if I was ever to understand.

"Come over here and talk to me in person."

"I'll be there in a few minutes," he responded eagerly.

I was excited about seeing him again. What the hell was going on with me? I didn't know if he was going to tell me I was the worst woman he'd ever been with, or if it was the worst sex. But I wasn't going to sit there and dwell on it. I needed to prepare myself for his visit.

I got up, brushed my teeth, and put on some nightclothes— something a little more appealing than the sweats I was wearing.

Just as I finished getting dressed, Johnny knocked at the door. I walked on wobbly legs to answer the door. I couldn't believe that I was so nervous. Johnny was no stranger to me. This was the man I both loved and hated.

When I opened the door, what I saw truly shocked me. The man who stood before me was no longer the strong, handsome man I knew, but just a shell of his former self. Johnny had lost weight, his face was much thinner, and his hair was no longer as full and healthy as I remembered.

"Come on in," I said.

"Thanks, Lonnie. I really needed to see you. I wasn't expecting you to answer the phone, let alone invite me over here."

"I know this. I just figured that if we were finally going to talk things out, it might as well be in person." I asked Johnny to have a seat. I still couldn't get over how different he looked. He looked broken.

Good.

I asked if he would like something to drink, and he asked for water. After I gave him his drink, I sat beside him. "Johnny, I must say, you don't look too well. What's been going on with you?"

"I haven't really been eating or sleeping too well lately."

I didn't feel all that much sympathy for him. I mean, I had suffered behind his behavior first. No matter how much I didn't like what I was seeing, part of me still felt he deserved to be going through whatever he was dealing with.

"OK, talk to me. Tell me why all this happened."

He set his water glass down, took my hands into his, and looked me dead in my eyes. I wasn't sure I wanted the physical contact just yet. It was a little too much for me to handle, so I pulled away my hands.

Johnny didn't seem fazed by this.

Good. Keep talking, brother.

"Listen, Lonnie, there were things going on with me that I couldn't share with anyone. I didn't know how to tell you that my business was going slow, and that the company was talking about downsizing."

"So what was the big deal? So you may have been out of work for a little while. That's not the end of the world. You have to come better than that with me."

"How could I tell you that I wouldn't be able to keep up with my share of everything around here? You have to understand that for someone like me who has never been without work, the prospect of not earning a living scared the hell out of me."

Again with the bull! This nut must think I'm stupid! "Please come off of it, John. First of all, I could handle the financial aspects of everything pertaining to this house by myself. Hell, I'm doing that now and was doing it long before I ever met you. Not to mention, the prospect of being out of work was just that, a prospect." He tried to interrupt me, but I held up my hand in protest. "If you had been laid off, you could have filed for unemployment, or better still, gone out and looked for another job. You have marketable skills, so don't sit there and hand me that crap about being scared. You had options! Now stop trying to play me and keep it funky."

He was dumbfounded. He looked at me as if none of this had ever occurred to him. I couldn't believe what I was seeing on his face. *Did I get myself involved with a stupid man? Nawwwwww, that couldn't be it.* Maybe he just didn't have any good sense, and somehow I'd missed that.

"Lonnie, I swear to you I was so busy panicking, I didn't think things through, at least not initially. I didn't. This all happened so fast. I mean, one day they mentioned cutbacks, and the next, it seemed as if it would all become reality very soon."

I didn't want to hear any more of his crap, so once again I interrupted. "OK, so tell me, where does your affair come into play?"

"Well, when I heard that the layoffs would most likely happen, I decided I needed a drink, a real drink, so I stopped off at the bar around the corner from work, and that's where I met Cherie. By the time she approached me, I was already drunk."

I vaguely remembered Johnny coming home drunk a few months back, because getting drunk was out of character for him. Maybe if I had thought about it more then, I would have questioned him about it further.

"Anyway, it was just some innocent flirtation at first, but as the night went on, she began to come on stronger. I'm sorry to say that I responded to her advances. Now believe me when I tell you that I'm not using being drunk as an excuse, but it did hinder me from making a better choice in that situation."

I sat there with my mouth hanging open. I didn't know what to say. I was too fucked up in that moment, because, as it turned out, John never did get laid off. The destruction of my life happened for no good reason. I only knew that I needed to keep my anger in check and listen.

"Although we did exchange cell numbers that night, nothing else happened. I didn't really plan to call her or see her again, but things between you and me weren't so great anymore. Not that I'm blaming you. It's just how it was. We weren't talking anymore about much of anything, and the laughter had all but deserted us. We were stagnant, and believe it or not, I was missing you."

I had to admit to myself that even though we were living in the same house, we had become strangers in a sense. There wasn't much going on between us, and there was no clear reason as to why the changes in our relationship had happened.

"Lonnie, are you listening to me?" he asked when I remained silent.

"Yes. Go on."

"About a week after I met her, Cherie started calling and kept calling. I guess you could say she wore me down. All I know is, I was lonely and stressing about my job, so when she insisted we get together, I went. The first night we only had dinner together, but she was giving me something I needed. She was talking to me. She was listening to me. And she was showing me so much attention and affection, I was feeling good again. Shit, she was feeding my ego, and I was eating that shit up. As you know, it eventually led to more."

Damn, that shit was the biggest cliché known to man. *She made him feel good again.* Oh please! Now I knew some men were weak, but I didn't know I was with one of them. This woman played him so easily. I wondered if maybe subconsciously he was indeed looking to step out on me, but I couldn't be sure about that.

Besides, his sorrow was written all over his face. I was taught that forgiveness was the only way to let go of the worst pain. I sat with my thoughts for a while before I responded.

"So, now that you've explained what happened, what do you expect from me?" I allowed him to take my hand.

"I don't know. I only know that I'm sorry I hurt you, and that my life is no good without you. If you could find it in your heart to forgive me, I'm hoping that we may be able to find our way back to one another."

I didn't know how to respond to that. I knew I could forgive him, but taking him back and giving him another chance to hurt me was something I wasn't so sure about. I told Johnny just that. I informed him it was going to take me some time to decide what I wanted to do, and he accepted this without an argument or any begging, and we left things that way. Then I escorted him to the front door and told him that I would call him once I'd made my decision.

Chapter 4

The decision to take John back wasn't something that came easily. Since I'd always considered myself such a hard ass—on the outside anyway—maybe instinctually I felt the need to save face. But I missed him terribly. The more time passed, the more I wanted my man back in my life. With time and a little healing, the betrayal didn't seem as bad. Crazy, right? The only issue for me was the fact that he had a baby on the way. I had to decide whether I could handle the fact that the man I loved—yes, I still loved him—had fathered a child with another woman. It wasn't that I wanted to have any children of my own at that time, but more that, this woman and her child—his child—would be a permanent part of our lives.

After a few weeks of wrestling with what I wanted to do and how much I could handle, I chose to give it another try with John. This might have been foolish, but at the time I believed he was genuinely sorry, and that I was mature enough to handle it. I also felt like what we once had was worth saving. I believed we had both learned not to be so complacent with our situation. The only real problem I foresaw was how my siblings would react to my choice. Once they were done with someone it would be a wrap forever. There was no way that this wasn't going to cause drama. I decided that I didn't have the balls to have that talk until after John moved back in.

I called his cell phone exactly three weeks after we had spoken.

I could hear his smile through the phone. "Hi, babe. I was beginning to think that I would never hear from you again. I'm glad you called. I hope you've decided to give us another chance."

"I've made my decision. I think we should try this again. It won't be easy, and there may be times when I won't make this easy for you. There's still a lot to deal with. I'm not sure how I'll react the first time I think about what you've done while you're in my presence. But if you bear with me, I'm sure I can get through this to get us back to a better place in our relationship."

"I understand that, and I can deal with it."

"Yeah, you say that now, but the moment I feel that you're not being honest with me about something, all hell is going to break loose."

"I know this, but I promise you everything is going to work out just fine between us."

Love sure does make you a dumb bitch on occasion. I walked my love-struck, dumb-ass self right back into that shit too. We agreed that John would start moving his things back into the house that evening.

When he arrived at the house, I was extremely happy to see him. I didn't expect to react that way, but whatever. It was what it was.

That first evening progressed slowly. We were both a little nervous with one another. I made a quick late dinner, and we sat down to talk for a while before bed. The anticipation of sharing my bed with this man again made me more nervous than I had ever been.

Once the moment arrived, Johnny wanted sex for sure. I wasn't surprised by this, but what did surprise me was the realization that I wasn't ready, or capable of going there with him. I obviously still had some residual effects of his affair lingering in my mind. How could I not? Not that much time had passed. I couldn't yet allow him to touch me. Given no choice in the matter, Johnny held me and we slept.

The next morning things were still a bit awkward between us. We managed to get through it with little communication. I guess he didn't know what to say to ease my anxiety, and I knew for sure that I didn't know what to say, so we left it alone.

I left Johnny and went in to work. The moment I arrived at my desk, I picked up the phone to call Sandy. I quickly told her about the night's events, especially my hesitance about having sex.

"It's only natural that you would not be completely comfortable in that situation, considering the circumstances," she said. "Just give it some time, *mami*. Everything will be fine."

"You're probably right. I'll just wait until I feel normal about things, whatever normal is in this situation."

"*Bien, mami*. Now what I want to know is, are you really sure this is what you want to do? I mean, he didn't pressure you into this reconciliation with his million and a half phone calls, did he?"

"Not at all. I really took my time and thought about everything that happened, and whether I could forgive him enough to try to work through it all. I sincerely think we have a shot at something better. And, believe me, I'm not stupid. I know it will take a lot of work and time if we are to succeed."

I don't think Sandy was convinced, but she didn't say so. If nothing else, we were always supportive of one another, even if we thought one was being stupid. After a few more minutes of catching up, we ended our call, promising to get together for lunch one day soon.

I tried to concentrate on my work, but it wasn't happening. I really wanted to figure out a way to get things back to as close to normal as possible between John and me. As it turned out, it wasn't as difficult as

I initially thought it would be.

By the end of the first week of our reconciliation, we had fallen back into our normal routine, and from there, things truly did seem to be better than the first time.

Johnny was being more attentive and spending more of his free time with only me. He didn't spend as much time as he used to with his friends, which was exactly what we needed at that time. And I had to spend a lot less time with Lena and our gay play cousin, Reggie. They were my partners in crime for sure. Tank was only around when it was time for the drama; otherwise, he was more interested in getting his hustle on. Every time my sister called I would beg off. I knew she was getting suspicious of my behavior, but Johnny and I needed that time and it was working for us.

We appeared to have gotten *us* back. We would talk with one another about any and everything. We went for walks, read books together, listened to music, and watched movies. We put all of ourselves into each other. It was necessary for us if we were to mend what had been broken.

The sex was even better than ever. John and I always had a pretty decent sex life, but the first time that I was capable of going there with him after his return, I got the surprise of my life. You see, John was one of the few men left in this world who wouldn't engage in oral sex. He would always say, "Lonnie, brothas don't do that." How old-school of him to believe that bullshit. But you can bet his black ass had no problem sticking his dick in my mouth every chance he got.

Nevertheless, the first time that man worked his way down my body and laid that warm tongue on my pussy, I damn near lost it. That "brotha" ate my pussy so good, I was climbing the walls and I felt like we were on our way to a blissful life together. Although, in the back of my mind, I wondered if this newfound sexual freedom came from his involvement with Cherie. Before her, I couldn't talk him into going there, but since her he was a professional pussy-eater? Come on now, what do you think? But with my capacity to live in denial when it suited my needs, I chose not to even explore that little revelation and went on with life like everything was perfect.

But as we all know, there is no such thing as a fairytale happy ending. My dumb ass was so busy enjoying our reunion, I wouldn't allow the thought of Cherie and her unborn child to enter my mind. In fact, whenever John tried to discuss how he wanted to handle this thing, I would shut him down by saying that we had plenty of time to deal with it later. Big mistake! I mean, come on now, what the hell was I thinking? Pregnant women eventually give birth.

Chapter 5

Johnny and I managed to last a good month before I had to come clean with Lena. She stopped by unannounced one Saturday and the shit hit the fan.

"What the fuck is that bastard doing here?" were the first words out of her mouth when she and Reggie came through the door.

Damn, I should've looked out the peephole first, I thought.

"Lele, please. I'm not in the mood."

"I don't give a damn what you're not in the mood for. Start explaining, Lonnelle."

Damn it! Whenever Lena called me by my given name, I knew she was serious.

"All right. Listen, I love him and I took him back. It's that simple."

"Yeah, your ass is simple all right."

"I know that's right Miss Thing," Reggie chimed in with his hands on his nonexistent hips.

"Shut up, Reggie!" Lena and I said in unison.

"Did you bump your fucking head and forget what he did to you?" Lena asked.

"No, of course not, but some things aren't all that cut and dry."

Lena shook her head in disgust. "Oh, no? Then you tell me what things *are* since you know so much."

"Well first of all, I know you need to bring it down. I love you, but check this out: I'm a grown-ass woman who can make her own choices.

"Oh, really?"

"Really, and second of all, everything in life isn't easy. Shit gets messy sometimes, especially relationships. And third, you need to learn how to lighten up some. Everything doesn't have to be a big-ass fight, Lele."

"Well damn, if that ain't the pot calling the kettle a black bitch. You're the one with the temper, Lonnie."

"Oh, and you don't have a temper too?"

"Hell no, I just like to fight. Shit, I'm good at it and I get bored easily. That's the difference, you little hussy."

I just laughed at my sister. She didn't have any damn sense.

"All right. Whatever, Lele. The bottom line is: I took him back and that's that. Now either respect my decision or bounce."

Lena turned to Reggie, "This bitch thinks she's tough."

Reggie whose ADHD had taken him off to faraway places, found his way back and said, "Uh huh, Miss Thing is growing up, chile."

"Damn, can y'all just leave please? We've got things to do."

"Yeah, all right, but there better not be no more bullshit from you or I will be back to set shit off up in here," Lena said to John.

He just smirked and left the room.

"OK, goodbye, bye, bye!" I said as I ushered Lena and Reggie to the front door.

No doubt whether or not she agreed with my decision, I knew Lena would leave me alone about it.

John and I had been enjoying each other for months when that dreaded phone call came. Cherie was in labor. Johnny looked as if his world was ending. I couldn't identify what his emotional state was, but what I saw scared me just a little. I wasn't sure if he was happy, scared, as I was, or just nervous. Like I said, I never wanted to discuss it, so I never asked him how he felt about his impending fatherhood. I know now how foolish that behavior was. Why screw up a good thing with reality when denial worked so well, right? Well, reality was about to kick me in my ass big time.

From the moment we arrived at the hospital, I could tell that things were going to go downhill from there. John headed toward the nurses' station and asked where he could find Cherie. At the mention of her name, a young woman dressed in pajama pants, a T-shirt, slippers, and a scarf tied around her head approached Johnny. My first thought was, *Damn! Another ghetto chick.*

It was three o'clock in the afternoon and this girl looked like she had just rolled out of bed. I was raised in this city all of my life. It wasn't written anywhere that just because we lived in the hood, we had to have a hood mentality. I was taught never to go out in public wearing bedclothes, and by no means did a woman step out the front door without her hair being done.

She approached Johnny with attitude. "You must be Johnny," she said.

"Yeah, and you are?"

"I'm Deja, Cherie's sister. So tell me, nigga, where the hell you been for the last few months?"

"Where I've been is none of your fuckin' business. I don't even know you, and whatever goes on between Cherie and me is our business."

Hands on hips and head wagging from side to side, Deja said, "Well, from what I can tell, you haven't been around to have any business with my sister at all. What? You think you can just knock her up and run back to your bitch without giving my sister a second thought? And don't think for one minute that your black ass is going to get off without paying for this kid you made!"

At this point I still stood back, debating whether I should make my presence known. Should I defend that *bitch* comment or just let it slide this time? My cooler head prevailed just as the doctor came out to speak to Deja.

John introduced himself to the doctor and asked how Cherie was doing. The doctor informed them both that all was going well, but that it would be a while before the baby was born. The doctor turned to leave, promising he would be back with any news.

Johnny took this moment to respond to Deja's comments about his part in the child's and Cherie's lives. "Like I said before, this is none of your business. Cherie knew from the door that I wasn't interested in anything serious with her. And when she got pregnant, the only thing that changed was the fact that we would have to co-parent. She knows I'll be there for the child for whatever he or she needs, but there is no love affair between us, and nothing is going to change that." Johnny turned to walk over to me but then he stopped and turned back to Deja. "By the way, it would be in your best interest never to call my woman out of her name again."

"Who the fuck do you think you are to be threatening me? Nigga, I swear I'll have you fucked up in a heartbeat!"

"Whatever," Johnny said, and kept it moving.

Deja just stared at his back as he walked away from her. That foolish girl had half the hospital looking at her like she was crazy, yet she didn't seem to notice or care. Obviously making a scene was a regular occurrence with chicks like her and Cherie.

"That chick looks like she brings a lot of drama," I said once Johnny reached my side. "I hope we won't have to deal with a bunch of nonsense from that family."

"Don't worry, babe. I'll keep things as smooth as possible in this situation. I just need to know I have you on my side. I mean, tell me, do you understand how important it is for me to be a part of my child's life, regardless of how this came about?"

"Yes, I understand, but just like I said, I can't deal with drama. Now don't you think you should go and check on Cherie yourself and at least let her know you're here?"

"Yeah, I guess I should." Johnny pecked me on the cheek and headed toward the labor room.

I sat down and grabbed a magazine. I looked up for a brief moment to find Deja giving me the evil eye, like she wanted to start some shit. That would have been a big mistake. I just smiled and went back to my magazine.

It was difficult for me to sit in that hospital waiting room with the realization that I was there with a man who was sharing a monumental moment in his life with another woman. He was becoming a father without me, and there was nothing I could do about it. Without a doubt I was jealous, hurt, and fearful of what the future held for us, but there was no way I was going to walk away. I had to be the bigger person in this situation. I chose to get back together with him, so I had to accept this child.

I never in my life thought I would be the kind of woman who would even consider being involved in something like this. I'd always said to myself and whoever would listen that if a man cheated on me, it would be over—no ifs, ands, or buts about it. Now there I was sitting in the hospital like a freaking idiot, waiting for a man who was in labor and delivery with some other chick. We were there for hours. I could do no more than sit there and stress, read magazines, nod off, and stress some more. It was a horrible day for me, but I had to keep that to myself. John would periodically come out to give me an update on how things were going. Like I really gave a damn. But I had to keep that to myself as well.

Now, don't get me wrong. I had no harsh feelings directed toward the baby, just the entire situation itself. None of this was what I wanted for my life, yet I walked myself right back into it. To say I was having major mixed emotions at this point would be an understatement.

I couldn't stand sitting there and waiting any longer. I got up, went outside, and called everyone I knew. However, my brother Tank was the only one who answered. I told him where I was and how I felt and he offered to come sit with me. That was a big surprise, but I accepted his offer. I didn't want to be alone with that situation.

Twenty minutes later I looked up to see Tank approaching me but before he could reach me I heard, "Jerry 'Tank' Devlin, you sorry-ass sack of shit!"

To my horror, that outburst came from Deja. I just shook my head. *Here we go again.*

Tank stopped on a dime and turned around slowly. "Deja, what are you doing here?"

"One of my sisters is having a baby. Anyway, all I want to know is when the fuck are you going to start taking care of your kid?" she yelled.

No, she didn't just say what I think she said! I screamed inside my own head. I stood up and stared at my brother, afraid of what I might hear next.

"You mean, *your* kid and any of ten other niggas'."

What?! The shouting match continued in my head but I was glued to my spot. No way was that conversation actually taking place!

"Tank, you know damned well Shakita is yours!" Deja yelled for everyone to hear. At that point I hustled my ass across the room. "What is this shit?" I asked, hoping Tank would convince me that I had heard wrong.

"Yo, Lon, this trick is trying to pin one of her babies on me. That shit ain't happening. She's a jump off. It was a hit it and quit it situation, so just ignore her ass."

Now I didn't know Deja from a can of spray paint, but I didn't necessarily like the way my brother was speaking about another woman. He was a natural born protector; therefore, his treatment of Deja and the possibility that he could be a father was extremely out of character. Thug or not, Tank loved women and children.

"Who the fuck you callin' a jump off?" Deja yelled some more.

And before Tank could react, she slapped him in the face. Tank barely flinched, but I was pissed. I reached around my brother and snatched that scarf off her head. I was going for her head.

"Bitch!" she yelled as she tried to cover her head. Tank grabbed me and ushered me out the door before security could kick us all out.

Once outside I asked, "Tank, is there any way she could be telling the truth? Is it at all possible?"

"Look, the jury's still out on that one." Tank began to chuckle. "Maybe I'll take her on the *Maury* show."

"That's not funny, boy! What if that child is yours?"

"Like I said, that's a big *if.* Anyway, why are you looking so upset about it?"

"T, that bitch Cherie is the sister she mentioned."

"Get the fuck out of here! Well, like I said, it was a hit it and quit it, so I didn't stick around to meet the family. Damn, it is a small-ass world for real, ain't it?" he laughed.

"Is everything a damned joke to you?"

"No, Lon. But damn, you need chill for real, yo."

"Damn, T, how can I chill? It's bad enough I have to deal with

Cherie and her shit, now you're telling me that one of that other crazy bitch's kids might be my niece!"

"Calm down, sis. Even if the kid is mine, that don't mean you have to deal with Deja."

Now unless he had some kind of master plan that he wasn't sharing, I didn't know why Tank believed that bullshit that he'd just told me. If he was indeed that kid's father, then our families would be connected by blood, which meant the bullshit would be never-ending.

Tank and I stayed outside until finally John came out looking exhausted and joyful.

"I have a son!" he said.

My heart broke at hearing his words. I don't know why, but something grabbed a hold of me, and it wasn't good. It was like some kind of omen telling me that no matter how much I tried to make things work with John, this relationship was going to end badly.

I just stared at him, not quite sure of what to say or how to react. For some reason, I was hoping the child would be a girl. I think I felt that a girl would somehow be less threatening to me, which of course was ridiculous, considering how fathers felt about their baby girls. I simply tried to hide my feelings from John, and I congratulated him.

Tank however, didn't say anything. He just kissed my cheek and left. It wasn't surprising that he didn't have any words for John. The surprise was that Deja didn't come out to bother Tank. I think she was scared of his giant ass. If I didn't know him, I would be too.

We hung around just a short time after that. Thankfully, there was no more drama from Deja, who pretty much kept her distance from me and John as well. Obviously, I had punked that ass.

Johnny wanted to see the baby again before we left, and I must admit that I wanted to see the child as well. I wanted to see if I could see John in his son.

About a half an hour later, the child was bundled up in his little baby crib in the nursery. I never thought such a thing could happen, but the moment I saw that beautiful little brown baby boy, I fell in love. *What the hell is this?* I wondered. I couldn't take my eyes off him. At that moment I realized that I wanted nothing more than to share this experience with John. All of my jealousy and hurt disappeared when I looked at that child. I wanted to be every bit a part of his life as John would be.

Chapter 6

The next few months were pretty uneventful. There was nothing more than daily visits with the baby, during which he slept, while his parents and I shared discomfort and uneasy conversations. Cherie wasn't too pleased that I'd accompany John on these visits. Her hostility toward me was evident, but I wasn't going to feed into her shit in the baby's presence. Nor was I going to stay away. John requested that I be with him, and that was exactly where I was going to be.

Anyway, it didn't take long for Cherie to realize that John wasn't going to leave me for her and the baby. Once again, DRAMA!

John was always there for his son—John Jr., no less—both emotionally and financially, but that wasn't good enough for Cherie. That fool began calling my house at all hours of the night for dumb shit. If the child sneezed, she called. If the child coughed, she called. If, in her opinion, the child's shit wasn't the right color, she called. And none of these so-called emergencies happened during daytime hours. Oh, no, it was always after midnight.

What pissed me off the most was the fact that John's dumb ass couldn't see this shit for what it was. Cherie was trying to worm her way back in with him. Her tactics were pathetic, and for a while I tried to let it go.

One night that bitch called when I had the worst headache ever. I was so not in the mood for any BS. As soon as I heard that phone ringing, I knew it was her. I rolled over and grabbed the receiver before John could get to it. "Hello!" I shouted.

"Oh, hey. I need to speak with Johnny."

"For what?" I yelled.

"I need him to come over here and help me."

"What is it you need help with?"

"The bathtub is stopped up, and I need to give Li'l John his bath."

I looked at the clock. It was one-freaking-thirty in the morning. I lost it right then. I damn sure lost the lady in me at that moment. "Listen, are you a fucking idiot, or do you think I am?" I asked. "There's no way in hell my man is coming over there. If you think for one minute that I don't know what your ass is up to, think again."

"You wait just one damn minute. I'm not up to anything. I just need some help here, and since his son is here, I don't see why you have a problem with John coming to help me out."

Now nobody called that man John but me. Don't ask me why that pissed me off so much, but it did. "First of all, it's *Johnny* to you and everybody else in the streets," I said. "And, second, what kind of person bathes a baby at one-thirty in the morning? Finally, John is not a fucking plumber. Call Roto-Rooter!" And then I banged on that bitch.

By now John was awake and staring at me. I gave him a look that said, *Don't even think about saying one word to me, or I'll kick the shit out of you.*

He rolled his eyes in exasperation then rolled his ass over and went back to sleep. He knew better than to fuck with me that night.

I turned off the ringer to the house phone, and got up and turned

off John's cell phone. That was it for the night.

The next morning at breakfast I decided that John and I needed to talk about Cherie. "John, I think you need to have a talk with Cherie about her late-night phone calls," I said.

"I know, but maybe it's because she's a new mother and she got that panicky thing going on."

I know I didn't just hear that stupid shit come out of this man's mouth. "Panicked new mother, my ass. The only reason that girl is calling here that late at night is because she wants you."

He looked at me as if I had lost my mind. "Lonnie, let that shit go. Cherie knows I'm not interested in her. I'm sure she's not trying to start anything."

"Oh, really? How can you be so sure about that?"

"Because she never says or does anything to give me the impression that she wants me back in that way. Besides, she'd be wasting her time any damn way."

"John, you can't be that dense. Think about her so-called emergencies and how minimal they truly are. I mean, come on now. She called last night because the bathtub was stopped up. Get real! You are not a freaking plumber!"

"I think you're overreacting, Lonnie, but I'll still speak to her and get this shit straight."

I let it go. Starting off my day in the same mood as my night ended wasn't what I wanted. I finished my breakfast and went to get dressed for work. I had no more words for John. Whether he believed Cherie was up to no good didn't matter. I knew better. I felt it, sensed it, and I knew it, damn it!

Halfway through the morning, my work phone rang. It was Cherie's sister, Deja.

"Lonnie, this is Deja, Cherie's sister. Or should I say, your niece's momma? I called to let you know that you'd better stop fucking with my sister, or your ass is going to be sorry."

I couldn't believe this fool was calling my job to threaten me. "Girl, please . . . I'm not afraid of you, or anyone else for that matter. Whatever is going on between your sister and me is between us, and if you ever call my fucking job again with this dumb shit, your ass is the one who's going to be sorry!" *Click!*

I picked up the phone and called John's cell.

"Hello," he answered.

"Hi, John. Deja just called me here at work and threatened me. You need to talk to Cherie and tell her that her sister had better back off with all the drama before she gets herself hurt."

"Hold up a minute. What are you talking about?"

"I just told you! Apparently Cherie relayed the conversation she and I had last night to her sister, and that bitch called here making threats. Now you're the one who needs to get this situation under control, because I won't be dealing with it."

Johnny was quiet for a few seconds. I suppose he didn't know what to say or do about it, but his black ass needed to figure it out soon.

"All right, babe, I'll talk to Cherie this evening," he said finally. "I need to stop by there to see the baby and make sure he has everything he needs."

Everything like what? What could he possibly need? I wondered. This man spent more than enough money on a child who was just a few months old. "Fine, just handle your business," I said, and ended the call. I knew John wasn't going to be able to handle this shit properly. There was no way these ghetto-ass chicks were going to act like they had any sense. If I had to call my family, this shit was going to get real ugly, real quick.

The moment I'd finished with John, I walked up to the reception area and asked Rose to screen all of my calls before putting them through to my desk. Enough was enough.

Chapter 7

During the following week my irritation with this baby momma situation grew. It was visiting day with the baby, and after the recent nonsense with the Johnson sisters, I didn't want to be bothered. Granted, I could have told him sooner, but I waited until thirty minutes before it was time to leave to let him know my plans.

We were at the kitchen table just finishing lunch when I said, "John, if you don't mind, I'm not going to Cherie's with you today."

He looked at me with disappointment. "Babe, I don't understand. I thought you loved being around my son."

I couldn't look him in the eye, so I got up and placed our used dishes in the sink. With my back turned to him, I said, "How can you expect me to sit there with that simple woman after everything that happened last week? Not to mention, you can't possibly think it's all right with her for me to go sitting up in her house like it's nothing."

"Lonnie"—He sighed—"I've already spoken to Cherie about that, and she's cool."

"What do you mean, she's cool?"

"She said it's OK if you come with me, and that she won't start any shit with you. Besides, I really don't want to deal with her bullshit by myself today. She's less likely to start stuff with me if you're there."

His eyes pleaded with me, but I knew this was probably a setup by Cherie. Nevertheless, I chose to go and support my man.

Not more than ten minutes into the visit, the drama started. Deja walked in, mean-mugging me instantly. No surprise there. Deja was two years younger than Cherie, but she herself had five children by the time she was twenty-two. One of which could be my brother's. I sure hoped that he wasn't one of the damn deadbeats. John had clued me in about this after their confrontation at the hospital. Apparently Cherie had told him all of the girl's business.

According to John, there were at least four fathers, of which only one bothered to try to help out Deja. Not having experienced anything like this in my own life, I did feel some sympathy for her. I knew it must be a difficult life to be solely responsible for five children.

I didn't think I would've been able to handle that kind of stress or pressure at that age. So her situation did explain her displays of ugly behavior. She just wasn't happy. I sat there staring at the little girl she called Shakita, trying to see if I could spot a family resemblance, but I couldn't. Maybe Tank was right and the child wasn't his.

But damn if sympathy, understanding, and any possible family ties didn't go right out the window the moment she started in on me.

Deja sat down across from me and let loose. "Why is your stank ass sitting up in my sister's house after you was talking shit last week? And don't think I forgot about that shit at the hospital either."

I tried to hold my tongue—which wasn't my forte—for the sake of the baby and the five little ones who'd followed Deja through the door, but come on now. Besides, the children didn't seem the least bit phased by their mother's attitude, tone, or language.

"Look, Deja, I'm trying to be respectful of the children in here right now, especially if one of them is my blood, but if you call me out of my name again, I'm going to give you the butt-kicking you've been asking for."

She jumped up and yelled, "Oh no! This bitch didn't just threaten me!"

"I sure did, and what?"

Before I could say another word, Deja leaped from the sofa and lunged at me. I wasn't so much afraid of her attack as I was shocked. Before I could move, she grabbed my hair, so I grabbed hers. Now, get this. We both grew up in the hood, where scrapping was no big deal, but the big knockdown, drag-out fight that you and I both were expecting didn't happen. Neither of us did more than hair pulling before Cherie and John pulled us apart.

"Deja, what the hell is wrong with you?" John screamed.

"What the hell is wrong with you, screaming at my sister like she's the one that's wrong?" Cherie screamed back.

"I'm going to kill that bitch!" I screamed.

And every kid in the house began screaming after that, so John and I got the hell out of there.

Chapter 8

By the time John and I got home, I still hadn't calmed down one bit. John went straight upstairs without a word and I went straight to the phone and called Lena.

"Hey girl, what's up with you?"

"I just came back from John's visit and that bitch Deja jumped on me!"

"What the fuck? Donna and Reggie are over here with me. Hold tight, we're on our way."

"No don't do that. I'm pissed and you best believe I'm going to be on Deja's ass real soon, but they got all of those kids there."

"So the fuck what, Lonnie? We ain't after no damn kids! Those bitches don't know when to stop, so it's time to show them what's what!" Lena yelled at me.

Before I could fix my lips to respond, she hung up and was undoubtedly on her way to my house. And no doubt with my sister on my side, I was going to go handle mine. I ran up stairs, changed my clothes and told John I was going to the store. By then he was so engrossed in his Phillies game, he didn't pay me any mind. He acted as if nothing had happened less than thirty minutes ago. Men!

Fifteen minutes later, Lena, Donna, who is our real cousin, and Reggie were pulling up in front of my house. I ran out and jumped in the back seat with Reggie.

"So Miss Thing, that skanky little fish jumped on you, huh?' Reggie asked.

I just nodded.

"Yeah, well we got something for the town whore," he continued.

I laughed, "Reggie, how you know she's a whore?"

"Chile please, she got like ten kids and fifteen baby daddies. I call that a whore for sure."

"So what do you have for them? You can't be out here hitting women," Donna said.

"Shit, I got my pepper spray locked and loaded."

"Good, 'cause you can't fight like a boy or a girl," Lena said.

We all laughed a little at Reggie, and by the time our laughter had subsided, we were pulling up in front of Cherie's house. As soon as I saw Cherie and Deja, my laughter died completely. All the rage I had been trying to contain since this whole thing began boiled to the surface. Flashes of all the drama and phone calls and the betrayal by John were rolling around in my head.

"Who's that other girl on the porch with them?" Donna asked.

"I don't know and it doesn't matter anyway. She's here, so she either gets her ass kicked or she gets her ass out of the way," I replied.

Where are all the kids? I wondered just before we all got out of the car and rushed the porch. Even though Deja was the one who'd started this particular episode, Cherie was the one I really wanted. Before any of them knew what was happening, I grabbed Cherie by her latest jacked up, homemade weave and started punching her in the face. I thought about her being with John, I punched that bitch. I thought about her having his baby, I punched that bitch. I thought about the phone calls,

I punched that bitch.

I believe Lena started swinging on Deja and Donna made a beeline for the unknown chick. I could hear her screaming, "I don't have anything to do with this!"

Donna didn't give a damn about something so trivial. She kept swinging. Sistergirl didn't even try to fight back; she just covered up and took the beating. Reggie had stayed down on the sidewalk and I could hear him screaming, "Fuck those bitches up!"

It was an all-out brawl within seconds. Fists, fake hair, and earrings were flying everywhere. Cherie was actually trying to go toe-to-toe with me, which pissed me off even more. I slammed her up against the door and knocked the wind out of her. I soon as I saw I had an advantage, I started kicking the shit out of her. For a second I thought she was screaming then, I realized it was coming from behind me. When I glanced around I realized it was Reggie. He always screamed like a little bitch. He came running because he saw one of Cherie's neighbors running up on the porch to jump in. Before the girl could even take a swing at anyone, Reggie was there in a flash with his pepper spray. I was trying to watch him and keep Cherie on the ground at the same time. That fool-ass Reggie started spraying that can like a freakin' maniac.

I left Cherie's ass lying there and got the hell out of the way. Donna followed my lead and we got the hell off that porch. Reggie's aim was terrible, and we all knew it. Unfortunately, Lena didn't react as quickly and Reggie's dramatic, over-hyped ass sprayed her too. Everybody on that porch was screaming, choking, and gagging. Reggie grabbed Lena, and as they stumbled down the steps he yelled, "Go start the car! Start the damn car!".

Donna jumped in the driver's seat and started the car. She sped off just as Reggie pulled the door closed. "Damn, bitch! We almost didn't make it in the car!" Reggie yelled at Donna.

"Shut up, diva. You're in here, aren't you?"

Lena was still screaming from the pepper spray while Reggie was screaming at Donna.

"I can't believe you maced me, you asshole!"

"Aw, I'm sorry, Lele. I didn't know which way to turn. I was just trying to stop that bitch from jumping in."

"Your ass should try not being so damned hysterical when shit goes down." Donna laughed. "Really, Reggie, you can be such a girl."

Chapter 9

We drove straight to our childhood home, which Lena had moved back into after our parents moved to Florida.

As soon as we got Lena's eyes flushed and she stopped cussing Reggie out, we called Tank. There was no doubt that Cherie and her family would retaliate. Not that my family gave a damn, but I had to be concerned because it was my house they would surely take their drama to.

As was the norm for me at that time, I allowed my temper to control my actions as opposed to thinking things through. It didn't really occur to me until just before Tank and his boys walked in that I still had to deal with John's reaction to what we had done. Because of him, Cherie was a part of our existence as a couple, and because of his son, I was going to have to answer for my actions.

"Lonnie, snap out of it. Are you listening to us?" Tank asked me.

"No, sorry, what's up?"

"Me and the guys are going to take you home and chill out there."

"What do you mean, chill out there? I don't want any bullshit between you and John."

"Girl, ain't nobody trippin' over that nigga. We just going to hang around out front and let our presence be known, that's all."

"That's all? Boy, y'all niggas are locked and loaded, aren't you?"

"You know how we roll, sis. Now let's go."

I kissed my family good-bye and followed my brother and his boys out the front door.

"Call us if you need us!" Lena yelled after us.

"That girl can hardly see. What she going to do?" Tank laughed.

"So you finally got a chance to spank that ass, huh Lon?" Clyde, my brother's best friend asked.

"I guess so." I didn't have more to say because I was mentally preparing myself to deal with John.

As soon as we pulled up to my house, I spotted John on the porch. He didn't look pleased, but at that point I realized that I really didn't care all that much.

"Look at this busta standing out there like he going to do something."

"Shut up, T. Y'all just do whatever it is you're going to do and I'll deal with him."

The moment I made it up onto the porch John said, "Lonnie, was all that really necessary?" Obviously Cherie had already called.

"Yeah, pretty much." There was that tough talk again.

"Where was my son while all of that bullshit was going on?"

"I don't know. He wasn't out on that porch saving his mom from getting her ass kicked." Damn y'all, sometimes I couldn't help myself.

Now I thought I knew that man pretty well, and although there were things he would blow off because he knew exactly who I was, I didn't think this would be one of them. All he said was, "OK."

Whatever. As long as I didn't have to go through any more shit that day, it was all good.

Later that night, I heard gunshots. I got up and opened the bedroom window and saw that Tank and the guys were still out there laughing and drinking.

"Tank! I know y'all asses ain't out here shooting like you in the wild fuckin' west!"

"Stop trippin', Lon. It ain't nothing."

"Stop trippin', my ass. If the cops show up here, I don't know y'all fools."

"What? That ain't right. You need to be thanking us for being here. Cherie and Deja just rode by here with a bunch of girls in the car. We just fired off a couple rounds in the air that's all. Word is that they don't have no dudes in that family and other niggas don't take them seriously enough to want to look out for 'em."

"So what's your point, T?"

"Just that if they think I might put a bullet in one of their asses, they'll lay off."

Tank may have been right about that. Those chicks might have thought they could turn this shit into an all-out war with me, Lena, and Donna, but throw my hard core brother and his thug friends into the mix, and it was a different story. Tank had a reputation for going balls out. He'd made quite a few guys shit their pants.

Cherie stopped calling my house, and, of course, I didn't go along on any more visits. I'm sure you're not surprised. Anyway, a couple of weeks passed without any drama, except for John coming home and complaining about the crap he had to now deal with because of the fight. Too damned bad. He created this shit.

For sure, one could say that I was suspicious by nature, but I would say, "I'm not stupid." That two-week break didn't mean anything. Cherie wasn't the type to let shit go. And she certainly wasn't the type to take an ass-whooping then turn around and have enough sense to know that she had met her match. Chicks like that would always come back for more. The thing I didn't know was exactly what she was up to. But it didn't take long for me to find out.

Chapter 10

I was on my way home from work, hungry and tired. Just as I pulled up to my house, I noticed Cherie's car parked across the street. I couldn't believe that chick had the nerve to show her face at my home. We'd already established that visits with the child were to be held at her house, so there was no reason for her to be there. I didn't have a problem with the baby being in my home. I loved that boy. I thought he was the most adorable little baby ever, but, of course, his mother didn't want me to have anything to do with him. So why was she there?

When I got out of the car, I could hear yelling coming from my house. I opened the door to find Cherie all up in John's face, screaming and yelling like she was some kind of nut.

"What the hell is going on in here?" I yelled.

Cherie spun around to face me. "Mind your own damn business! This is between me and my baby's daddy!" Then she had the nerve to turn back to John, dismissing me.

I saw red. As if it wasn't bad enough dealing with this girl's bullshit phone calls, now I had to come home and deal with drama in my own home. Hell no! I grabbed that bitch by the back of her head and dragged her to the front door, kicking and screaming, and there wasn't a damn thing she could do about it. I had a viselike grip on her weave, and she was practically on her ass while I was dragging her.

Once I got to the front door, I slung her across the porch and waited for her to get up. It was time to whoop her ass once and for all.

Just as she found her way to her feet, John came out and grabbed me. *This brother had better learn who he should be grabbing in these situations.* I swore, for one split second, I thought about clocking him too.

"Lonnie, please don't get into this with her."

"Why is this person in my house? I expect her ignorant ass to be disrespectful, but not you."

"I didn't invite her over here. She just showed—"

Before he could finish his statement, Cherie was up and all over his back, trying to get to me, screaming at the top of her lungs about how she was going to fuck me up. She didn't scare me. I grew up in Camden just like she did, and I'd spent the majority of my early years kicking ass.

John turned and grabbed her arms. Then he pulled her off my porch and down the sidewalk. Somehow he managed to calm her down, while I stood on the porch and watched them for a few minutes.

The moment he came back in and closed the door, I asked him again, "Why was that girl in my house?"

"She came over here asking me for money. She said J.J. needed some diapers and formula, but I told her no, because I just gave her money for those things two days ago. And before you ask, I don't know what she did with the money."

I sat on the sofa looking at this fool like he had two heads. I swear, I never knew how little common sense he had. He truly acted as if someone had to spell things out for him all the time. How did I miss that? "John, isn't it obvious to you what's going on? Either she spent the money on herself, or she wanted to see you and just needed an excuse. Take your pick."

"Lonnie, go ahead with that shit. As bold as that girl is, if she really wanted me, she'd put it out there, and she hasn't said a word to me."

"Of course, she won't. She wants you to want her. She's pissed because she can't believe that you won't pursue her."

John stood there shaking his head in disbelief.

"Whatever the hell it is, it had better stop. I can't live with this nonsense, and I won't be telling you this again."

"Whatever, Lonnie." He turned and walked away.

I had no choice but to let it go in that moment, but I wasn't going to continue to deal with this crap for too long. I just couldn't.

As I headed for the kitchen to start dinner, it hit me that I had just spoken to John like he was a child. It's no wonder he walked away from me. I also realized that I had been doing that shit to him ever since the baby was born. Apparently I harbored more resentment toward him than I realized.

I noticed too that John had let me get that off. Although he didn't like arguing or conflict, he would at least hold his own whenever we fought about anything. But since his cheating was discovered, it was becoming more evident that he was holding his tongue. I'm sure it was because he still felt guilty about everything that had gone down and thought it was more important for him to try to keep the peace.

We were in bed that night, and I had just nodded off to sleep when I heard what sounded like crashing glass. By the time my head cleared, John was up and running. I ran down the stairs behind him and found my front window shattered and a brick lying on the living room floor.

I couldn't even go off. I just stood there staring at the mess in disbelief, wondering if staying with this man was worth all this trouble.

"Find a way to fix this shit," I said. "I'm going to bed." And I left him standing there looking stupid.

I went back to bed wondering how I was going to deal with all this shit realistically. I had to consider that the only way to have peace in my life would be to let John go. I loved him dearly, but my patience was wearing thin. By the time he came back to bed, I was asleep.

The next morning wasn't good for us at all. I didn't have anything to say, and he didn't know what to say. The tension between us was a bit too much for either of us to handle.

During the course of the day, I received several hang-up phone calls. I knew who the culprit was, but there really wasn't anything I could do about it. Cherie definitely got something out of it, though, because she managed to ruin my day. I was completely frustrated by the time I got off work.

As I approached my car in the parking lot that night, I noticed that something wasn't quite right about the way it was sitting. As I got closer, I realized that my driver's side tires had been slashed. I couldn't believe my eyes. I was so upset, I couldn't even scream, cuss, or cry. I just stood there in shock.

Finally I called that dumb-ass John and told him what happened. Then I called the police to make a report. They arrived shortly before the tow truck. I wasted no time telling them that I knew Cherie had committed this act of vandalism. I told them about the incident the night before at my house and of the phone calls earlier that day.

I was physically and emotionally drained by the time I got home.

John was on the phone arguing with Cherie. Apparently the police had already gone to see her. Of course, she denied everything, and since I had no proof that it was her ignorant ass who fucked up my car, there really wasn't any way to deal with this legally. I had to eat the cost of the repairs. Actually, John had to eat the cost. After all, he was the reason for all of this craziness. He spent the entire evening apologizing for Cherie.

At one that morning, the phone rang. I could have slit my wrists. John answered, spoke for a couple of minutes, and informed me that he was going to Cherie's to deal with this shit once and for all. I didn't say a word. It was about time this nigga got his balls back. Maybe it might actually work if he made a sincere effort to deal with it, as opposed to blowing things off.

John returned home two hours later. I didn't have the energy to ask him how things went with Cherie, and he didn't volunteer any information. He simply went to sleep.

The next morning at breakfast I noticed John had some scratches on his arms. I was afraid to ask him what had gone down last night, but I had to know. He truly looked defeated.

"John, what the hell happened?"

"That crazy girl attacked me as soon as I got there. She was ranting and raving about the police showing up at her door."

"So?"

"She swears she didn't have anything to do with your car being damaged."

"Don't tell me you believed her."

"Of course, I didn't. That's why we got into the scuffle."

"You know she's vindictive enough to press charges against you. Did you hit her?"

"No, I'd never do that. Besides, I don't think she would go that far. But you were right, she does want me to start fucking with her again. Once I got her off me and calmed her ass down, she tried to talk me into staying with her."

"I knew it! That bitch is shameless. She honestly thought you would just stay out all night like it was nothing?"

"I guess so. The bottom line is, she's not going to stop acting like a fool unless she gets her way. That's become obvious to me."

"So what are you trying to say?"

"She's saying that if I don't break up with you and go back to her, she's going to leave the state and take my son with her."

"I know you're not falling for that bullshit."

"I don't know. The only thing I do know is that she is not going to take my son away from me. I'm not having that shit. But knowing Cherie, I do think that she'll just take off with him. She has family all over the South. Trying to fight her legally would be a waste of time, and chasing her ass all over the country is not something I have time for."

I was shocked. Was this guy sitting here telling me that he was seriously considering going back with that girl over some stupid-ass threats? Would he really leave me just to avoid having to battle for his son? He was weaker than I thought. *Again, how'd I miss this?* I wondered. *Damn! Love really is blind.*

I must have been in shock, because I felt like I couldn't function, so I called out of work. There was no way I was going to get any work done that day anyway. I lay around the house all day until I got a call from the tire place saying my car was ready. Picking up my car was pretty much all I could manage to do that day.

The next day things got worse for me. Ten seconds after I had gotten into the office, my supervisor called me into her office.

"Close the door," Logan said. "There's been a complaint made against you."

I couldn't believe it. How could someone make a complaint against me when I only worked in the clerical department? It wasn't like I dealt with the public on a regular basis.

Logan smiled.

"Why are you grinning so hard?" I asked her.

"Because you should see your face.

"Ha! Ha! So, tell me, what was the complaint?"

"First of all, it's obvious it's a bunch of bull. The anonymous caller stated, and I quote, 'Ms. Devlin misused her authority as a caseworker to harass my family.'"

"But I'm not a caseworker."

"Exactly. There's no way I could take that nonsense seriously. It was obvious that this was something personal."

Obviously, this was Cherie again. Not only was this girl harassing me, but now she had the nerve to try to fuck with my livelihood. That was it for me.

I called John and told him that if he couldn't find a way to control his baby's momma so that I could have peace in my life, he was going to have to leave my home and my life.

I knew as well as he did that there was no way he could control that woman. I had to make a decision that would be best for me. That was my responsibility, not his. I had to weigh whether holding on to this man was worth the stress and frustration this woman was bringing into my life.

After another week of the bullshit phone calls, I had had enough. I had to tell John to leave my home. We were sitting in the living room watching television, and I decided just to lay it all on the line.

"John, I have to tell you, I can no longer deal with things the way they are. I feel that the only way for me to have some peace in my life is to end this relationship. I do still love you very much, but I don't see things getting any better, and I simply can't handle this any longer."

"Lonnie, I agree."

To say I was shocked by his response would be an understatement. Was this man actually going to let me go without a fight?

"I know how you feel about drama of any kind, and for you to have to deal with it on a daily basis is not right. It's more important to me that you be happy, and the truth is, Cherie isn't going to change. The best thing to do is to remove you from her line of fire."

I sat there with my mouth hanging open. I may have put it out there, but how could this man give up on us so easily? He obviously had been thinking about this longer than I had.

The coward didn't stay around long enough for me to say anything else. It was a done deal. I mean, *Damn!* I had to make a decision, but dude acted as if losing me didn't mean anything.

The way I saw it, I felt that after the child got older and Cherie had maybe grown up some, we could probably get back together.

John packed his shit and bounced that night. Now I knew the truth. He never really gave a damn about me. He was just like the others—self-absorbed and useless. Cherie had to mean more to him than I ever thought. No, it never occurred to me that he might actually be leaving because he really wanted me to be happy. He wanted that bitch.

Even though I was relieved after John had been gone for a few days, I couldn't just stop loving him. It didn't matter that this breakup was the best thing for me; that was beside the point. Even after I had time to think and realize that the relationship was only going to get worse, I still missed him.

Getting over him, though, wasn't as hard as I thought it was going to be. The relief I felt at not having to deal with Cherie and the drama anymore made his absence easier to deal with. Not to mention, he'd walked out so easily. I was still pissed about that for a long time, but apparently anger did help to heal a broken heart.

During the next twelve months, I heard from John occasionally, but nothing had changed. I couldn't forget our last time together and how he left. It was definitely over. I had lost respect for him as a man, and there was no coming back from that.

Around this time I got a call from one of our mutual friends, Sam, telling me that John and Cherie had gotten married. I was stunned. I knew a lot could happen in a year, but it still struck me hard. I had spoken to John a few months earlier, and he'd never mentioned anything. I wondered how he could choose such a messed up person like Cherie to be his wife. I was over John, but I still harbored some hatred for Cherie and her behavior.

All I could do was hope that I never ran into the two of them together. No matter how much time had passed, I wasn't sure if I could handle that.

Chapter 11

THE PRESENT

It had been two years since I'd gone through all of that bullshit with John and Cherie. Although I dated occasionally during that time, I couldn't get serious with anyone. If I had to admit it to myself, that situation had changed me. I'd lost some of my edge. I still talked tough, but honestly, I was afraid. Afraid to open myself to anything or anyone in any way that mattered. My spirit was weakened in ways I wouldn't know of until it was too late.

There had been some changes in my siblings as well. My sister Lena had calmed down considerably after her love of the fight had caused her to lose her job, which subsequently led to her being out of work for a year and a half. She was just now getting back on her feet. That girl did more whining than a little bit, especially after her unemployment checks ran out.

Nevertheless, she began to understand what was wrong in her choice to act a fool. She actually did a lot of growing up. Personally, I think it had more to do with her falling for a guy named Devon, who refused to put up with her bullshit. He called her on everything she did.

She'd never admit that he was the main reason for the change, though. She took all the credit for turning her attitude around. Yeah, right. She didn't want to lose that man. Besides, I honestly believed that, like me, Lena wanted to live a more peaceful life.

Now Tank, on the other hand, was a slightly different story. He had always been loud and intimidating, which served him well in the city. All he had to do was flex his build and that menacing stare of his, and most people would wisely leave his ass alone.

Shortly after I got rid of John, Tank ran up against someone who didn't back down. Which, of course, pissed him off even more, and my brother beat dude senseless. That altercation landed him in jail. He served a year and a half of a three-year sentence. Upon his release six months ago, Tank decided to work harder at getting his life together as well. The first thing he did was finally have a paternity test done with Deja. Guess what, people? I now have a three-year-old niece named Shakita. Oh and hell no, I still don't have shit to do with Deja because of it. Certainly, without the influence of my brother and sister's nonsense I have become the softer, kinder Lonnie I've always known was in me, but I'm not that damned soft and kind.

I'll never forget the day we found out the truth about the child. Tank called me to come over to Lena's, where he had been staying since his release. I had barely gotten in the door before Lena thrust the paternity test results in my face.

"Here, read this!" I focused and read, 99.999% probability of paternity.

"Damn! That little girl is yours?!"

"I thought for sure that Deja was lying," he said.

"Ain't that some shit?" Lena asked.

"To say the least." I was a little stunned by the results myself. On the one occasion that I saw the child, I really didn't think that she was my brother's. There was no resemblance whatsoever. Obviously looks don't mean anything.

"Wow! So T, what are you going to do?"

"I called Deja and asked her to bring Shakita over here."

"And he know damned well I don't want that bitch in my house," Lena interjected.

"Yeah, but Lele, this isn't about you. Our brother has a child that he has been ignoring for years."

"Yeah, so?"

"So let him deal with this however he needs to."

"Yeah, OK, but if she says one thing wrong, I'm straight going back to my old ways and I'm fuckin' her up."

"Whatever, Lele. Finish what you were saying, T."

"I was just going to say that I feel really bad about all this. No matter how hardheaded I was and ignored mom and dad on the regular, I still had two parents who were there for me. I've been doing dumb shit for years, but after that prison shit, I'm starting to really understand some things."

"Things like what?" I asked.

"Like a grown man being locked up like a fuckin' animal is no way to live. Dad would always say, there's better things to do than run the streets and act a fool for no good reason. He was right. There's nothing better than having freedom, and I plan to use that freedom to make better choices."

"So what does all that have to do with you being that trick's baby daddy?" Lena asked.

"What I'm saying, Lena, is that it's time to grow up and be a man. And, the first thing is to get to know my daughter."

Tank had barely finished speaking and Deja was knocking on the door. My brother let her and the child in, but no one said anything.

I think we were all stuck for a minute. Finally Tank knelt down and offered his hand and introduced himself to the girl.

She stared at him for a second before she accepted his hand and said, "Hi, Daddy."

Shakita had the sweetest little girl voice, and my heart melted a little in that moment. Tank pulled the child into his arms and kept repeating, "I'm sorry, I'm sorry."

Damn if I knew my brother could be so emotional about anything. I shed a couple of tears at his show of emotion. Lena looked bored by it all and Deja actually seemed relieved. I wondered if there might be a little more to that chick than I originally thought.

So that's how the Devlins and Johnsons became connected for life. The world really is too small, or at least the city of Camden is. Bizarre!

Anyway, Tank wanted a fresh start and to get to know his daughter. Deja allowed him to take Shakita down to Florida to meet my parents and they hadn't come back yet. He said Deja didn't mind. No surprise there; she had one less mouth to feed.

I missed my brother a great deal. I also missed Reggie and Donna a lot. Reggie had gotten seriously involved in the drag scene and spent a lot of time touring and doing different shows. My cousin Donna got promoted to a services rep for a car company and they transferred her to Chicago.

Yes, life had changed and we had grown in the last two years, but sometimes I missed the craziness of having them all around.

As much as I liked working in child protective services, it could get hectic, and today was going to be a long day. I had a ton of paperwork on my desk that I had to get it done by the end of the day, since it was Friday.

As I stopped outside to pick up my newspaper, the sun was shining brightly, and the temperature was already warm, which lifted my spirits immediately. I loved the spring and summer months. Just like the flowers, plants, and trees, the spring gave me a sense of rebirth.

I stood there for a moment and took a deep breath. As I exhaled, the warmth of the sun relieved me of any stress I felt about the work piled on my desk. All things seemed possible in moments like this.

Shortly after I arrived at work, my supervisor, Logan, advised me and my coworkers that we would be having a unit meeting that afternoon. I was good with that. It was Friday, and I would rather sit around talking and laughing with my unit members instead of sitting in front of my computer staring at the screen and pretending to work. I sat down, logged on, and proceeded to get some work done.

I was a good two hours into knocking out some of my paperwork when my phone rang. It was my "sometimes friend," Sandy. I called her that because, as long as she was free, she was up my behind. Every time I turned around, she wanted to go out and do something together. That was, until she got a man. Then she couldn't remember my number or my name, unless of course she was having some kind of drama with the man of the hour. But I couldn't really hold that against her because seriously, Sandy truly was my girl and always had my back, no matter what. When I had man drama of my own, she was the one who held me up. All my wild-ass family wanted to do was fight about it.

Sandy and I had met seven years earlier when she rented the house next door to mine. At first I wasn't too fond of her. She talked too loudly and too much. She was the opposite of my quiet, keep-it-to-myself nature. At least that's how I tried to be. Frankly, I thought she was a little flaky. Nevertheless, I made it a point to get to know my new neighbor because, with all of her loudness, she was funny and always spoke to me whenever we crossed paths.

I eventually got around to inviting her over for a drink, and to my surprise, I learned that underneath all of her rowdiness, she truly was a down-to-earth woman with a big heart. Her strong and independent nature was something I greatly admired. In fact, I believed I possessed those same qualities. Most importantly, she didn't do stuck-up, and neither did I. Our friendship had grown from that first invite. We enjoyed some of the best times together and had seen one another through some of the worst times of our lives. Our families had even bonded.

Sandy had this way of going off "Puerto Rican mamacita style," and would have me in stitches. That girl would get to cussing and fussing about something, but I would only catch half of what she was ranting about because the other half of it would be in Spanish.

Seven years later, Sandy Martinez was still one of the closest friends I had, and no matter her faults or mine, I knew she was in it with me for the long haul.

"What's up with you?" I asked her.

"Not much, *mami*. I was just calling to ask you how to get an application for your job."

"Oh yeah? For whom?"

"My neighbor Niki just got laid off, and she needs something right away."

"OK, I can get one from my supervisor, but I can't say if there's going to be any openings. We're pretty full right now."

"That's fine. All I promised to do was to see if I could get the application. I'll talk to you later."

"All right. Bye."

That girl was too much. Like I said, she only called if there was some man drama or if she needed something, but that was cool. I loved that girl, no matter what.

With Sandy forgotten, I got back to work.

But before I could even get back in the flow, Malik Reese came by and plopped his ass on my desk, nearly knocking over my cup of coffee. "Hey, Lonnie."

"Hi, Malik. What's up with you?" I asked, rolling my eyes at his near spill.

"Not much. How's everything going?"

"Pretty good. I'm just trying to get some of this work off my desk."

"Oh, OK. That's what's up. I'll talk to you later."

As Malik walked away from my desk, I thought, *If this guy doesn't just say what he really wants to say to me, the next time he stops by here, I'm going to tell him to just keep it moving.*

I knew this man was trying to holler, because most days he tried to push up on me. I was flattered by the attention. But then there were other days when he backed off big time. I got confused by his behavior, but all he had to do was say the word, and I would be on it. Fear and insecurities notwithstanding.

Malik Reese was fine as hell. He was tall with dark brown skin, and he had the most intense honey-colored eyes. He wore his head shaved bald. Sometimes it would turn me on just to imagine holding on to that head. I would have no problem spending time with him.

Aside from all of that, Malik was one of very few men I called a friend. When we weren't flirting, he and I had some of the best conversations. I truly enjoyed him as a person. Not to mention, he kept me laughing, which was the best thing of all.

The next time he makes one of his little comments or insinuations about us getting together, I'll respond in the positive to see how he'll react to that.

No sooner than I thought this, Malik was coming back.

"Lonnie, I meant to tell you that you look very nice today," he said.

"Thank you."

"So, tell me . . . you must have a date after work, huh?"

"No, not at all. Sometimes I like to look nice just for myself."

"Well, I was hoping you would say that there was no one waiting to see you this evening, because I'd like to be the one you look so special for."

I was totally blown away by that comment. His flirting was one thing, but for him to come right out and say he was checking for me completely took me by surprise.

"It can be any way you want it to be," I said, expecting him to back down like he usually did when I was so direct.

But to my further surprise, he asked me, "When could we get together?"

Normally I wouldn't even consider getting with someone I worked with, but what the heck? This man was fine and, as far as I knew, single. That was good enough for me. "That's up to you, sweetie. I'm ready for whatever."

The look on his face was a combination of joy and uncertainty, like he was happy he had a shot, but not quite sure how to proceed. I didn't know what to make of this, so I gave him my cell phone number and told him, "The ball is in your court."

"OK, I'll call you," he said, and then he went on about his business.

By the time I got back into the flow of my work, it was time for me to go to lunch. I had to get moving, so I could run some errands, get a bite to eat, and be back in time for the unit meeting.

At one-thirty my unit coworkers and our supervisor were gathered in the meeting room. Logan was the coolest supervisor anyone could have. On the outside, she was the stereotypical white girl—blond hair, blue eyes, big boobs, and a flat ass—but her personality was the best. Logan had our backs and kept us cracking up with her tirades about our off-the-wall coworkers.

My co-worker Asia sat next to me like she always did and immediately stuck her cell phone in my face. "Look at this!"

Once my eyes focused, I screamed, "Oh my God! Whose dick is that? Is that real?" It was huge! I forgot where I was while staring at that thing, until the entire room fell out laughing hysterically. Well, everyone except Rose. She was old school and not happy at all with my language.

"Sorry Rose," I said when I noticed the look on her face.

"Who the hell is that?" I whispered to Asia.

"That's that nigga Pop I met last week."

"Last week and he's already sending you porn shots? You're such a whore, I bet you asked for it."

"I know, right?" she said, and we both fell out laughing.

Asia and I were still laughing when Logan and got down to business. As always, the main topic on the agenda was employee abuse of time.

"If you're going to be longer than an hour for your lunch, you have to let me know," Logan said. "Every time one of you is not where you're supposed to be and someone comes looking for you, they all come and ask me. Ladies and gentlemen, I can't cover your behinds if I don't know what you're doing."

Of course everyone agreed to behave, and that was that.

Logan then asked if anyone had anything else to discuss, and as usual, there were more complaints about the caseworkers not knowing how to do their own jobs and running to the rest of us to clean up after them.

We were considered support staff, but we did just as much as, if not more, than those workers who worked directly with the families. And complaining about it wasn't anything new. Our unit meetings pretty much always went this way. It was really just a venue for us to vent. We stayed on our game, so unless there were any changes in duties, there wasn't much to meet about. Once a month we just needed to get together and let it all out.

The last order of business was Logan's announcement that a new person would be starting on Monday. Asia and I finally stopped giggling about that picture when we heard that.

"Good," Asia said. "We could use another body around here."

Asia was my girl too. We had started working at the agency within weeks of one another and had become mad cool from the door.

"Since this was just sprung on me at the last minute, I'm not exactly sure what I'll have her do," Logan said. "I'll just probably start her on the phones. Rose, I'll need you to train her."

"That's fine," Rose replied. "What's her name?"

"Cherie Johnson."

The giggles left me completely in that moment. Asia looked at me and I looked at her.

"Not *that* Cherie Johnson," she said.

"This can't be happening to me." I whispered to myself.

And in that moment I saw red. It couldn't be the same Cherie Johnson I knew. Because if it was, I didn't know how in the hell I was going to be able to work with that witch . . . at least, without hurting her up in there.

My head started spinning, my body began to overheat, and I swear I broke out into a sweat. The rage and disbelief I was feeling must have shown all over my face.

Logan asked, "You all right, Lonnie?"

I could barely answer her. "I'm just a little tired," I said.

That was a good enough answer for her to simply let it go, and my coworkers continued on with their chatting and laughing while I sat there in shock and disbelief that I had to deal with that bitch in my life again.

Chapter 12

After getting the news that Cherie Johnson would soon be back in my life, I needed a drink or two. As soon as Asia and I got back to my desk, I called Lena and Reggie and told them what was up. They agreed to meet us at their favorite bar for happy hour.

I ran into my sister's arms the moment I spotted her sitting at the bar. She had been so wrapped up in her man, I hadn't seen her in weeks.

"Hey, baby sis. I know your ass is fucked up about this Cherie shit."

"Hell yeah. Can you believe it?"

"No, I can't, but all I know is, she better not start her shit again."

"She don't want another beat down," Reggie said as he hugged me and Asia.

"What's up Miss Asia? I ain't seen you in months, you little fish." Reggie laughed.

"Stop calling me a damn fish, Reggie. You just hatin' because you can't get rid of that piece you got swinging between your legs," Asia joked.

"Not funny Miss Thing, not funny at all," Reggie said semi-seriously. We all knew Reggie would much rather have been born female. When he wasn't on tour, he spent his weekends doing drag shows over in

Philly, and, truth be told, he transformed into one of the prettiest women I had ever seen.

"All right now you two knock it off. We came here to get our drink on, what y'all having?" I asked.

"Long Islands," Lena replied.

"Damn, I can't handle that. Let me just get one of my fruity, girly drinks," I responded.

"You're such a punk, Lonnie. I'm having what y'all having," Asia said to Lena.

Lena barely let me get a sip of my Parrot Bay and pineapple before she started questioning me. "OK Lon, what are you going to do about this Cherie shit?"

"Honestly, I don't know. I've spent the last two years getting beyond the bullshit and drama. I don't know how I'm going to go back to that. I like the peaceful existence I've created for myself. I don't want to give that up," I explained.

"I know one thing," Asia interjected, "she better not start no shit up in that office. She'll find out real quick, she can't get that off. We will break her ass in."

"Thanks for having my back, tough little one."

"Well, all I can say is, I hope Miss Girl got a better weave now," Reggie said.

"That's all that matters to you, crazy boy? Hey, Reggie, maybe you can loan her one of your wigs." Lena laughed like that was one of the funniest jokes ever told. She was obviously starting to feel her liquor.

"Hell yeah, I could teach her a thing or two about being a lady," Reggie said and broke into his runway strut.

We all fell out laughing at the spectacle Reggie was making. Everything he said seemed to be funnier than it was because he spoke with a classic gay-boy lisp.

76 Denise Coleman

"You're a damned fool, Reggie!" Asia laughed. "Do the twirl, do the twirl!

Reggie commenced to spinning around in the bar like he was Tyra Banks or some damned body. After a just few spins however, he staggered over to the bar. "Whew chile, I done made myself dizzy."

"You're out of your mind, Reggie."

We spent so much time laughing at Reggie and his antics that night, none of us gave Cherie another thought. Happy hour was a good idea. That was, until Deja walked in one of her girls. As soon as she got within earshot, Reggie yelled, "Hey, Miss Girl, did your sister tighten up her weave yet?"

Lena and Asia cracked up, of course.

Deja didn't say a word. She just rolled her eyes and kept on walking. She was obviously pissed, but what was she going to do? She hadn't forgotten how bad Lena had beaten that ass. And no, our newly discovered family ties hadn't lessened the animosity.

Like I said, I hadn't seen Cherie since John had left, and this was probably only the second time I'd laid eyes on Deja since then. I bet that part of the reason Tank took off was so he wouldn't have to deal with that simple girl.

"Leave that girl alone, Reggie," I admonished. "We're trying to live drama free, remember?"

"Sure, sure, whatever."

"OK, you two so called drama-free sisters, what was it like to find out that one of Deja's kids is y'all's niece? I'm still trippin' over that myself," Asia said.

"Well, apparently, Lonnie over there had more time than I did to absorb that little tidbit, seeing as Deja spilled those beans way back when Cherie was becoming her man's baby momma," Lena said sarcastically.

"Oooh, Miss Thing, you knew all that time and didn't say anything?" Reggie asked.

"OK, in my defense, no, I didn't know for sure. Tank said it was a hit-and-quit thing, and since I couldn't see any resemblance in the girl, I let it go."

"So what, nut? You still should've said something. If it was my family, I wouldn't have been able to keep that to myself," Asia declared.

"Oh please, that's because you can't hold water about anything anyway. I'm going to say it again. In my defense, I was going through some shit back then. I didn't give a damn about Tank and Deja's, 'she's yours,' 'no, she's not' crap!"

"You know, Miss Thing, sometimes you can be a mess," Reggie said.

"Whatever, girly girl."

"Forget about Lonnie, let me answer the damn question," Lena slurred.

Although at that point she had been so quiet, I thought that she was oblivious to what was going on around her.

"Again, we hardly had a chance to absorb that news before Tank took off with the kid. Anyway, we don't know the little girl yet, and that still won't change shit when we do get to know her. Those bitches fucked with my sister, and I still can't stand either one of them," Lena stated with finality, then got up, walked over to the table Deja shared with her friend, and poured what was left of her fourth drink on Deja's head.

Deja screamed and her girl jumped up ready to throw hands. Reggie screamed his girly bitch scream and ran over to grab Lena.

Asia and I could only sit there and laugh, more at Reggie than at the look on Deja's face. That damned alcohol was burning her eyes. Reggie pulled Lena back over to her seat and the bartender said, "Lena, take your drunk ass home. I'm not having that shit in here tonight."

"I got her. Don't worry, we're leaving, Sammy," I said and stood Lena up so we could leave.

"Aw, bitch, I was just starting to get a buzz. When are you going to learn how to act?" Asia whined.

"Obviously not tonight," Lena slurred some more and snatched her purse off the bar. She had the nerve to have an attitude like she did nothing wrong.

"Let's just go, y'all. So sis, you managed to go two whole years without getting us kicked out of anywhere. That's a record for you, huh, girl? I'm proud of you."

"Shut up, Lonnie, it's not funny. I didn't even get to finish my drink."

"Fool, you didn't have a drink to finish. It's dripping down Deja's forehead," I said.

"Now that was some funny shit. That little fish sitting there looking like a wet dog." Reggie laughed as we exited the bar.

"Lonnie, how are these two drunks going to get home?"

"I'm going to call them a cab, then I'm going to take you back to your car."

"That's cool. So, do you feel any better?"

"Sure I do, for now. But I wish those two drinks could keep me knocked out for the weekend so I don't have to think about this mess."

"Oh well, too bad you can't have that dream come true."

"Whatever, smart ass. I just want to go home and sleep.

"I understand, but whatever happens, like always, I've got your back."

"I know you do. Damn, Asia, this shit is going to be weird."

"Right? I can't wait to see how she's going to act on Monday."

"To tell you the truth, I'm kind of curious about that myself. I wonder if she's changed any. I have. Hell, even Lena has changed. OK well, she's still working on it." I laughed. "Anyway, we're all capable of growing, right?"

"Yes, we can, girl, and we'll find out if Cherie's one of those capable beings on Monday. Now call the cab so these nuts can go," Asia said as she pointed to Lena and Reggie sitting on the curb like two orphaned children.

After I placed Lena and Reggie in the cab, I dropped Asia off and went home.

Chapter 13

After getting home from the bar, my anxiety returned. I couldn't, for the life of me, calm down. Just the thought of having to work with her was wearing me out. Of course I knew how to behave at work, but never before had I been in a situation like this. What if she was still just as crazy as she was two years ago?

I had spent so much time and energy focused on my own life, fortunately, I never ran into her or John, and if any of my friends or his had any gossip about the two of them, I refused to listen to it. I didn't even know if they were still married. All I could say for sure was that I didn't want that man after all this time, and I didn't want to deal with any drama at work. I'd lived pretty much drama-free since removing myself from John, and I couldn't imagine going back to the bad shit.

I tried to do some reading to keep my mind off what might happen on Monday, but that didn't work. I listened to music in an effort to relax, and that didn't work. I watched TV and tried to sleep the weekend away, but that didn't work either.

By the time Monday morning rolled around, I was exhausted and not in the mood for anything. I had stressed myself out so badly, I called out of work. I wasn't ready to face this nut. *Eight freakin' hours a day with this chick in my presence. What the hell am I going to do?*

I called Sandy and told her what was going on. She stressed to me how important it was for me to treat Cherie just as I would any other coworker, no matter how difficult it might be for me, and that it would be foolish to lose my job over her.

Sandy, always my voice of reason, was right. I couldn't allow this woman—and I use the term loosely—to interfere with my life or my work.

I hadn't seen Sandy in a while since she'd moved across town, so I asked her to come and spend her lunch hour with me. She didn't hesitate, especially after I promised to make some of her favorite dishes. Sandy was a hell of a cook herself, and when we were neighbors, she taught me how to make rice and beans, *pastelillos*, and fried bananas. That girl had my ass turned out on Spanish food.

When Sandy arrived, I greeted her with a big hug. "Look at you. You look great, with your little tiny self!" I said.

Sandy was a petit, dark-haired woman with blue freakin' eyes.

I would always question, "Where did your Puerto Rican ass get those blues eyes from?"

She would just laugh and say, "Why you hatin', *mami*? Because your black men love these baby blues?"

I could only laugh with her because it was true. For reasons neither of us understood, black men were always after Sandy, yet Hispanic men never seemed to give her a second glance. Although I would never say it to her, I thought it had more to do with that sister-girl booty she was carrying around. Shit, brothers saw that before their eyes ever went near her face.

"Thanks, *mami*. You look exhausted. This Cherie shit is really wearing you out."

"It is. But, for now, it's all about the food. Let's eat!"

"OK, Lonnie. It better taste as good as it smells."

"Ha! Ha! Let's go." I escorted Sandy to the dining room where we could sit and enjoy our meal.

When we were done eating, Sandy gave me her stamp of approval. I was so damn proud of myself. I don't think I had ever cooked Spanish for Sandy before that day.

We had such a good time catching up with one another, Cherie's name never came up.

Before Sandy left, she suggested that I do a lot of praying on the situation. It couldn't hurt, so that was exactly what I did.

By the time I woke up on Tuesday morning, I was feeling a little better. I didn't know what the day would bring, but whatever it was, I could deal.

The first thing I did Tuesday morning when I arrived at work was to speak to Logan.

"Logan, I hope this isn't out of line, but for personal reasons, I can't train this Cherie person in anything. I do, however, understand that we have to work together, and I will do my best to behave. I just need you to understand that I would rather keep my distance as much as possible."

"I don't have a problem with that, if this is what it takes to keep things running smoothly. Anyway, Rose is training her."

I thanked her and went back to my desk. I could only sit there for a few minutes because I was still reeling about the fact that that bitch would be working there.

I walked over to Asia's desk.

"Hey, Lonnie. How are feeling today? "

"I can't sit still. Damn! Can you believe this shit? I actually have to work with that nut. I still can't wrap my head around this craziness."

"Girl, I don't know. One thing's for sure, I'd be in here fucking her up every time she looked at me."

Asia was sitting there with a look on her face that said she meant those words from the bottom of her heart. And I believed her. She would go off way quicker than I would.

We talked for a few more minutes then I went back to my desk.

I couldn't have been at my desk for more than thirty minutes when Cherie came walking by. That bitch had the nerve to stop long enough for me to look up, and then she rolled her pop eyes at me.

Aww, shit, here comes the drama in my life again, I thought.

At that moment I decided to start keeping a record of every little incident with her, no matter how small. If I was going to have to deal with a lot of shit, it wasn't going to be for too long. Fortunately for me, Cherie was going to be working the phones, which meant she was stuck there most of the day, with the exception of breaks and lunch. Since I rarely had a reason to go near that area, there was little chance of me running into her often.

I really didn't see her much that first week, but just like before, I had the same vibe I did about her two years ago. Obviously, she hadn't changed a bit. It never fails to amaze me how people in this world live their lives without any growth.

Because of people like Cherie, I'd become even more grateful for my parents. They taught us to learn from whatever experiences we had—good or bad, but especially bad. Growth was what gave people wisdom, strength, and courage in this life. Even if there was no one in a person's life to teach this valuable lesson, I would imagine that the person would get tired of nothing ever changing. It was beyond me that some people were not capable of coming to the conclusion that it was up to them to fix or change whatever needed to be fixed or changed. I guess to do that, they'd have to believe that something was wrong in the first place.

Chapter 14

The following week, Logan decided that Cherie would do more than just answer phones, and would be trained by different people for different tasks. I again requested that Logan not put me in such a messed up situation. She agreed that Cherie didn't need to learn how to do any of my particular duties. Seniority helped. Otherwise, I may not have been able to get that request granted.

On day three Cherie was working with Bridgette at the desk next to mine. She took every opportunity she had to roll her eyes at me.

How immature is this fool? I wondered.

Just before lunch, she did it again.

I calmly leaned over Bridgette's desk and grabbed that bitch by her throat. "I don't know what your problem is, but you should probably try growing up. This petty crap will never work with me."

She couldn't say a thing after that. She was too busy choking. I got up and went on about my business. Who the hell was she going to tell? Nobody else was around.

Friday rolled around, and Cherie was now doing her training with Melissa at the desk opposite mine. I woke up in a bad mood, so this day wasn't the day to be messing with me. Every time Melissa got up from her desk, Cherie would make some kind of snide remark.

"So, Lonnie, still no kids, huh?" she asked one time.

I ignored her. I didn't give a damn about having any kids.

She came at me again. "Well, my John Jr. looks just like his daddy."

I ignored her some more, all the while writing down everything she said. It didn't matter how small or stupid; I was keeping track of the bull. Hell, it didn't even matter that I had already found out that John had left her ass over a year ago. Truth or lies, I was keeping track for my own benefit.

"Anyway, last night while John and I were in bed, I mentioned to him that you weren't looking too well," she said. "I told him you were looking a little old and tired these days."

That was it! "Look, bitch, I don't give two shits about what you and your man—whoever that is—talk about, because we both know that John has *been* gone. If you know what's good for you, you'll stop playing these stupid little high school games with me. And, oh yeah, wasn't it you that I fucked up on your own porch?"

She looked at me dumbfounded. In a city this small, how could she not think that I would find out about her and John being over? And she damn sure didn't have anything to say about that beat down.

She just smirked at me and continued whatever the hell she was working on.

I was steaming mad when I got home that night. I was so hot under the collar, I jumped into the pool as soon as I got to my house. I needed to cool down, relax, and figure out a way to get that fool out of my life for the second time. I wish I knew how to be sneaky and conniving. These qualities would have helped me tremendously, but unfortunately or fortunately, depending on how you looked at it, I never developed the ability to be a manipulating bitch. Straightforward was how I played everything.

By the time I'd finished in the pool and dried off, I had come to the conclusion that straightforward was exactly the way to handle my dilemma. Cherie was a freaking nut case, and eventually, if I played my cards right, that fool would screw herself over. The best thing for me to do was let her be. All I had to do was continue doing what I was supposed to do at work to cover my own ass, in addition to keeping track of her nonsense.

The following Monday, I went to work with a new sense of purpose. I was sure Cherie would screw herself up. I informed each of my unit members who she was. Considering most of them were part of my life two years ago, they all had my back. I wasn't concerned with any of them repeating anything I said to her. These women were my friends, my family away from home. I had also asked that none of them treat her badly on my behalf. I simply suggested that they watch their own backs with that snake.

As I was headed to the ladies' room one day, that witch bumped into me. I wasn't expecting the situation to get physical, but that one incident changed my way of thinking immediately. Keeping a lid on my temper was a done deal. I shoved Cherie into the ladies' room and pinned her up against the wall with my forearm pressing on her throat. I could've choked the life out of her dumb ass.

"What the fuck is your problem? I've already kicked your ass once, you got that dumb-ass man you wanted so badly, and now two years later, you still can't let this bullshit go?"

Cherie struggled beneath me, trying to free herself from my grip. It seemed like she had something to say, then it dawned on me that I should probably let her go if I wanted to hear her response.

I stepped back to give her some space. Hands on hips, tapping my foot impatiently, I waited for her to finish choking and sputtering.

"Well, what the hell is your problem? I mean damn, you won, what the hell else do you want?"

"You know what, Lonnie? I'm not even going to do this with you."

"Not do this with me? Bitch, you've been doing this with me from day one."

"OK, I hate your fuckin' guts! Is that good enough for you?" she yelled.

"No, dumb ass, that's obvious." I exhaled loudly, completely exhausted by it all. "Look, the bottom line is this is all so fucking ridiculous. It should've been a done deal two years ago."

Cherie didn't say anything. She just stood there staring at the floor. I didn't really know what to make of her silence. Hopefully, she was considering finally let this crap go. So I stood and waited until her silence became eerie.

For a brief moment I thought about trying to make amends with her. Maybe then I'd have some peace, but, what she said next blew me away.

"You don't get it, Lonnie, or maybe you're just playing at being stupid."

"What the hell are you talking about?"

Cherie leaned against the wall and crossed her arms over her chest like she planned to stay a while. "You honestly believe that I actually wanted John. Well guess what? I didn't."

What did she just say? I questioned silently.

As if she'd read my mind, she continued. "You heard me right. I never wanted Johnny Rowe."

I pulled it together then because that statement had mad questions running through my mind. "If you never wanted him then, what the hell has all of this shit been about? Who puts that much energy into keeping up the drama over a man they never wanted?"

"It's real simple. I wanted you to hurt as much as you hurt me."

With that statement I was even more confused. "When did I ever hurt you Cherie? I didn't even know you before that mess with John."

"Oh no? So you're trying to tell me that you don't know a guy named Darnell Prescott?"

I just stared at her, searching the recesses of my mind for a Darnell Prescott. I came up empty. "Who the fuck is Darnell Prescott?"

Cherie gave me a look that was pure crazy. "Liar!" she yelled. "You know exactly who I'm talking about!"

"No, really I don't."

Cherie shook her head in disbelief and began pacing the ladies' room like a caged animal. I had been calling her a crazy bitch all along, but what I saw before me really was nuts. All I could do was try to pull her back in the moment with me.

"Cherie, Cherie," I said. "Stay here with me. Tell me who this Darnell Prescott is." I had to take a hold of her arms to stop her from pacing. I held on until she made eye contact with me.

Slowly she seemed to find her way back. She blinked several times as if she were awaking from a long daydream.

"You really don't remember him?" she asked. "You dated him in high school."

"High school? That was twelve years ago," I said, astonished that she thought she even knew me all of those years ago. I was positive I didn't know her back then. She was from Centerville and I was from North Camden. She went to the High and I went to Wilson.

"Damn it, Lonnie, you ripped my life apart back then, and you don't even remember it?"

This conversation was getting more bizarre by the minute. I'd ripped *her* life apart?

"Listen, Cherie, I have no idea what you're talking about, but I'd like to understand. But to be real with you, I'm getting bored with this entire scene. So either clue me in right now or I'm out." Maybe if she realized that she didn't have an audience anymore, she'd get to the point.

"All right then, let me break it down for you."

Damn, damn, damn! Just as she was about to spill her story, a coworker walked in and Cherie clammed up. Fuck that! I grabbed that girl by her arm and escorted her to my desk so I could grab my car keys.

"Lonnie, you better let me go!"

"Hell no! We're going to finish this right now. Let's go to my car."

Asia, who was just coming past my desk, stopped dead in her tracks when noticed me holding on to Cherie.

"What did this bitch do now, Lonnie?"

"Mind your fucking business, Asia!" Cherie said, spitting venom at my girl.

"Bitch, I'll bash your fuckin' skull in!" Asia retaliated.

"OK now, y'all need to keep it down. Asia, we can't get into this right now. Cherie and I are going outside. I'll talk to you when I get back."

"Yeah, OK," Asia said just before she leaned closer to Cherie and said, "You better watch your back."

I stopped Cherie from jumping bad by taking her arm again and walking her to the elevators.

Chapter 15

Once we were in the car, I asked Cherie to continue with what she was trying to tell me. "All right, Cherie, talk to me."

"I'm going to start by saying, I don't believe that you don't remember Darnell."

"Whatever. Just get on with it."

"Me and Darnell were going together back then. That boy was everything to me. Whenever I was with him, I was happy. When I was with him I could get away from the bullshit going on at home. We didn't have a dad at our house, and my mom was always drunk."

I couldn't believe she was telling me, of all people, her personal family business! She stopped to exhale. I was listening intently, trying to figure out where her story was going before she got there.

She continued, "Darnell took me away from all of that. For the first time, I felt free. I thought I was going to have a future worth living. Darnell promised me that he would marry me and take me away from there. He was the first person to show me unconditional love, and he never judged me by my family and home life. He even gave me a promise ring. My whole world revolved around that boy. I loved him more than I thought was possible." As she spoke, I could see Cherie remembering those times. She smiled at those memories. Then her face reflected a mixture of sadness and longing. I felt for her in that moment, although I still had no idea what any of it had to do with me.

"Everything was perfect for about a year," she continued. "Then suddenly, things began to change. It started with him calling less and less. Or we would make plans but he wouldn't show up. His reasons never made any sense, but I held on. I would spend my time trying to figure out what I had done wrong or how to make him happy so we would be close again. He was pulling away from me. Nothing I did seemed to help, so I decided to find out what was going on with him.

"Me and my girls started investigating, and guess what we found out?" Cherie's face changed to rage when she asked that question.

"What?" I asked still baffled.

"You!"

"Me? Where the hell did you find me?"

"We found out from some guy he hung with that every day after school, he was hanging up North."

"So?"

"So, he was going to see some girl."

"Again, so? Who was the girl?"

"It was you. Damn it, Lonnie! Stop playing dumb!"

I giggled a little because she was serious and I still didn't remember any Darnell Prescott.

"I swear, I'm not playing with you. I don't know that guy."

"Come on now Lonnie, are you trying to tell me you never messed with anybody named Darnell?"

"Look girl, I only remember two boys at my school named Darnell, and neither one's last name was Prescott."

"He didn't go to Wilson, he went to the high with me!" she yelled, clearly fed up with my ignorance. I sat there searching my memory again. I started replaying times when I may have had the opportunity to meet people from the high. There weren't many since they were our rivals. We didn't socialize with the enemy.

After a few minutes of searching, it hit me. "Oh my God! Darnell Prescott, kind of short, light skinned dude, pretty hair?"

"Yeah, that's him."

"Wow! I'd forgotten all about that guy. We met at the turkey game my junior year. But wait a minute, Cherie, I only went out with him twice."

"You're a fucking liar, Lonnie!"

Damn, she just keeps yelling at me.

"If you only went out twice, then why was he always hanging up North Camden, and we lived all the way in Centerville? Tell me that!"

This bitch was serious.

"I really don't know, but I do know it wasn't for me. Look, the bottom line is, I didn't know anything about him having a girlfriend the two times I saw him. Anyway, we went to the movies, I figured out that he was gay, and that was that."

"Gay!"

"Yeah, damn it, gay! Who's playing dumb now? And stop yelling at me! Let me tell you something. Cherie, unlike you, I don't go after other women's men. I don't do it now, and I certainly didn't do it then. Even if I was that type, why on earth would I be chasing after a boy who clearly liked guys as much as any girl did? So whatever happened between you and that boy, it didn't have shit to do with me."

"You're full of shit, Lonnie. Darnell was not gay."

"Sure he was. You must've been a front for him. Obviously that was his M.O. at the time. Anyway, how stupid were you not to figure that out?"

"Fuck you!"

"Whatever." I chuckled. "I'm curious. How did you come up with my name anyway? I would think that all of your spying would have led you to another guy for sure. Especially since I wasn't actually dealing with him."

"That was easy; girls always gossip. Anyway, I heard your name one time too many, so I got a copy of y'all's yearbook."

I sat there shaking my head, just dumbfounded at this ridiculous woman. Was she really still trippin' over some stupid guy that didn't even want girls in the first place? Then it all hit me like a ton of bricks.

"You mean to tell me that, you caused the destruction of my relationship because of some stupid-ass high school boy that, until two minutes ago, I didn't even remember?"

"He was mine, damn it! And guess how I found your ass that time?"

"I can't imagine, Cherie. Why don't you just tell me how you found me?" I couldn't believe that I was sitting there participating in that girl's psychosis.

"Eww, wait!" I stopped her. "Did you and the gay boy actually have sex?"

"Yeah, damn it! For the last time he wasn't gay!"

"Fine, whatever you say." I giggled.

"Anyway, I saw you and John at the club one night. I knew you as soon as I spotted you, so I decided that it was finally time to make you pay. I went after your man just like you did mine." She said that shit like she was proud of what she'd done.

"Bitch, are you crazy?" I screamed.

"Crazy ain't got nothing to do with this, and I'll keep causing trouble in your life if I want to." She then gave me this sinister smile and said, "I'm going to get you, Lonnie."

"Not if I get you first. Now get your crazy ass out of my car before I kick you in your fucking throat."

She just laughed and cackled at me like a witch and got out.

Sure, someone else may have been afraid of that little display and denial about the true nature of whatever went on between her and Darnell, but I wasn't. No, I didn't have any experience dealing with real life nuts, but get this: I didn't need any. You see, as far as I was concerned, Cherie was full of shit. She almost pulled me in with that bullshit story. I don't know what purpose it served, but it was obvious she needed to come up with something to justify still fucking with me after all this time.

Maybe she thought that if I was convinced that she was psychotic or something that she could intimidate me. I don't know what it was, but I was going to make damn sure it wasn't going to work.

Chapter 16

True to her word, she started fucking with me and in the silliest way possible. It started with little things happening. One Monday morning I went in to find all of my family photos and knickknacks lying strewn all over my desk. I just stood there looking at the mess, wondering what the hell had happened. Then the tiny light went on. *That fucking Cherie*! I simply put everything back as I'd had it and started my day.

I knew I needed to let the small stuff slide. I wasn't going to let her get a rise out of me. But damn, it was the annoying shit that bugged me the most. I still made note of what she did in my "book of bullshit." If I ignored the stupidity, Cherie would get the message that I refused to play her little games. But of course, this dumb bitch didn't have the intelligence to figure that out on her own.

I called my confidante, Asia, over to my desk to let her know what was going on. Asia came over and sat on the edge of my desk.

"Guess what that silly girl did."

"What did she do now?"

"That fool turned all of my pictures and shit upside down."

"No, she didn't!"

"Of course, she did. That girl ain't got no sense. Anyway, I'm just going to ignore that craziness."

"Good for you. Now tell me what happened with you two yesterday."

"Oh yeah, where did you disappear to? By the time I came back up here, you were gone."

"My mom called. I had to run her to a doctor's appointment, so I just took the rest of the day off."

"Oh, OK." I proceeded to fill Asia in on the conversation I'd had with Cherie. I told her about the hard core grudge she had over some bullshit she'd made up in her head.

"Oh my goodness. That girl really is crazy. Lonnie, you can't let that nutty bitch pull you into any more of her shit."

"I know it. Anyway, I'll do my best to behave, but I can't make any promises. You know how I get when I can't take any more."

"Yes, I know, but please try to hold it together. And if you can't, I got your back." Asia laughed.

"I will. I promise."

No sooner than I'd said those words, Cherie came strolling by. She stopped and looked me and Asia up and down.

Asia tripped on her. "What the fuck are you looking at?"

"I know you not talking to me," Cherie said.

"Yes, the fuck I am. And if you know what's good for you, you'll get your dumb ass away from my desk."

"What?"

"You heard me, bitch. Kick rocks."

Cherie walked off in a huff. She knew not to fuck with Asia.

Asia and I fell out laughing and high-fived one another after Cherie left.

After I went back to my desk, I tried to return to my work, knowing full well that no matter how much I tried to ignore Cherie, I had a temper of my own, and could only take so much.

Every morning that week I came in to find the same situation at my desk. By Friday I decided to tell Logan what Cherie was up to. And just like with Asia, I let Logan know I wasn't going to be dealing with this shit for much longer. Logan said that she would speak to Cherie about my allegations.

I went to back to work as usual, and later that day Logan informed me that she had spoken to Cherie, who denied having anything to do with messing with my things. A normal person would have laid off for a while, but not Cherie. She decided to take another approach to her harassment.

On Monday I was typing some forms to be sent out, and when I went to retrieve my work from the printer, all my shit was gone. Guess who had just walked by the printer a few minutes earlier? I looked around and found my letters in the damn trashcan. I could have killed that witch right there on the spot. That was it for me. Fuck with knickknacks, fine! But don't ever fuck with my work. I took my job seriously, so the worst thing someone could do was try to mess that up.

I sat at my desk, pissed off, but trying to calm down. Since that wasn't working, I decided to take a break and go outside to walk off my anger.

I was sitting in my car still trying to calm down when Malik, who was just getting back from lunch, came by. I rolled down the window as he approached my car.

"Hi, Lonnie. Why are you sitting here alone?"

"I just needed to take a minute to calm down from some bull that's going on. Why don't you get in and sit with me?"

Malik jumped in as soon as the door was unlocked.

"So what's up, Lonnie? What kind of bull are you dealing with?"

"Actually, I'd rather not talk about that. I'd much rather have a distraction from that. So tell me, Malik, what's been going on with you?"

He sat back and got comfortable in his seat. I knew this fool didn't think we were going to be sitting out there all afternoon.

"Not much, really. I've been a little busy with my work these last few weeks. You know I've been out for a couple of weeks, so I had a lot to catch up on."

"Yeah, I knew I hadn't seen you. Is everything all right?" I asked.

"Oh, yeah, just fine. I just needed to handle some personal business, that's all."

"Cool. As long as everything worked out the way you wanted it to, that's all that matters."

Malik and I were cool, but I wasn't about to delve into his personal business. He would share if and when he felt like it. Besides, if I pushed, he might take it the wrong way. I didn't want to deal with that right then.

I missed him coming by and confusing the hell out of me with his hot-and-cold behavior. He kept me guessing, not to mention that this kind of weirdness from him kept me laughing too. I never knew when to take him seriously, but for whatever reason, this worked for me, because I was always comfortable with him. And of course he was real easy to look at too. That always helped.

We sat quietly in the car for a while longer, lost in our own thoughts. Neither of us really wanted to talk about our issues. I suppose we just wanted not to talk together.

It was time to go back inside and face the drama.

Chapter 17

Other things began to get a little weird for me at work after a while. I started to notice that people who I used to be cool with were now acting a little funny with me. Tamika, one of the caseworkers, was the first.

On occasion I would go to her desk to talk and see what was up with her and her dramatic-ass life. Tamika and I had always been good with each other. She was always open and friendly, and ready to laugh with me. However, on this particular day, when I sat down next to her, I noticed she was a bit standoffish.

"Hey, girl. What's up?"

She barely acknowledged my presence.

I just chalked it up to her having a bad morning. "So how are you? I haven't spoken to you in a while. I was just wondering how you've been."

"I'm busy," she said, never looking at me. "I don't have time to socialize right now."

I didn't so much mind what she said as much as I minded the way she'd said it. That girl gave me much attitude. You would have thought I had screwed her man, with all that bass in her voice.

I went right back to my desk, wondering what the hell was wrong with Tamika, or what it was that I could have possibly done to upset her. I hadn't seen her in a few days, so I had to think back to the last time we spoke. I knew for sure that we hadn't had any misunderstandings.

I called Asia's line and let her in on what had just happened.

"What the hell is wrong with her?" she asked.

"I don't know. How has she been acting with you?"

"The same as usual, I guess, but I haven't really seen her too much either."

"Oh well, I don't know what to say about it. I'm just going to stay away from her. I don't need the bullshit with yet another person in this office."

"I know that's right. Whatever it is, she'll get over it."

"True. Let me get back to work. I have a lot of stuff sitting here today. I'll talk to you later." I disconnected our call and tried to focus again.

Even though I didn't care what Tamika's problem was, I didn't like being mistreated for no apparent reason. I thought we were cool enough that if she had a problem with me, she would come to me and speak to me about it, as opposed to acting so damned stank. I wasn't too stressed about it, though. It was just not in my nature to be overly concerned with someone else's shit. Hell, I had my own crap to deal with. I would get to the bottom of this when I felt like it, and no sooner.

My morning went by pretty uneventfully after that episode. That was, until just before lunchtime. I had to take some paperwork over to Tamika for her signature, and the moment I walked up to her desk, that bitch gave me mad attitude and snatched the papers out of my hand. I could not believe it. I nearly slapped the shit out of her.

I didn't even bother to ask her what the hell her problem was. I bent down close to her ear and simply said, "If you ever snatch something from me again, I'm going to fuck you up!" I couldn't have sounded or looked more menacing. The look on Tamika's face let me know I had gotten my point across, and that she would think twice about playing with me again.

It didn't take much for me to cut someone off, and right then and there the minor friendship I had with Miss Tamika Talley was a done deal. Although deep inside I knew Cherie had in some way caused this minor drama, it made no difference to me. I was done. I didn't handle being disrespected well, no matter who it came from.

I was back at my desk when Tamika came by a few minutes later.

"Lonnie, can I speak to you for a moment?" she asked.

"What is it?"

"Look, I just came to apologize for my behavior earlier. I just had a lot on my mind, and I shouldn't have taken it out on you."

"Don't try to play me for stupid. I know damn well you got some bullshit going on with Cherie, and just let me say, I'm not for it. Now we're done. Get away from my desk."

It took all I had not to laugh at the look on her face. She started stuttering like she had something to say, but she couldn't get it out. Dead giveaway that I had hit the nail on the head about her and Cherie.

Thinking Cherie might chill with her shit was a mistake. She was right back at it,; she just used another tactic. Who knows what kind of bullshit she said to Tamika to influence this change in her behavior toward me?

After a moment Tamika gave up and walked away with her tail and her pride tucked between her fat legs. She actually acted shocked by my comments. Please, everybody in this piece knew how I could get, especially her. She'd seen me in action before.

At one point in time, I was laying people out at least once a week, and then I went right back to work as if nothing had happened. I could dismiss silly bitches in a heartbeat. I knew what real friendship was, so there was no need to trip over these fools at work.

I did, however, begin to wonder just how far Cherie's crap would go before it ended. The fact that she and I were working in the same place at all still had me tripping. Not to mention, we now had a niece in common. I mean, damn! Was I living under some kind of crazy drama curse or what?

Another few weeks went by without any more nonsense from Cherie and whoever her cohorts might have been. Maybe my prayers worked.

Chapter 18

Just as October rolled around, I noticed a change in Cherie's demeanor. She began coming in to work looking like a hot mess. She stopped getting her hair done, and was wearing that shit natural, but not in a good way. She would come in with wrinkled or smelly clothes, and on one particular day I noticed she had on run-over shoes. Now how in the hell did a pair of shoes that were practically new a month ago become run-over when she didn't even wear them every day? It was the strangest shit. I mean, this chick seemed to have fallen apart overnight.

Everyone began talking about her. And, of course, there was more speculation than fact. The fools in that place had the girl on her last leg of some fatal disease, or smoking crack in the parking lot on her lunch hour. (She wouldn't have been the first.) It got quite ridiculous real quick. Regardless, it was hard for me to work up much sympathy for her. My hatred might have dissipated, but my dislike of the bitch still remained intact.

After another week or so, I really began to take note of her appearance, and she was looking really bad. I knew she was a tacky woman, but she really was coming across like a street person. To see someone falling apart right before your eyes wasn't something I took pleasure in, no matter how much I didn't like her. I honestly began to feel bad for the girl. I wondered what could have happened in her life to take her to such an ugly place.

Cherie walked by my desk one afternoon, and when I looked up, we made eye contact. What I saw in her eyes pulled on my heartstrings just a little, and I do mean, just a little. I recognized sadness.

My dislike began to subside. Not that I planned to reach out to her in any way, but I didn't feel the desire to punish her any more. It looked as if life itself was taking care of that.

Later on that same day, I went over to Asia's desk to find out if she knew what might be going on with Cherie.

"What's up, girl?" I asked as I took a seat.

"Not much. Same old shit. What's up with you?"

"Absolutely nothing. I saw Cherie earlier and that chick looks pitiful. I know you know something. Why is she falling apart right before our eyes?"

Asia pulled her chair closer to mine and began spilling everything she knew. That girl stayed in the gossip. She usually knew everything that went on in and out of the office. "Girl, I heard she's been messing with this guy that ain't no damn good, and he's taking her ass through it. He supposedly has two baby mommas that both bring mad drama. Other bitches are calling his phone and shit. And I heard he was some petty hustler, not really making loot. Oh, and get this, the reason she's tripping so bad is that this fool is actually in love with the nut. Can you believe her?"

I was shocked. I sat there shaking my head and thinking, *What goes around, comes around.* "Get the fuck outta here!" I said. "That bitch is going through tripping like that over some dude? Please! Well, guess what? Whatever sympathy I may have had for that chick this morning is gone now. She took me through the same shit, and now it's coming back to bite her in the ass. Not only do I have zero sympathy for her, I have no respect for a woman who lets a man pull her down like that. She's walking around here looking cracked out. Ain't no dick that good!"

Asia sat there laughing her head off at my mini tirade. "Lonnie, your ass is crazy."

"Shiiitt! I don't know why. I mean what I say. That's what she gets." I got up and went back to my desk, wondering why I even gave an ounce of concern to that foolish woman.

When I got home later that night there was a message on my voicemail from John saying he had been thinking about me and wondering how I was doing. I couldn't believe it. *What the hell has gotten into him after all this time?*

For whatever reason, I wasn't opposed to hearing from him. Maybe it was just the loneliness taking over, or maybe enough time had passed that I was no longer thinking of him as a weak coward. Or it could've simply been a juvenile way for me to get back at Cherie for her shit. Who the hell knew?

Although he did leave a number, I wasn't going to be the one doing the calling. But I decided that if he called again, I would at least speak to him.

Three days after the first message, John called again. This time he was brave enough to call when he knew I'd be home. Lena was over to have dinner with me. We were in the middle of cooking dinner when the phone rang.

"Hello," I answered.

"Hello, Lonnie. How are you?"

"I'm fine. Just a little surprised to hear from you. It's been a long time."

"That's true. I just called to see how you're doing. You've been popping into my mind a lot lately."

"Is that so?"

"Yes, that's so."

I could hear some amusement in his voice. "Well, in that case, I'm doing just fine, but still wondering why you called."

Now I don't know if Lena had some kind of super Spidy senses or what, but she butted in so fast I couldn't believe it.

"I know that's not that punk-ass John you're talking to."

"Hold on for a minute," I said to him. I placed my hand over the receiver and turned to Lena. "How could you possibly know that?"

"Your voice changes whenever you talk to a man, so that was obvious. Then I asked myself, who could it be because, you ain't seeing nobody. Then that jerk popped into my head."

"Oh, so you didn't actually know it was him?"

"Of course not, dumb-ass little sis. I ain't got no ESP; you just told me."

"Lele, you fuckin' weirdo, shut up, OK?"

She just laughed. "Guess what? I'm not going to say anything else about it. I think you're wiser now and wouldn't dare make the same mistake again."

Whoa! Was that my Lena Devlin talking like a wise, mature and calm woman? I was talking to John and she wasn't spazzin' out? It must have been a full moon.

Lena was right; I was wiser and I was not going to make this easy on him. I hadn't forgotten any of the hell I went through with that man and his baby momma. Not to mention, five days out of the week, I still had to deal with that girl.

"So where were we?" I asked him. "Oh, right. I was asking you why you called."

He cleared his throat. I could feel his hesitation through the phone.

"I guess you could say I couldn't help myself," he said. "Like I said, you were heavy on my mind. The truth is, I never really stopped thinking about you."

I suppose I should have been flattered. I wasn't. I felt absolutely nothing for that man in that moment. "I don't know what you want me to say to that. I could tell you that I've thought about you occasionally, but it doesn't mean anything. I certainly haven't given any thought to calling you. Not that I could, since I have no idea where you've been since your divorce."

He laughed a little. "I know, I know. I've been out of the state for the last year. I just got back to Jersey a couple weeks ago."

I heard through the grapevine that he had left town, but I didn't know where or why. "So where were you? And what were you doing?"

"I was down in Georgia setting up a business system for a new company my boy Jay started. I enjoyed the state so much that I decided to stay for a while."

I tried not to make my next question sound harsh, but I think it came out like that anyway. "So why did you come back?" I knew John was a little taken aback by my question, because he didn't answer immediately.

"I missed home."

I don't know what I expected him to say, but it wasn't that. Maybe I wanted him to say it was because of me. It had been so long since I had been with anyone, my ego probably needed some stroking. I got over that minor ego-downer right quick and promptly changed the subject.

"So what are you up to now?"

"Well, I'm thinking about starting my own business, and I'd like to do that here at home."

"That sounds good to me. What type of business?"

I could hear Lena suck her teeth in the background. As long as she didn't say anything, I'd ignore her.

"Actually, I'm not really sure. I just know that now is the time for me to do something for myself. I feel the need to establish something substantial for my future, and now I'm finally in a position to accomplish this."

"Good luck with that. I hope everything works out for you."

Believe it or not, I actually meant that sincerely. I mean, hell, even though I didn't really want to be bothered with the man, I wished the best for him. I couldn't hold on to a grudge. I tried, but I just couldn't. What would have been the point? We were done. Besides, I once loved him completely, so hatred wouldn't be my way.

Talking to John made me realize that I was not just over him, but also over the pain his actions had caused me. I also realized I was no longer afraid to invest myself in someone else. I had spent the majority of the time since we'd broken up staying away from men most of the time, fearing that there would be no man out there who wouldn't be a selfish asshole. But with time, my fears began to dissipate.

After our conversation, I started to remember how good it was to share my life with someone when things were going well. Although I hadn't decided to take an active approach to getting back out there, I knew at this point that I was at least open to the possibility of being with someone.

With that in mind, I also made the decision to make some changes in other areas of my life. My work had always been important to me. At least, doing my best at whatever I was doing was important. But I had been slacking on my duties and feeling a little uninterested. I made a choice to put more effort into everything in my life. I needed to get out of the rut I was in.

I even decided to take Cherie and any thought of her off my radar. What was in the past would remain in the past as long as she left me the hell alone. I wasn't sure how I was going to accomplish all the changes, but the truth was, I was going to do it, no matter what it took.

The first thing I chose to do with my life was to take an exercise class. I wasn't really into working out, so I felt that I had better find something that would get me excited, or at least hold my interest. I went online and found a pole dancing class. Now that excited me. I figured I could release some built-up sexual frustration by getting in touch with my inner sex kitten, as well as getting a good workout a couple days a week. It was a win-win situation.

Chapter 19

A week after I found the class I had my first session. The place wasn't difficult to find. It was in Center City, Philadelphia, not too far from home. Once I got there, it wasn't exactly what I expected it to be. Actually, I wasn't sure what I expected it to be. The spot was small. There were six poles set up in the center of the room, which looked like a dance studio, and there were about twelve women in the class. My first thought was, *I should have taken one of the private sessions.* I chose to make the best of this new situation, and shortly after we got to work, I found that I was having a good time.

A bunch of women acting a fool together was always a good time. There was no room for modesty, and certainly no room to take oneself seriously. Not to mention, I was working muscles that I didn't even know existed.

It was a great new experience for me, and in the process I made a new friend from North Philly. Tracey was truly hilarious. She had this light about her that was contagious. We bonded almost instantly over that damn pole. I tended to be goofy in certain situations myself, and learning to pole dance was definitely one of those goofy situations. We spent the majority of our time laughing, which made holding on to the pole a bit difficult. We didn't really learn how to do shit that first day, but we had a ball nonetheless.

In between sliding down that damn pole and laughing at the spectacle we were making of ourselves, Tracey and I decided to have lunch together after the class. It was refreshing to have someone so full of life to hang out with.

We decided on Geno's for our meal. While eating our chicken cheese steaks, I learned that Tracey was a paralegal for a firm in Center City. She was childless, had just gotten out of a bad marriage, and was looking to make some changes in her life.

What impressed me the most about her was that, considering the drama she had gone through with her husband, she wasn't bitter about it. I could've taken lessons from her on that subject.

After lunch we decided to keep in touch. I could sense that this would turn out to be a lifelong friendship.

As much as I loved my friends and my sister, they all tended to dwell in negativity a little too much, which was starting to wear on me. I certainly wasn't trying to get rid of them, but I needed to be around more people who tried to remain in a positive place, no matter what the stressors in their lives. I wasn't actively looking to make new friends, but doing so was more in tune with my new attitude about the direction in which I wanted my life to go.

It didn't take long for me to realize that my thoughts about Tracey were correct. She called me a couple of days later just to talk.

As it turned out, we had a lot more in common than we initially realized, especially our troubles with men. It may have seemed to us as if our shit was special, but we both knew that the things we had gone through with the opposite sex were nothing different than what many other women went through. We were on the phone for at least two hours, talking and laughing about the hell that men had put us through.

Tracey had been married to a man who was verbally and mentally abusive. He would take every opportunity to make her feel ugly, useless, and unworthy. He projected all of his insecurities onto her until she was completely demeaned and torn down. In that moment my situation with John and Cherie didn't seem nearly as bad. Not that I could dismiss the pain it caused me, but when a person who vowed to protect a woman's soul could hurt her so deeply in the most disrespectful manner, it couldn't be an easy thing from which to recover.

I asked her, "Tracey, tell me, how did you recover from such a huge betrayal?"

"It wasn't easy by any means. I cried a great deal and did a lot of prayer. And, I must say, prayer is the driving force in my life, and that gets me through everything."

"Wow! You said that with so much joy in voice. Prayer alone got you through something so deep?"

"Yes, indeed. Lonnie, I'm a practicing Buddhist, and because of my practice I've grown stronger, wiser, and more forgiving than I'd ever thought possible."

Tracey's revelation about her religious choice surprised me. "Buddhism, huh? I've heard of it, but I don't know much about that religion. Tell me a little about it, Trace."

"Basically, a coworker introduced me to the practice about ten years ago. And the basic premise of Buddhism is faith in the mystic law. This simply means that everything in the universe is connected, and from the moment one begins chanting *Nam-myoho-renge-kyo*, the universe begins working to move your life in the direction it's meant to go."

"OK, girl. I guess that makes sense. But how did that help you to get over your husband's awful treatment of you?"

"That too is quite simple, honey. The more I prayed on the situation, the more I began to see things clearly. Chanting is like polishing the mirror to your life and your nature. I came to understand that my husband's issues had nothing to do with me, and that staying married to that man wouldn't lead me to the happiness I was searching for. That was solely on me. Lonnie, once you begin to see your life clearly, you cannot ignore the obvious. Therefore, your actions automatically reflect your truths."

Tracey said this with so much joy and peace in her voice, I couldn't doubt the benefits of her chosen form of prayer. "That's deep. So let me get this right. You're saying that chanting helps you take a step outside of yourself? You're not stuck in your own head, and that's how you get to the clarity?"

"Exactly! So many people stay in relationships or situations that have gone bad because they cannot remove themselves from their inner turmoil, which is the main thing that keeps them stuck in the first place."

"Wow! That does make a lot of sense. I really appreciate the perspective."

"You're very welcome, honey."

Although I sometimes still felt the pain of John's betrayal, it wasn't enough to upset me or to even regret having ever gotten involved in the first place. No matter how much I didn't want to be with him anymore, I was no longer in a place where I didn't want to be with anyone. By the time I'd met Tracey, I was looking forward to all the good things life had to offer, and making a new girlfriend seemed like a hell of a good start to me.

Tracey and I soon began to make it a point to have lunch together at least once a week. No matter what was going on at work, or how busy we were, we would meet to eat, laugh, and act a fool. It was during this time that I came to understand why she had become so important to me as a friend. Although she was only a couple of years older than me, she possessed the kind of wisdom you'd get from a mom. She also had this comforting nature that my own mother didn't have. Certainly, I didn't need a replacement for my mom, but since I couldn't spend more time with her, Tracey's friendship gave me some of what I was missing. Lena always had my back, but she definitely was not motherly.

My life finally seemed to be coming together. I had my old friends, I had my new friend, and my crazy sister, and for the time being, Cherie didn't faze me. And, to top it all off, I was headed for a promotion at work—a higher title and more money. Although I couldn't complain about what I was already making, more money meant I could do a lot more for my future, when I would have a family of my own.

Chapter 20

Things in my love life unexpectedly started to turn around one morning when I got to work and found an envelope sitting in my chair. I opened it and was shocked to see that it was a card from Malik. I damn near fell out of my chair. It was a thinking-of-you card. Inside Malik wrote that he was having a hard time keeping me off his mind, and that if I was open to it, he would like to start spending time with me outside of work.

I sat there staring at that card, my mouth hanging open. I didn't know what to think. Although we'd continued to flirt with one another occasionally, it had never gone past that. I had pretty much accepted that this would be the extent of anything between us, and had long since given up trying to figure out why he would come on so strong one minute then back off the next.

Once the shock wore off, I ran to see if Asia was at her desk yet. I was actually shaking, although I couldn't figure out why.

Asia was just sitting down when I got there. "What's up?" she asked.

I slammed the card down on her desk and said, "Read this!"

Asia picked up the card and began reading. Her face registered the same shock mine did when I'd read it. I couldn't help laughing at her expression.

"Call the cops! What the hell?"

"I don't know! Why didn't he just speak with me face to face? What the hell is he up to?"

Asia laughed. "What makes you think he's up to something? Maybe that nigga's finally finished playing and didn't have the balls to tell you to your face."

"He's a grown-ass man, and I know damn well I don't make that fool nervous."

"Yes, you do make him nervous. Look, bitch, this guy is checking for you. Now stop trippin' and go talk to his ass. As far as I'm concerned, as fine as that man is, you'd better go for it."

I couldn't stop smiling. I was definitely excited at the prospect of getting to know Malik on a different level. After all, my decision to go for it with someone had already been made. "You're right," I told Asia. "I'm going to call and invite him to lunch."

"Hell, yeah! Go for it!"

I went back to my desk and tried to focus on my work, which was a wasted effort. I couldn't get my thoughts together. *Forget this,* I thought. I picked up the phone and called Malik, who answered almost immediately.

"Hi, Malik. This is Lonnie."

"Hi, Lonnie. How are you?"

I could hear the smile in his voice. My pulse began to race. This man was actually happy to hear from me. "I'm fine, Malik. I was just calling to let you know that I received your card."

"Oh, OK. So tell me, do you think you'd be interested in the two of us getting to know one another better?"

"I'm not sure. I mean, I don't really know what to make of your behavior."

"What do you mean, Lonnie?"

"Well, one minute you come on strong, and the next minute you back off. Now you come at me like getting closer means so much to you. How do you expect me to understand where you're coming from, when your behavior is so erratic? For me, this card and everything it suggests comes from out left field."

For a moment he didn't speak at all. I was beginning to wonder if he was trying to come up with some BS to sell me. He spoke up after what seemed like an eternity.

"I know my behavior has been a little strange. There's a reason for that, and I'd like the opportunity to explain it all to you."

"OK, Malik. Why don't we go out to lunch together? This way we can have some privacy and not have to deal with these nosy-ass people around this office. I'd like to clear the air and find out where you're really coming from."

"That sounds perfect."

We agreed to do lunch at one o'clock. With that done, I tried again to get some work done, but for the life of me, I couldn't calm down. I spent the entire morning spinning my wheels, trying to figure out what was truly on Malik's mind, as well as his explanation for his curious actions.

At about twelve fifty-five Malik called my desk and asked if I was ready to go. He said he would get his car and meet me in front of the building. I gathered my things and went down to meet him. We chose to go to The Pub.

Once we were on the road, I asked him, "What's up? What's all this about?"

"Let me just come right out and tell you, I'm really feeling you."

Again, I was blown away by this admission. His statement, body language, and facial expression were all so sincere and intense, it really threw me off.

"Malik, where's all of this coming from?"

"Lonnie, the truth is, I was attracted to you the first time I saw you. When we started talking and getting to know one another a little better, I became even more attracted to you."

"OK, so, explain why you kept turning it on, then turning it off."

Just then, we pulled into the restaurant parking lot.

"Why don't we just go in and get settled at our table? I'll tell you everything then."

Shortly after we were seated and had placed our orders, Malik said, "Lonnie, not too many people in our office know this, but when I first came to work at the agency, I was married. Actually, up until a few months ago, I was still married."

Although I wasn't expecting to hear that, I wasn't all that surprised either. It did explain some of his behavior. At least it explained why he would back off so suddenly, especially during those times when I would give him a positive response. I nodded and allowed him to continue talking.

"My marriage was already a mess when I came to work here, and when I started to get to know you, I couldn't stop myself from wanting more. That's the reason I sometimes went beyond flirting. Even though I wanted you to respond to me, I never really thought you would. On those occasions when you did let me know you were interested, the reality of my situation would hit me. No matter how bad things were at home, I couldn't be disloyal to my marriage vows. My interest in you goes beyond just physical attraction. I knew there was no way to pursue an emotional relationship with a woman while I still had a wife at home."

Whoa! My head was in orbit now. I knew we were really cool and had a good vibe going between us, but this guy was sitting there talking about emotional involvement, and he was serious.

Malik Reese was hot as hell! He was sexy, funny, and intelligent. And he was a beautiful chocolate brown complexion. I was crazy about chocolate men—the darker, the better. Hell, yeah! I was ready to get closer to this one.

Malik was looking at me with anticipation, almost as if he was expecting me to say something negative, or afraid that I wasn't feeling anything he was saying to me. "Are you all right?"

"Yes. I'm just a bit stunned by all of this."

"Why is that? I know I've gone back and forth, but I thought you could tell I was feeling you in this way."

"Maybe a little, but to be honest, I didn't think too much about it either way. For the last few years I've been focused on myself. Actually, I should say that I've been oblivious to men. That would be more accurate."

He simply nodded.

"Malik, I'm truly flattered by what you've said. I'm also impressed by the sincerity with which you've expressed yourself."

He smiled that smile again. "Does this mean you might be interested in pursuing a relationship with me?"

For one brief moment I thought about trying to play it cool, but what would have been the point of that? This man was sitting there offering me the very thing I wanted in my life. It didn't matter that it came from an unexpected source. The chance to get to know a man romantically again after all this time was exactly what I wanted.

I waited for the waitress to set our food down. "One question, Malik. You said your marriage was a mess, and now you're already divorced. What was there to be loyal to?"

"That's a fair question. Even though the marriage was over, I let her stay until she could find a place."

"Wait. Why did she have to be the one to move out?"

"Well, it's quite simple. The house was mine before I met her. And the reason I remained loyal to the vows was because of my moms and pops. For most of my life, I didn't have my dad, because of his cheating. When Moms found out, she put him out. I know shit happens, but once he was out of the house, he never looked back. So, I guess, because of the way things had gone down with them, I wanted to avoid complications as much as possible. Getting involved with someone else while she was still around just would've started some shit."

"Understood. But damn, that's messed up what your dad did to y'all."

"Yeah, but we've worked it out. All has been forgiven for the most part. Now, Miss Lonnie, tell me, are you interested or not?"

"I am interested. The only apprehension I feel is about getting involved with someone I work with. I don't know if you do, but I can see all of the ways in which this could become problematic for us. We work with some nosy-ass people."

He laughed. "You sure are right about that. Honestly, though, I hadn't really given that much thought. I guess we should keep our business to ourselves as much as possible, but I certainly won't be changing my mind about getting closer to you."

This guy sure as hell knew how to turn it on. My only thought was to go for it.

"All right. I agree we should keep this just between the two of us. My only question is, What do we do now?"

"I suppose we should start with a first date, maybe go out to dinner or a movie," he suggested.

Although I had asked, it felt as if Malik was moving a bit too quickly for me. I had no explanation for this feeling. He wasn't a stranger. I was game to get involved with this man, and if I wanted to label it, we were already technically on a lunch date. I must say that I did have a tendency to start tripping in situations like this. I was willing and unwilling at the same time. There was something holding me back. What it could have been, I don't know. I was truly interested and excited about the prospect of being with Malik, but for whatever reason, when he mentioned an actual date, my nerves took over big time. Fear actually had a grip on my soul.

Malik must have noticed my hesitation. "Maybe we shouldn't rush this. It might be better for both of us if we go slowly. Besides, I'm newly single, and I am coming on a little strong, asking for so much so fast."

"I agree. We're good at being friendly. Maybe we should concentrate on becoming friends. If we both want this to go further, I think we'd have a better chance at making it work if we build a foundation based on friendship first."

Malik agreed, and in spite of my apprehension, I was determined to release my fears and at least move forward with a first date. I figured a movie would be appropriate for friends. We were already comfortable enough with one another not to feel any pressure to converse. We certainly would be at ease sitting through a movie together in silence.

Just as our dessert was being placed in front of us, I said, "So, OK, Malik, tell me what it is you like about me."

"Well, the first thing I noticed was how fuckin' hot you were with the short twists in your hair."

"You men are so visual. I mean, damn, can't you all be attracted to more substantial qualities?"

"Get real, Lonnie. How the hell is a nigga supposed to know if y'all have substantial qualities when we first see you? Think about that."

I laughed. "All right, all right, smart ass. That makes sense. Keep talking."

"Anyway, we do become attracted to other things later on, after we get to know y'all better. But seriously, I really started to check you out more when you cut your hair and went natural."

While I was sitting there listening to Malik talk, I noticed for the first time that he had this intense edginess. That shit turned me on to him a little more.

"OK, Malik, let me tell you what I like about you."

"Spill it."

"First of all, I like the way you scrunch up your forehead when you're in deep thought. Actually, you look like you're pissed when you do that. I remember the first time I saw you do that. I had asked you a question about a case, and you gave me that look. For a second, I thought you wanted to kick my ass!"

Malik started laughing. "You have no idea how many people I've scared with that look. I can't help it, though. I must have been born with the furrowed brow. So what else did you like?"

"All right. I don't know if you've noticed it, but whenever you get frustrated, you rub both of your hands over your head from front to back. I think those little habits are endearing. Oh yeah, and one more thing, and this is the most important. I like your conversation. You always have something significant to say, as opposed to just talking for the hell of it." I let out a long breath. "That's it." I leaned back in my chair.

Malik just sat there staring at me with his honey-colored eyes. He stared like he could see right through me. I half-expected to become unnerved by that stare the longer it went on, but instead, it had my mind drifting off to places it didn't need to be going. My skin began to tingle a little bit while I waited for him to speak.

Luckily for me, the waitress came to ask if we were ready for our check before I could say something I shouldn't say because of the heat I was experiencing. While Malik gave his attention to the waitress, I took that moment to pull myself back.

"All right now, Malik, tell me what else you like about me."

"Damn, woman! Fishing for compliments, huh? I didn't think that was your style."

"Listen, smart ass. I gave you several things. Now you better come up with something more significant than you like my new hairstyle."

He sat there for a second with that mischievous grin on his face. Then he reached across the table, took my hand in his, and leaned in real close like he had a secret to tell. "Let me keep it real with you, Lonnie. I liked our friendship from the minute it developed. But everything about you makes my dick hard."

As soon as he said that, my panties got wet. "Here you go with the dirty-ass mind." "I laughed.

"Let me finish, woman. The way your eyes have that twinkly thing when you laugh gets me hot. That juicy, squeezable ass makes me want to grab hold and never let go of it. Oh, and I just want to throw those long-ass legs up over my shoulders. That's real. Now, as far as any other attraction goes, you're funny, turn-on. You're hella strong, turn-on. And intelligence has always been the biggest turn-on for me. Is that enough for you?"

Hell yeah. That was good enough for me! I was going to have one hell of a time not rushing into bed with this one.

Chapter 21

Malik and I agreed to have our first date that upcoming Friday. By Thursday I was more nervous than I'd ever been about anything in my life. I tried to call Lena, but she didn't answer. It was cool because I needed to call Sandy and let her know what was going on in my world. I thought about calling Tracey to tell her, especially since we hadn't spoken in about a week, but today I wanted to discuss my nerves and fears with someone who'd known me longer. I figured that because of our history, Sandy might have a little more insight into what was bothering me.

As soon as I got home from work, I headed straight for the telephone. I dialed Sandy's number, and thank goodness, she picked up right away.

"Hey, Sandy. What's up?"

"Not much, *mami*. I'm just sitting here relaxing and trying to decide what to have for dinner. What's up with you, girl?"

"I have something I need to discuss with you. Do you have time to talk?"

"Sure I do. What's up?"

"Now, I know I told you about my friend at work, Malik, right?"

"Yeah, he's the hot *papi chulo* that you're always laughing with."

"Yup, that's him. Well, earlier this week he left a card on my chair telling me about how much he likes me and wants to get to know me better. Actually, he said he wants to start a relationship with me."

Sandy gasped and then started laughing. "That's great, *mami*! Did you even have a clue that he was feeling you like that?"

"Hell, no! I mean, I told you he would flirt sometimes or come on strong, but then he would change his tune, so I had no idea. We went to lunch the other day, and he explained that his behavior was erratic because he was married up until a few months ago."

"Married? *¡Ay Dios mío!* These damn men are something else. OK, but then that does makes sense. He was feeling you and couldn't really do anything about it, even if he wanted to. So tell me, how do you feel about him?"

"Girl, that's my problem. I'm feeling Malik a lot, and you know I've made the decision that it's time for me to get back in the game of romance. But now that we've agreed to start seeing one another, I'm terrified. The worst thing about my fear is that I have no idea where it comes from."

I sat back, kicked off my shoes, and waited for Sandy to lay something deep on me. I was hoping for some of that girlfriend wisdom.

"What the hell is your problem, *mami*?"

I couldn't help but laugh at Sandy's simple ass. "Fool! That's why I'm calling you. I don't know what the hell my problem is. Help!"

"*¡Ay Dios mío, mami!* I don't know what you're so afraid of. I think you should stop tripping. Go for it and just enjoy it while it lasts."

Enjoy it while it lasts. Something about that while-it-lasts comment set me on edge. It only served to intensify my anxiety about dating Malik. I realized in that moment that talking to Sandy was no help.

In fact, she was making me more anxious. Her attitude toward these situations was always, "just go for it." But I tended to be a little more cautious with men, and I had to pay attention to my feelings. There was a reason I was going through this crap, and I needed to understand it if I was going to be able to get closer to Malik.

"All right, San, I'll do my best to stop tripping, but for now I really have to get off this phone. I have a lot of shit to do. I'll talk to you later."

"OK, *mami*, but if you need to talk some more, just give me a call."

With that comment, I ended the connection and stared at the phone like it had lost its mind. My girl wasn't any help at all, and believe me, she thought she was. Of that I was sure. Obviously I was wrong about history facilitating insight. Sandy didn't have a clue. I loved her, but her knowing me for so long didn't mean she could give me insight into myself if she didn't have any damn sense in the first place. I had momentarily forgotten that minor detail about my girl. Although she didn't help, she sure did put a smile on my face. Sandy just being Sandy usually did that.

Feeling somewhat more relaxed, I grabbed the mail and went upstairs to change my clothes. As soon as I got to my room, the phone rang. If it was Sandy calling back, I wasn't going to answer. I couldn't talk to that nut any more this evening.

"Hey, Tracey. What's up?"

"Not much. I was wondering if you'd like to go out to dinner with me tonight."

I didn't hesitate for a moment. I still needed someone to talk to, and getting out for an evening sounded good to me. "That sounds good. What time do you want to go?"

"How does seven sound?"

"Perfect! I need a little time to unwind. Where did you have in mind? And should I meet you there?"

After Tracey and I decided on a restaurant, I took a quick shower and lay down. I needed to relax. Tripping over my date with Malik was actually wearing my ass out.

I lounged around for a short while then dressed and left to meet Tracey in Center City. I arrived a few minutes after she did. One of the things I liked most about Tracey was that she greeted everyone with a big smile. This was not something that I was used to. It seemed as if no one else in the world mattered when she directed that smile toward me. I'd always wanted to have the ability to make everyone I came in contact with feel as if they were special, and this woman did just that.

As I sat down, I noticed Tracey staring at me with an odd expression on her face. Before I could say a word, she jumped right in. "What's up, Lonnie? You don't look too happy. There's a bit of sadness behind your eyes that I noticed the moment you walked into this place."

I was dumbfounded. I didn't feel sad, but it blew my mind that Tracey could read me so well, especially since I didn't think I was putting anything out there.

"What do you mean, I look sad? I'm not sad at all. I do have some things on my mind, but it's more confusion than anything else."

"OK, maybe sad wasn't the right word, but I'm telling you, I can tell when you're not quite yourself. You carry it in your eyes."

"Tracey, how is that even possible? We haven't known each other that long."

"I know, but when we met, you were being your true self—no pretenses, no putting on of any kind. Maybe, because it was just a bunch of women in the class, and we were all so comfortable with exactly who we were in that setting. I saw the good and fun nature you have from day one. That's why I was drawn to you."

It was a damn shame. This girl knew me better than I knew myself. Or she at least saw things in me that I had forgotten existed. I'd spent most of the last few years on auto pilot, not really living much at all, and not really noticing that some parts of me were shut down.

"Thanks, Tracey. You've just reminded me of the Lonnie I had forgotten about. I haven't necessarily been unhappy, just a bit off. Actually, if I remember correctly, the day we met I did feel more like myself than I had in a long time. It's amazing how I hadn't even noticed the difference in me since that situation with John. In many areas of my life, I was just going through the motions." I took a deep breath. "OK, so you know I've been aware enough to want to make some changes. Well, there's been a new development with Malik from work."

"What kind of new development?"

I filled Tracey in on the events of the week and our impending first date. That crazy woman squealed so loudly, everyone in the restaurant looked our way. That outburst surprised me a little because Sandy was always composed and proper out in public.

"Girl, calm your simple ass down."

She laughed. "OK, OK, I'm fine now."

"Good. May I finish what I was saying?"

Tracey nodded, giving me her full attention.

"Our first date is tomorrow, and I'm scared as hell to go out with him."

"Didn't you tell me you were attracted to this man?"

"Yes. That's why I'm so confused. Why would I be terrified of a simple movie date with someone I want to get closer to? I mean, it's just a movie, and I want to turn tail and run."

Tracey set down her water glass and smiled at me like I was some kind of nut case. Before she could say anything, the waitress came to take our orders. We both decided on fish and fries.

With that done, Tracey began to break me down to me. "Lonnie, it's only natural that after all of the time you've spent alone, you would be a little nervous about dating someone. I'm sure that some of your anxiety probably has a lot to do with all the crap you went through with John. It took me a few years to start dating again after the things I went through with my ex husband, and when I did, I found it hard to trust any man. That situation had me almost hating men, and I know for sure I hated that one. Heck, if I saw that man lying in the middle of the street on fire, I wouldn't urinate on his behind to put him out."

I burst out laughing in the middle of the restaurant. I could tell this woman meant that shit from the bottom of her heart. Tracey never used curse words, but she sure could get her anger across without them.

"Now, Tracey, that was harsh. I thought you had forgiven him."

"I did. I was still very angry about it back then."

"Oh, OK." I was still laughing.

"Lonnie, would you stop that darn laughing? I'm not finished. Now it's very difficult to put yourself out there and be vulnerable after you've been hurt so deeply. OK, now I'm finished."

I laughed some more before I got serious again.

"Girl, I have to say that I hadn't even thought about it that way. It never occurred to me that my past issues with John were in the way. I mean, I was so excited about the prospect of being with Malik, it didn't make sense that I would be suffering from fear."

"It seems to me that the only reason you couldn't see it for what it was is because you're not on the outside of the situation. You're living it, so you can't remove yourself from it and look at things objectively."

I was so grateful at that moment to have Tracey as a friend. It all seemed so simple now. Her objectivity was exactly what I needed.

By the end of dinner, I was feeling a lot more relaxed and at peace about my upcoming date with Malik. Maybe if I was lucky, this thing with him could turn out to be something wonderful. It was about damn time. I deserved some happiness in my life.

Chapter 22

Although my conversation with Tracey did help me to see things a little clearer, by the time I arrived back home, my anxiety had returned tenfold. I knew my mom was the only one who could get me closer to releasing the craziness going on inside me, and a visit with my parents was long overdue. Unfortunately, I didn't have time for that, because the two people who meant the most to me in the world were retired and living out of state. Nevertheless, I needed my mother's guidance and my father's comfort, so a phone call had to suffice.

Macey and Lamont Devlin have always been the kind of parents that all children should be blessed with. My father was a sanitation worker who worked hard every day of his life to provide for his family, and he never had a harsh word for anyone, especially his family. He was the provider, our hero, and the giver of comfort.

My mom, on the other hand, was a piece of work. Now, don't get me wrong. My siblings and I were now, and had always been, crazy about that woman. She was a nut in the best possible way. She was loud, funny, and straightforward—never one to pull punches or spare feelings, no matter what the situation. No doubt, a lot of her had rubbed off on Tank and Lena.

I'll never forget her advice after the first time a boy broke my heart. I was eleven years old and madly in love with Timothy Little. Every day he would walk me home from school and hold my hand. After two weeks together, my every thought was of Timmy. But by the end of week four, that boy shattered my eleven-year-old heart when he walked into the lunchroom hand-in-hand with Kelly Young, my worst enemy.

I couldn't bear to sit in the lunchroom and watch them together, so I ran and cried the entire three blocks it took me to get home. Fortunately for me, my mom was home from work that day. I hurled myself in the front door and right into her, almost knocking her over. She must have thought the police were after me, the way I came rushing through the door.

"My God, Lonnie! What's wrong? What happened?"

I couldn't speak. Tears flowing and snot running, I was lost in pre-teen hell.

My mom slid herself into the chair with me and put her arms around me. She rocked and consoled me until I had at least stopped crying.

Finally I told her what Timmy had done.

She said, "Girl, dry your eyes and forget about that dumb-ass boy."

Although I knew my mom kept it funky—like I said, my father was the comforter—hearing the harshness in her voice shook me. Couldn't she see I was distraught? My world was coming to an end.

"Lonnie, you're eleven years old. That boy is not the last boy you'll love in this lifetime. Besides, he's a little bum any damn way. He ain't shit, won't be shit, and you don't need him. Now go wash your face and take your ass back to school."

Knowing I wasn't going to get any sympathy from my mom, I did as I was told and went upstairs to wash my face. From that moment on, I knew that if I was looking for sympathy, my mom wasn't the one to go to. But if I was looking for the truth, point-blank, Macey definitely was the one.

Right now, I needed the truth, I needed to be strong, and I needed to get over my fears, so I knew a call to my mom was necessary. I hadn't spoken with my parents in a couple of weeks, and I was missing them like crazy.

As soon as I got settled in my house, I picked up the phone and dialed their number. I was so happy when I heard my mom's voice on the other end of the line.

"Hi, Mommy. How are you?"

"Hey, baby girl! I'm good. How are you?"

"Missing you and Daddy. Where's he at anyway?"

"That father of yours is out running the streets with that old fool, Bernie. You know this is their bowling night."

"Oh, yeah. I forgot. So everything's OK with you and Dad? You guys don't need anything, do you?"

"No, not a thing. We're fine, but I sure do appreciate you asking."

"No problem."

I figured, *Why beat around the bush?* Small talk wasn't my purpose tonight. I might as well get right to the point. I was sure my mother would appreciate that. "So, OK, Mommy, here's the thing. I've been trippin' about this guy I know at work. His name is Malik. He's hot as hell, he's smart, and we laugh a lot. Actually, I would say he's a friend. The problem is, he wants us to get closer, so he asked me out on a date. Well, let me correct myself. That's not the problem. The problem is that I'm terrified."

"Girl, take a breath!"

"Oh, sorry. I was just trying to get it all out. Mommy, I don't know what's wrong with me. Malik is someone I really want to get closer to, but ever since he asked me out, I've been afraid to go for it."

"Lonnie, you went through a lot with that sorry-ass John. It's no wonder you're apprehensive about possibly opening your heart to another man."

"That's exactly what Tracey said to me."

"Oh, yeah? How's she's doing? And has she met your sister yet? Maybe some of her ways will rub off on that girl."

"She's good, but Mommy, this is about me now, not her or your other daughter. Besides, Lele's just fine as she is." I always felt the need to defend my sister against my mother's opinions of her behavior. She was too harsh considering she'd created that monster. I think my mom was bothered because Lena was so very much like her. She reminded her of things she didn't like about herself.

"OK child, this is about you. Anyway, I'm still glad you have a new friend, and from what you've told me, she sounds like a good person to have around."

"She really is, Mommy. So, anyway, back to me. I understand why I'm feeling this way. I need to know how to make it stop."

My mother took a deep breath as if she was losing patience with me. "You know, Lonnie, sometimes you can really be a pain in the ass. Stop trippin', as the saying goes."

I had to laugh. My mom had never been corny, but every time she spoke to me like my friends did, it sounded funny as hell. She could curse you out like a sailor, but slang wasn't her thing. I didn't think so.

"Ok, no more trippin'. But, for real, what do I do?"

"The only thing you can do is date the man. You feel what you feel about him and about dating him. If you focus on enjoying him, with time, you'll feel more comfortable with getting closer to him."

I did my best to absorb what my mom was saying. She really was right, after all. My apprehension most definitely was about John and the situation with Cherie, who I still had to face every day. I decided

I would throw caution to the wind, and would do my best to relieve myself of this fear.

"You're right, Mommy. I'm going to try. Thanks for that."

"You're welcome, Lonnelle."

"So, where's Tank? I want to talk to him."

"He took Shakita to one of those kiddy restaurants for dinner. I can't believe he has that child out this late."

"So Mom, really, what's she like?"

"Well to tell you the truth, she's a great little girl. She's kind of quiet, but she's well behaved and very bright." My mom laughed a little and said, "I have to say, though, I didn't know what to expect considering the child has your wild-ass brother and that simple woman for parents."

I had to laugh a little about that myself. Maybe the child had dodged a big old crazy bullet. "That's so true. Tank as a father is funny. He sure isn't anything like Daddy, is he?'

"No, he is not! Actually, you are the only one who inherited your dad's kind heart. Who knows, if my two nuts hadn't teased and tortured you so much, you might not have that temper of yours."

"Maybe, but we'll never know. Besides, I'm not that bad anymore anyway."

"Whatever you say, Lonnelle."

"Anyway, tell me what Tank is like as a father."

"You may find this hard to believe, but he's actually pretty good with her. I know he's as crazy about her as your dad and I are. She is a joy to have around. That's half the battle right there. Just because he was always rough doesn't mean your dad and I didn't try to set an example. I think some things actually sank in that boy's head."

"Wow, impressive. All right, Mommy, I have to go now, but tell T I said I'll call him."

"Take care, sweetie, and remember: go get that man."

After I finished speaking with my mother, it occurred to me that maybe I should try to make peace with Cherie for the sake of our shared niece, who was obviously becoming a true member of the family. She hadn't been fucking with me, so maybe. In the meantime, trying to let go and get closer to Malik was going to be my focus.

Chapter 23

Two seconds after I put my head to the pillow that night, my phone rang. I was pleasantly surprised to hear Malik on the line.

"Lonnie, are you in bed yet?" he asked.

"Yes, but I'm not asleep yet. I just laid down a second ago. What's up?"

"Nothing. I just felt this strong need to say good night to you. I hope that's OK with you."

"Sure, it is. I think it's very sweet that you were thinking about me."

"Woman, I think about you a lot. That's just how it is."

"I didn't know that, but I'm impressed that you could be straight and tell me that. Most men would have kept that sort of thing to themselves. You know how y'all always be trying to play hard." I laughed.

"I know, I know, but check this. I'm not your typical man. I believe in keeping it funky at all times. As far as I'm concerned, this eliminates the nonsense and leaves little room for misunderstandings."

Is this brotha for real? I wondered.

It was rare to find a man in this world not afraid to express exactly what he felt, even if it was something small like the fact that he was thinking about me. For most guys, telling a woman something like that was a sign of weakness. If only those fools knew how much women loved for guys to share. Men and women would get along a lot better if men had the courage to express their emotional selves. Women would certainly be more impressed and have more respect for men.

"Malik, I must say, I like that way of thinking. It matters very much to me that you're a man who can allow himself to feel, and that you're one who can share that with me."

"Just realize that, in being open with you, I'm not trying hard to impress you. I just want you to know who I am."

"I understand, and I appreciate that. Anyway, Malik, I'm getting sleepy, but before I let you go, I want to tell you that I'm looking forward to our date tomorrow."

"Me too, precious lady. Rest well, and I'll see you at work tomorrow."

"You do the same. Good night, Malik."

"Wait, Lonnie. One more thing before you hang up."

"What's that?"

"Do you want to have phone sex?"

I busted out laughing. "Man, get off the damn phone."

"Good night, precious lady." He laughed.

I broke the connection first and then rolled over with the biggest, goofiest grin on my face. First of all, he had called me when I least expected it, and I loved that shit. Secondly, I could seriously get used to a man that fine calling me *precious* anything on the regular. Plus, like always, he made me laugh.

The next day I woke up with a new attitude about dating Malik. I felt like a kid with a new toy. The same smile I took to sleep was the same one I woke up with and carried through my morning routine. I couldn't wait to get to work just so I could look at him. I really wanted to be in his presence. I had no true explanation as to why I flipped my feelings about him so drastically, considering only yesterday I was still freaking out about dating him at all. The only thing I could come up with was that something about his tone and the manner in which he spoke to me last night touched something inside me. Some part of me needed something special, and although I couldn't put my finger on exactly what that special thing was, Malik at least put a fingernail on it.

The minute I got to my desk, Malik stepped up behind me. "Good morning, Lonnie. How did you sleep?"

"I slept very well, and you?"

"I slept OK. It would've been better if you had phone sex with me."

I punched him in the arm. "I'ma knock you out!"

"But, for real, though . . . I had the most beautiful dream."

"Oh, really? What was that dream about?" I asked, a stupid grin on my face.

"A precious lady named Lonnie."

It better not have been a damn sex dream, I thought. *We won't be getting that familiar too soon.*

"She had the loveliest brown eyes and the sweetest smile."

That was more like it. It was good for him that he went in the direction he did with his dream talk, because I was prepared to shut him down.

I stayed in the moment with him. "Did she now? Is there more about this precious lady named Lonnie?"

"Nope, that's it. She smiled at me, went on about her business, and then I woke up." Malik stood there with this stupid-ass grin on his face, trying not to laugh.

I slapped him on the arm. "Very funny, Malik. Don't be in here teasing me, boy."

"I'm sorry. Just messing with you, but, for real, after I spoke to you, I had the most peaceful sleep. It's been a while since I had some stress-free slumber."

"Really? Why is that?"

"My divorce and all of the drama with my ex was causing a lot of stress in my life, so my nights were pretty restless."

"Oh, that makes sense. You know, sometimes I forget about you going through a divorce, especially since I didn't even know you were married until it was over."

Malik had this sheepish look on his face after that comment. I didn't mean anything by it. It was simply the truth.

"I know that. Besides, all that matters now is that it's over and I have no regrets about it. So tell me, precious, are you ready for our date tonight?"

"Yes, I am, but I thought we agreed to keep our business to ourselves around here. If you don't learn how to whisper, we shouldn't have these discussions in the office."

Fortunately, no one was around to hear our conversation, and Malik agreed again to keep a low profile.

My day went by uneventfully. Work was light, but time went by quickly. I actually spent more time thinking about Malik than anything else. I was really looking forward to going out with him. My change of heart was blowing my mind.

The only negative about our situation would be trying to keep Asia quiet. When it came to men, she and I always shared what was going on, and since she had been in on all of this from the beginning, I couldn't keep it from her. But she had a tendency to run off at the mouth, and although she meant no harm, that girl would accidentally tell your business before she realized she'd done it. I had to make sure she understood how important it was for her to keep her mouth shut. If Malik and I were going to have a fighting chance at actually building a strong relationship, we needed to start with just us. No outside interference was needed.

Malik and I both wanted our thing to begin and remain in peace. We both knew from witnessing other workplace relationships that a work family could cause the most problems for a couple. Admittedly, there were those who would be supportive and root for us every step of the way, but sadly, there would always be haters, with a capital *H*! And we all knew those bitches—male and female—would try to throw salt every chance they got.

Chapter 24

I went straight home from work to get ready for my evening with Malik. I took special care in preparing myself. I wanted this man to know that he was going out with a woman who knew how to present herself to a man. He would be proud to have me on his arm.

I grabbed my favorite pair of jeans, which hugged me in all the right places. Couple those with a royal blue halter-top that clung perfectly to my body, and the highest, skinniest heels I had, I was looking hot. Yes, Malik would be pleased.

We agreed on seven o'clock, and Malik did not disappoint. He was ringing my doorbell at exactly seven. When I heard that bell, my nerves went into overdrive, but the moment I opened the door and saw him standing there just as fine as he wanted to be, I relaxed. Something in his facial expression told me all was well. This was the same man who was already my friend. With him I would be safe.

I smiled. "Come on in. You're right on time. I just need another minute and I'll be ready."

Malik followed me into the living room. "Lonnie, precious lady, you look absolutely lovely this evening. You know what? Fuck that, you look hot!"

All I could do was blush. I was afraid to turn around and face the man for fear that he would see that he was getting to me. I just kept walking toward the closet to grab my wrap and said, "Thank you," over my shoulder.

Malik took the lead and made the plans for our date. We went to dinner at a nice Italian restaurant in Cherry Hill. I was pleasantly surprised, because I thought we were just doing a movie, and Italian food just happened to be my favorite.

After we were seated, I asked him about it.

"Malik, how did you know Italian is my favorite food? Did I tell you that already?"

"No, you didn't. It just so happens that it's my favorite as well."

I smiled and took a sip of my water while he just sat there with this Cheshire grin on his face, watching my every move. I must admit, I was a little unnerved by this attention, but certainly not enough to upset me. I guess I could say I was feeling like a young girl on her first date.

"OK, Malik, why are you grinning so hard at me?" I finally asked.

"I'm just happy to be here with you. I know you probably think I'm moving kind of fast, but the truth is, I've been feeling you for a while now, and I'm grateful to have this opportunity to get to know you better."

"I am extremely flattered, but you make it sound like I'm something you find unattainable. I'm just a woman with faults and flaws just like anyone else."

He continued to smile at me. "Woman, I'm not trying to put you up on a pedestal or make you live up to some expectation that is impossible for a human being to reach. I simply like what I see, and I like who you are. I've noticed your strength of character, and I've also noticed your joyful nature. Do you realize that you smile and laugh more than anyone else in that office?"

"No, I hadn't realized that. Are you for real? I do that? The strange thing is, I've always thought that I was putting my attitude on display. I've never been able to hide my feelings, and with some of the things I've gone through, especially with Cherie, I would've bet my last dime that the entire office could see my ugliness."

Malik gave me a puzzled look. "What's been going on with you and Cherie?"

I told him it was a long story, but he was willing to listen to it all, so I told him everything. By the time I'd finished speaking, our dessert was being served.

Malik sat back in his chair and stared at me for what seemed like an hour. "Wow, babe! I had no idea you were going through anything with her. So she's a real bitch, huh?"

"Yeah, pretty much. But actually she hasn't bothered me in a while. I think that maybe she's had enough of the drama."

"I sure hope so. Damn! I know it must have fucked you up big time to have your ex's baby momma turn back up in your world as a coworker."

"It sure did. I mean, of all the tests to have to deal with in this life, that's one I could have done without."

"No shit! So how is it with her there now? I mean, I haven't noticed anything between you two."

"That's because you sit on another floor. For now the game-playing has stopped, which is odd because not too long ago she was determined to make my life a living hell. But there are times when we pass each other and she'll give me a stupid look, or sometimes she even says some snide remark under her breath. I simply ignore the bitch, because if I don't, I'll have to act a fool, and that won't be good for me for more reasons than I can tell you right now."

"I agree. The best thing to do is keep your distance as much as possible, but don't you ever wonder why she backed off?"

"Not really, because I think she's going through something with the man she's with and she's all caught up in that right now. No doubt, that if that passes, she'll start again."

"I guess you'll take a break however you can get it huh?"

"True that."

As it turned out, Malik and I had a lot of things in common. We enjoyed many of the same things, which I felt helped in building a solid foundation between two people. But then again, John and I had many things in common too, and look how that turned out. Maybe I'd better start paying attention to other things such as character and integrity, of which Malik appeared to have plenty, if his refusal to pursue me while he was still married was any indication.

Malik and I enjoyed our conversation so much, we wanted to continue. Therefore, we decided to a movie the next time. During the ride back to my house I couldn't help but wonder about Malik's marriage, so I asked him what had led to his divorce. He didn't seem bothered at all by my curiosity.

"Well," he said, "my ex and I got married too young, and for the wrong reasons. At the time we simply thought it was the thing to do. At least I did anyway. Believe it or not, I wasn't always this suave, chivalrous man you see before you."

"Nooo, you're kidding, right? Say it isn't so!"

"OK, knock it off, Lonnie. I'm being serious," Malik said, humor in his voice.

"All right, go ahead and finish what you were saying."

"I told you before that I went to Howard University. Well, when I got down there and got a taste of freedom, I went buck-ass wild. I mean, everywhere I turned there were women, all shapes, sizes, and colors. Yo, this was my first time having real, true freedom. Because it was just me and my mom, she kept me close. She kept me in line with her strictness. So, anyway, at Howard there was more temptation than I knew what to do with."

I sat there in his car, intrigued.

"I started chasing women like I had never seen or had one before. I started smoking weed with my roommate and drinking like a damn fish. I got so fucked up in the lack of rules and restraints, I barely passed my classes. I still don't know how I managed that."

"So you were just a hot mess, huh?"

"Yeah, babe, I was. During my second year I got drunk and beat down this nigga that was trying to holla at this chick I messing with. I got expelled for a semester. I was charged with assault and did two years probation."

"Damn! So you really were a straight bad boy for a while there."

"I was, and I liked it a lot. I spent my childhood being a good guy, doing everything my mom told me to do, you know, getting good grades and being respectful at all times. My mom would always tell me that there was nothing out there in the streets for me, but there was always that little voice telling me, yes, there was. And when I was down there in D.C. acting a fool, I felt like myself finally. Ain't that some shit? I believed that a tree-smoking, beer-guzzling womanizer was the real me." Malik chuckled.

"Well, I don't know, Malik. Sometimes I can see some intensity in you . . . this little bit of an edge that always seems to be lingering just under the surface."

"Really?"

"Yes, but I've watched you and gotten to know you a little, and I think that maybe that wild guy is a part of you. But, the kind and gentlemanly you is very much who you are as well. We're all multidimensional. The thing is, as we grow, we find a balance."

"You're right. I couldn't have said it better myself."

"OK, so tell me, brotha, how did you pull yourself together?"

We pulled up in front of my house just as I'd asked that question.

Malik turned off the car. "Get this. By my senior year, I was a little steadier. I had cut down on the bullshit and was dealing with only one girl. I was actually tired of acting a fool. Getting kicked out of school and having to report to a probation officer was more than I wanted to deal with at the time. I wanted a future, and all of that combined with knowing that I was breaking my mom's heart slowed me down. But the one thing that straightened my ass out completely was my girl telling me she was pregnant."

"What?"

"Yup. It was a lie, and I'll tell you that long story some other time, but dealing with all that bullshit gave me the final kick in the ass I needed to get my act together once and for all. So by the time I'd met my wife, I was looking to settle down and live a quiet life. I didn't want any more bullshit in my life. I asked, she said yes, and we did it. But after a few years we found out that we really didn't share the same interests anymore. She no longer wanted to be a wife. Being settled down didn't fit into the type of life she had envisioned for herself. I would say her goals and desires changed, and mine hadn't. After all of that other shit, I liked the idea of being married with children. Fortunately for me, she didn't want that."

"What do you mean, fortunately, Malik?"

"Isn't it obvious? If she and I both still wanted the same things, I wouldn't have been able to pursue you, and I know I want to be with you."

Whoa! He doesn't stop. I had no words for that one, so I just let that statement ride. I looked at the clock on the dash, and noticed it was after ten o'clock. I was tired and ready to get some sleep. I told Malik I wanted to call it a night, and he walked me to my front door.

I wasn't quite sure, but I thought Malik wanted me to invite him inside. Hell, no! There was no way in hell I'd be playing the whore. Dating was one thing, but allowing a man to invade my body too soon was a definite no-no. I thanked him for a nice evening, politely kissed him on the cheek, and sent him on his way.

Chapter 25

The very next day I woke up with a smile on my face, excited at the prospect of being with Malik. I had to share my new found romance with my sister. As of late, I hadn't had the opportunity to share the details of my life with her, so I called.

"Hey Lele!"

"Hey, goofball, why are you talking so loud?"

"I'm just happy, I guess."

"Happy about what so early in the morning?"

"I met a man. No, let me correct that. I went on my first date with a friend of mine from work."

"So apparently, you had a great time, but what I want to know is why I am just now hearing about this guy?"

"Well it's a long story and I want you to spend the day with me so I can tell you all about it."

"What, he must be the shit, huh?"

"So far. Are you going to go out with me or not?"

"That depends on what you have planned. It better be good enough for me to leave this hot assed man lying here without me."

"Illlll, Lele. I don't need to picture all of that. I want to go to the mall and shop and maybe have lunch with you."

"OK! You knew all you had to do was mention shop. I'm there. Besides, there is something I want to talk to you about as well."

"Cool, pick me up at eleven."

"Sounds good, I'll see you then."

Lena and I spent our first two hours hitting our favorite stores. I really wanted to update my wardrobe now that I had someone to date.

"All right, Lon, my feet are killing me and I'm starving. Let's hit the food court so we can sit down and you can tell me all about this new man."

"OK."

We ordered bourbon chicken and found a corner table.

"All right, girl. Talk to me. Who is this guy?"

"Well, his name is Malik Reese and he's fine as hell!"

Lena laughed. "Look at you gushing over a man. I haven't seen you like this in forever."

"I know, but I really like this one. I have to tell you, though, I was terrified to even go out with him at first."

"Really, why?"

"Because of John and Cherie, but I talked to Mommy, Sandy, and Tracey and they all said the same thing: 'Stop being scared and go for it.'"

"Wait a minute, you talked to everybody but me? Even Tracey? You hardly know that girl."

"Sorry Lele, don't get all bent out of shape. I actually tried to talk to you first, but you didn't answer or call me back. I didn't trip about that, so don't you trip on me." I could see the wheels turning like she was actually debating about giving me a hard time.

"All right, I'm going to let you have that one. I have been missing in action myself lately."

I proceeded to fill her in about everything that had transpired in the last few weeks. Lena was very supportive and encouraging about the situation. The longer she was with Devon, the calmer she was becoming. I only wondered if she'd stay that way. I sure hoped so.

"That's really good, Lon. I'm glad you finally met a good guy. As much as you've always tried to hide it, I know how much you want to live the picket fence life."

"This is true. So, Lele, you said you wanted to talk to me about something. What's up?"

Lena took a moment to finish her soda before she spoke. "I ran into Deja the other day."

"Aw damn, don't tell me you got into it with that girl."

"No, as a matter of fact, I didn't. I saw her at Pathmark and guess what?"

"What?"

"She approached me first."

"Get the hell out of here! What did she say?"

"She said, 'Hey Lena,' without an ounce of malice in her voice."

"What the hell?"

"Will you shut up and let me finish?"

"Will you shut up and get to it?" I laughed.

"Anyway, she stopped me and asked if we could talk. I started to slap the shit out of her just for the hell of it but, I decided against that."

"Oh really? Why?"

"'Cause Devon was with me and I would've had to hear his mouth. Anyway, she said that she wanted to talk about Shakita."

"OK, what else?"

"She said that since Tank stepped up to do the right thing, she was thinking that she should try to appreciate the fact that at least one of

152

her kids has a family that gives a damn."

"Wow! Where the hell did that come from?"

"Girl, I don't know, but it fucked my head up."

"You mean to tell me she wants a truce? That's funny considering the last time she saw you she wound up wearing your drink."

"She sure did, but get this: I actually told her it was cool with me."

"No, you didn't!"

"Yes I did, Lon. The truth is, I'm tired of the drama in my own life, most of which I create myself. I sometimes wonder if I would have accomplished more in my life by now if I hadn't been such a mess." Lena never ceased to amaze me. More and more lately, she was transforming into an adult.

"Damn, Lele, what's gotten into you?"

"I don't know, but I do know that for the first time I have a man worth having around , and I was also thinking that by now I should have a family."

"Girl, I didn't even know you wanted a family."

"I can understand why you would think that. I spent my entire life being a ball busting brawler, but I only did that because I thought if I was hard, then people wouldn't bother you and Tank."

"What the hell are you saying? That the only reason you bullied was for us?"

"Kind of, but I also liked it a little too. Shit, people left me alone too. That was a plus. Anyway, Mommy always made me believe that it was my job to protect y'all when we were outside the house, so I did. I guess maybe I was over the top with it."

"You think?"

"Yeah, hussy, I think."

"Good for you. Now tell me, what does this thing with Deja mean? Are y'all trying to be friends or what?"

"Oh, God no! I'm not that evolved. It just means that I won't be fucking with her every time I see her and I guess that we'll at least be cordial to one another. Honestly, I don't really have a problem with that. Deja never actually did anything to me. That craziness was all about you and Cherie. By the way, what's she been up to?"

"I don't really know. She's been changing up on me. You remember I told you about that crap she told me about that boy Darnell?"

Lena nodded.

"Well, if she was really messed up like she pretended to be, she would still be fuckin' with me, but she's not. At least not anything major."

"That is odd. Do you think she's had enough?"

"No, because she's enlisted some other people in her shit, but it's no big deal. I guess she decided to go in a different direction with her nonsense with that move. Maybe she thought it would get to me if she turned people against me. Or it could be that she's so messed up over some guy that she can't focus on pestering me. I don't really know."

"Oh well, as long as she doesn't get stupid, she'll be safe."

"Now see, you just finished talking about turning over a new leaf and here you are ready to do battle."

"What can I say? Old habits die hard. Anyway, I'm glad you met a nice man and I hope it works out for you."

"Thanks Lele, I hope so too."

We spent the rest of the afternoon window shopping and laughing like we did when we were kids. I hadn't realized how much I was missing my sister, and getting to know the new and improved Lena was a treat.

Chapter 26

T he rest of my weekend dragged. I could not seem to find enough to do to make the time go by quicker. Malik called me several times that weekend just to talk, but it bothered me a little that not once did he ask to spend any more time with me.

Our first official date was so comfortable and easy, and I was feeling really good about having this man in my life. That was, until my own insecurities and issues from the past began to interfere.

Now it did take me a minute for me to start trippin'. In fact, we were going along just great, spending a great deal of time together, outside of the office, of course. I truly enjoyed his presence in my life, more than any other man before him. We laughed and we talked about everything. When we weren't on the phone, we were together. We both loved movies, so we would go to the theater every Friday night. We even liked our popcorn the same way: with extra butter, lightly salted.

We were together for about three months when he spoke to my parents for the first time and expressed to them how he felt about me.

I never knew a man to be as open as Malik. He never disguised his feelings, no matter what they were. He was true to who he was—open, feeling, and caring. The opinions of others didn't matter either. He was one of those take-me-as-I-am people, and that, I truly appreciated. Malik was becoming my best friend.

Because of his mentality, I began to feel more comfortable with allowing all of myself to be exposed—the good, the bad, and the crazy. Normal, everyday crazy, but crazy nonetheless, although my brand of crazy did keep us both laughing. The bottom line was that no matter what was happening in my life, I could share it all with Malik without hesitation and without fear of him judging me or changing his feelings and thoughts about me. This kind of security in a relationship was exactly what I needed and had longed for. But for someone like me who had never felt this safe with any man other than my father, of course I thought that Malik was too good to be true.

Malik and I had plans to go out to dinner. When he arrived at my house to pick me up, he greeted me with a kiss. This kiss was different. It had a passion behind it that wasn't there before; consuming me in a way I didn't know was possible. When my body began to tingle all the way down to my toes, I knew dinner wasn't going to happen that night.

There was not much discussion. Malik and I looked at one another, and our eyes said it all.

He simply asked, "Are you sure about this?"

I nodded, and he followed me upstairs.

Malik laid me across the bed as soon as we entered my bedroom. He unbuttoned my blouse and began kissing my breasts through the fabric of my bra. After only a few moments of this exquisite torture, he slowly lowered my bra straps and began caressing my nipples with his tongue. As he lifted his head, his thumb made several passes across my full, erect nipples as he watched the way my skin responded to his touch.

Again he bent his head down and took my nipple into his mouth. Responding to the wave of sexual electricity that ran through me, I arched my body up off the bed. *Damn!* I was soaking wet already.

Malik then began to run his hands over my stomach and around to the inside of my thighs. He pulled off my jeans and panties and slowly he found the sweetest part of me with his fingers. I whimpered from the pleasure of his touch. He gently used his fingers to make my passion swell as he continued to play, making my clit pulse, grow, and throb with anticipation.

I reached for him, taking his piece into my hand. I felt him growing and throbbing in unison with me. And just when I couldn't take another moment of him teasing my pussy, he placed the palms of his hands on my knees and pushed them apart. He lowered his head, and with his mouth found my center, moving his tongue inside me.

Just as I was on the verge of coming, he removed his tongue, using it to taste my thighs. He worked his way back up to my mouth, exploring every inch of me in the process, again giving me access to his dick. It was huge!

I took him into my hand, rubbing, squeezing, and needing to mix the flavor of him with the flavor of me that he'd left on my tongue. I slid my body down lower until my lips reached him. I began licking the rim of his head and shaft. Softly sucking his balls, I took all of him into my mouth.

Malik trembled from the pleasure my mouth was giving him. He removed himself and rolled me onto my stomach. Very tenderly he entered me from behind, taking his time, inch by wonderful inch, until my body had accepted all of him.

I began to meet his long, slow, strong thrusts. I wanted to come, but I fought it because I wanted more. I wanted everything he had to offer.

Malik said, "Babe, you're so tight and wet, I don't want to stop."

I was so caught up in the passion, and my breathing was so ragged, the only words I could form were, "Don't stop, ever."

Just as those words escaped my mouth, Malik pulled out of me and turned me back onto my back. With his fingers, he again opened me; teasing me and making me beg him to fill me. To fuck me long and hard.

He rode me slowly at first, then faster and harder, thrusting deeper and deeper into me. I was losing my mind. Entwined in heat, sweat, passion, and a lust that was so intense and electric, it consumed us until we were completely lost in our powerful physical connection. Malik and I exploded together on wave after wave of ecstasy, unable to breathe from the fire we had just created.

Malik found his voice first. "Damn, girl! That was the shit. I knew that pussy would be good, but damn! I didn't know your ass was that hot."

I had to laugh at that. Malik was right. That shit was so hot, romantic words were not necessary at that time. Real and raw truth was good enough for me.

That night was the most extraordinary night of my life. That man touched me in ways and places in my soul that no other had ever done before. Malik knew instinctively how to please me. That night was the first time he expressed to me how much he really loved me. I knew then that I was truly in love and that I would never be the same.

So I started trippin', secretly questioning everything about this man. I hadn't yet said a word to him about any of my thoughts, but I began to question his sincerity. I found it hard to believe that he loved me like he said he did. I no longer believed that he would always be there for me. And that's when my insecurities began to surface.

Every time another woman was in Malik's presence, I got hot under the collar. I was literally waiting for him to cheat. There was no doubt in my mind that he would.

We were at the movie theater when we had our first argument over my jealousy. I accused him of flirting with the ticket girl.

This wouldn't be the last time I accused him of being interested in other women. Fortunately for me, Malik was patient with me and understanding of my fear of betrayal.

I had all of this turmoil going on inside me, and to make matters worse, things at work began to get ugly again. More specifically, things with that damn Cherie began to get ugly again. It was bad enough that I was no longer relaxed in my situation with Malik, but then I had to start dealing with that bitch again. Cherie had decided that it was up to her to spread me and Malik's business, even though she didn't know what our business was.

It was mid-July before anybody at work found out about Malik and me. That in itself was shocking, considering how nosy folks were. Although we chose to keep our business to ourselves at work, we certainly didn't try to hide out in public. But, somehow, for the last few months we had not once run into anyone from work. Not a soul. We went to the movies, concerts, restaurants, and even walks in the park, and yet we never saw anyone we knew from the office. What actually got us caught was pure speculation on Cherie's part.

One day Cherie, of all people, walked by Malik and me while we were talking in the hall at work. Now it wasn't unusual to see two coworkers conversing at any given time, in any given place in this office, so neither of us thought anything of it. That was, until we started getting questioned by others in the office. Some people came straight out and asked us what was up, while others didn't say anything but would give us those stupid I-know-your-secret looks.

After about a week of the silliness, Malik wanted to come by my house to discuss how to handle the work situation. I decided I'd cook dinner for him, and we could talk and maybe watch a movie. We needed some in-the-house time anyway. It seemed as if we were always out in the world doing something.

I was setting the table when he arrived.

He kissed me on the cheek as he entered. "Hey, baby," he said.

"Hey, yourself," I responded. "Dinner's ready, if you'd like to sit down now."

"Sure, that's fine. I'm starving because I didn't have lunch today. I had too many errands to run; things I couldn't put off any longer."

My first thought to that comment was, *Oh, really? I wonder what her name is.* My head snapped up as if someone had slapped me. *Where the hell did that come from?* I immediately pulled myself back to reality. I didn't want to explore which of my insecurities may have led to that thought.

Malik came back from washing his hands and sat down at the dining room table. I served his meal and sat down across from him.

"Well, Miss Lonnie, how do you think we should handle this situation at work?"

"What do mean, handle it? As far as I'm concerned, there is no situation at work. Whether we confirm or deny our involvement is irrelevant. Once those people there get a hold of something, they don't let it go. So whether we tell the truth or continue to keep our business to ourselves, there's going to be talk either way."

"That sure is true. I guess we could stay quiet about our relationship, but truthfully, at this point I really don't give a fuck. We made the choice to keep it to ourselves only in an effort to be able to enjoy just us for as long as possible. But, what the hell? We have friends there, and no one is being malicious. They're just being their regular nosy selves."

"You're right. This really isn't a big deal. I was just surprised that people were coming at us like we had won the damned lottery or something. Actually, Malik, it's a little sad. Don't you think?"

He looked at me with this half-smile on his face. "Why do you call it sad?"

"Because these people don't have anything else to think about. I mean, they act as if they're excited about us, but the reality is that our personal life won't affect theirs in any way."

"I know it. Our peoples need to get a life, huh?"

"Exactly! Anyway, you can say whatever you choose, and I'll simply respond in whatever way I feel like responding at the moment."

"Sounds good to me, precious."

Malik and I finished our dinner, washed the dishes, and sat down to watch movies. We chilled on the couch for the rest of the evening. I loved being cuddled up with this man. One of my favorite things was the way he would lay my head in his lap and twiddle with my hair. I felt so safe. This was the first evening in a while that we chose to spend inside. I liked that he enjoyed being outdoors and doing different things with me, but us just being together was what I needed at the moment.

When we awoke the following morning, I got the best surprise—breakfast in bed. And as if that wasn't enough, Malik invited me to Sunday dinner at his mother's house. Now I knew he cared for me, but to invite me to his very first woman's house was a big deal. I hadn't really absorbed that he was feeling me like that. This was the man's mother, for goodness' sake; a man's first true love. Talk about having a nervous breakdown. I damn near choked on my eggs when he said that.

Malik started patting me on my back. "Are you all right?"

"Yeah, I'm fine. You just caught me off guard, that's all."

"Caught you off guard, how? It's only dinner."

"Malik, it's not only dinner. It's dinner with your mom. This is major."

He just laughed.

"Stop laughing. It's not funny. I know you well enough by now to know that you don't introduce just anyone to your mother."

"This is true, but you had to know that this day was coming. I've never misled you about my intentions toward you, and this, as far as I'm concerned, is just the next step. So stop trippin', woman."

Malik was right. I needed to stop the silliness. I was a grown woman who was confident in who she was. Also, this man had been making it clear to me for the last few months that he wasn't dating me just for the sake of dating. He had definite plans about a future with me, and meeting his mother was naturally a part of those plans.

"You're right, Malik. I'll just be myself, and she'll love me as much as you do."

He kissed me on the forehead, took my tray, and headed downstairs to clean up whatever mess he'd made in my kitchen.

Truth be told, I put on a show of false confidence for Malik, but for real, my ass was nervous as hell. I didn't usually care whether a man's mother liked me. Hell, I never even cared whether I met the mom. This time, however, was very different. Malik had come to mean so much to me, so it was important that I made a good impression on his mom.

I spent the rest of the morning trying to hide my anxiety from Malik, although I was sure he could tell I wasn't acting like myself. We relaxed for the remainder of the morning, and then at around two o'clock, we began getting ready for dinner.

While we were getting dressed, Malik filled me in on some things about his mom. He told me that the best way to describe her would be "soft and warm." That description put me a little at ease. Considering that my own mother didn't do soft or warm, I knew I would like to have someone like that in my life. I also knew that if I could grow to love Malik's mom, it certainly wouldn't take away any of the love I felt for my own mother. Never.

Malik also told me that his mother, whose name was Jewel, was one of the funniest people he knew. That also put me at ease. No matter what I might be going through in life, laughter had always come easily to me, and if Miss Jewel's sense of humor was the real deal, I knew we would be fast friends.

We had barely gotten in the front door of Malik's childhood home before his mother started showering me with love. She greeted me with a hug, one of those comforting, make-you-believe-everything-will-be-all-right hugs. Yes, I loved her instantly, and she took to me as well. This woman looked into my eyes in a way that told me, *If my son brought you to me, I already know you're good and special.* She never had to voice those words to me, though. I saw them, and I felt them. From that point on, it was all good.

Over one of the best soul food dinners I'd ever eaten, Malik's mom entertained me with his childhood misadventures. Once when Malik was six years old, he decided that his neighbor wasn't feeding his dog enough, so he got it into his head that he would adopt the dog, without permission, of course, and take care of it himself. He hid that dog under his back porch for a week before anyone found out. When Ms. Jewel discovered what Malik had done, he cried and begged his mom to sue Mr. Leroy for neglect. Maybe that was why he got into the child protective services business.

By the time we were done with dinner, I knew as much about Malik the boy as I did about Malik the man. We left Ms. Jewel's house with the promise to get together again very soon.

I couldn't have asked for my first meeting with Malik's mom to go any better. I was comfortable enough to be open, to be myself, and not to be concerned about being accepted. Considering I had never cared about any man's mom's thoughts of me, the fact that this meant so much to me was a bit of a mind-blower.

After Malik dropped me off at home, I chilled in a bubble bath for a while, replaying the events of the day in my head. I was overwhelmed with happiness. The last few months with Malik had been exactly what I wanted in a relationship, my insecurities notwithstanding. I had nothing concrete to support my insecurities, and when I was thinking rationally, I knew he wasn't like John at all and would never cheat on me.

Chapter 27

That night I went through my nightly routine with a smile on my face and joy in my heart. That was, until I settled down in bed. I grabbed the book I was reading and tried to get into it, but two pages into reading, I lost focus. Anxiety began to consume me. It hit me that I had been home for at least an hour and a half, yet I hadn't heard a word from Malik. He always called to let me know that he'd made it home safely. My anxiety grew with each passing moment.

Not once did I think that Malik might have had car trouble or anything of the sort. My mind immediately went to him being with another woman. I convinced myself he was playing me, and that taking me to meet his mother was simply a ploy to throw me off his slimy, doggie trail, to lull me into a false sense of security.

That bastard! I thought. Well, that nigga wasn't getting that shit off on me. Just like with John, I was going to be watching his ass, and I would catch him. And this time around, I wouldn't be walking away without leaving an impression. If this man was doing what I thought he was doing, he was going to pay. I planned to make his black ass suffer.

Totally heated, I picked up the phone and dialed his cell. It went straight to voicemail. Malik never turned that damn phone off. Once again, it was on.

For the rest of the night I tossed and turned and fumed. No matter how hard I tried to shake my thoughts of betrayal, I couldn't. I simply got more and more angry. It didn't help that Malik had told me about his past behavior with women.

When I did finally fall asleep, it couldn't have been more than three hours before that damn alarm clock started ringing.

When I dragged myself out of bed, I felt no better than I did the previous night. My thoughts about what Malik was doing hadn't changed, and my anger didn't subside in the least. I was so pissed, I couldn't see or think straight. I had no appetite because my stomach was doing flip-flops.

I don't even remember getting in my car and driving to work.

I arrived at work ten minutes late. I just couldn't get it together. I sat down at my desk and put my head down. I was suffering from a headache and nausea, which only intensified with the realization that I still hadn't heard a word from that man.

I started calling his desk at nine fifteen. No answer. It took me until my lunch hour to accept that he wasn't in the office, and more than likely wasn't coming in at all. This devastated me. I had to get the hell out of there.

Would he actually go so far as to not come to work to avoid me? What is it he was doing that he couldn't call and say anything?

I called Logan's office and told her I wasn't feeling well and went home. Two hours after I got home, I was still staring at my cell phone, willing it to ring. But, like the saying goes, a watched phone never rang. I turned it off, trying to convince myself that I was fine, and that I wouldn't be chained to it.

Fuck him! I don't need him, and life would be just as good without him.

Shit, I was happy before I met him.

Yeah, right. I spent the next hour turning the phone on and off, begging God for a message from Malik whenever I turned it on. The last time I checked the phone it was three fifteen in the afternoon. I started crying and didn't stop until I was so exhausted that I fell asleep.

When I awoke, it was four A.M., and once again I was in tears. I checked the caller ID and my cell. Still nothing.

By now I was terrified about what might have happened to him. Who could I call? There was no one. I didn't know Ms. Jewel's telephone number, so I couldn't call her, and besides, what would I say that wouldn't have me making a fool of myself? What if Malik was fine and simply decided that he didn't want me anymore? Maybe he had found someone he thought was better. With that thought, my crying began all over again. I realized then that there was no one I could call. My sister would have gone right back to 'kick ass' mode, and anyone else would have told me I was overreacting. Besides, I was too embarrassed by my feelings to tell anyone else. I felt so alone in this.

There was no way I could make it into work that day. Tuesday passed in a haze for me. I don't remember anything more than crying, sleeping, and suffering through it all. By evening I was determined to pull myself together. I had suffered over John, but never had I fallen apart so completely. This would not do. I was not this person. Malik was not going to get that out of me. It was time to shake it off.

I got up at six, took a shower, and went down to make myself some dinner. I had to force down some leftover soup. I believed that if I could eat, then I was OK.

After I ate, I walked around my house. I walked in circles, thinking, trying to figure out just what I had done wrong. Where and how did I miss such a huge character flaw in yet another man? I chastised myself for being so stupid. How could I spend all of this time alone and still turn around and pick the wrong damn man again? He'd fooled me so completely.

I questioned my good sense and my intelligence. What was missing in me that I could be so gullible? The only answer I could come up with was that I wanted to be loved more than I could ever admit. I wanted a family of my own. What my parents had was always so beautiful and affectionate. I was raised in good and true love. I craved that so much, deep down inside, I couldn't stand another moment of this life without it. And I thought Malik was the one.

Still I hadn't come to any conclusions about who Malik was or his intentions after an hour of walking around in circles, so I gave up. Besides, I was only succeeding in making myself dizzy.

I was halfway upstairs when I heard my cell phone ring. I thought it might be one of my friends or family members who hadn't heard from me, and I didn't want to be bothered. I didn't want anyone to see or hear me like this. Nothing had ever embarrassed me more than the thought that I had chosen another loser. How could things go from so good to so bad in an instant?

I went upstairs to the linen closet to get some fresh sheets. As I was taking the used sheets off the bed, my cell's message alert went off, and right then, a vibe swept over me. It was Malik. Everything in my being told me I would hear his voice on that message. Never in my life had I felt such a strong connection to another person. Not until Malik. I sat down on the edge of my bed and wrapped my arms around my body. I sat rocking back and forth for a long moment before I could listen to the voicemail.

Surprisingly, relief swept through my body when I heard his voice on the other end of the phone. I had no idea where the anger went.

"Hey, babe, I know you must be worried sick," he said. "I'm so sorry to put you through that. I just needed some time to clear my head.

Please, call me. I'd like to come over to talk to you."

I closed the phone and sat there staring at the floor. I didn't know what to do. Call him? Maybe. I was stuck. My entire body and my senses were numb. I was relieved that Malik had called, but more than my concern for what was going on with him, I was concerned with my reaction to his disappearance. I had completely lost it, and his phone call did nothing to alleviate the depression I had fallen into. In a matter of two days, I was completed devastated by his absence. My right mind knew this wasn't a normal reaction.

Since I wasn't capable of making a decision, I lay down on the bed and closed my eyes. I tried desperately to calm my racing pulse. I tried to visualize something peaceful, but I failed. My mind as well as my pulse continued to race. I thought I was having a heart attack.

I don't know how long I was there when I heard a banging noise. It wasn't until then that I realized that I had fallen asleep. I looked at the clock to find that it was after nine. There was that banging noise again. Someone was at my front door, but there was no way in hell I was going to answer it. I was in no condition to see anyone. The only positive was that I had showered, so I wasn't funky, but I still looked like hell.

I stayed still, hoping that whoever was down there would get the hint and go the hell home. No such luck.

After a few minutes of knocking, I heard Malik calling my name. I jumped up and looked around as if he was in there with me. I knew better, but I couldn't stop looking from side to side. In the midst of my ridiculous terror, I could hear Malik getting louder. I also noted the desperation in his voice. Not to mention, it occurred to me that my neighbors could also hear that fool making such a racket. Because of this, I decided against my better judgment to let him in.

Emotionally I wasn't prepared to see or speak to him, but if I didn't, there was little chance of me pulling myself together. Whether or not I wanted to hear what he had to say about his absence, I needed to listen for my own good.

I did my best to gather myself and went down to open the door. I was shocked to find Malik standing there looking just as messed up as me.

"Lonnie, baby, can I come in?"

The sadness in his voice was also etched on his face. Seeing this broke my heart in an entirely different way. What I saw and heard scared me. What had this man been going through?

"Come on in, Malik." I led him into the dining room, and we sat across from one another at the table.

For a long moment neither of us spoke. We sat there staring at one another. I had no intention of speaking first anyway. I wasn't the one who took off. This man owed me an explanation. At that thought something shifted in me. Feelings of anger and rage began to take over, and I began to feel stronger. The last couple of days of despair were slowing melting away as my outrage at his behavior surfaced.

"Where the hell have you been?" I screamed. "How dare you walk out on me without so much as a *Fuck you, Lonnie*! Why? Why would you do this to me? To us?" By now I was crying hysterically.

"Lonnie, please calm down."

How can he expect me to calm down? I wondered.

Malik walked around the table and put his arms around me.

I sobbed even more. It hit me like a ton of bricks. I loved this man more than I thought was humanly possible. Malik truly *was* the one, and just the thought of not having him in my life had caused complete emotional devastation. This scared the crap out of me.

Malik stood me up, sat down in my seat, and placed me in his lap, all the while never breaking physical contact with me. He wrapped his arms around me and began to speak.

"Precious lady, let me start by saying, I love you more than life itself.

Yes, before now I knew I loved you, but to this degree was a total shock to me."

I tried to calm down my crying in an effort to absorb Malik's words.

"The other night after I dropped you off, I was headed home, replaying in my mind the events of this past weekend. Lonnie, the reality of how much you mean to me hit me so hard, and I'm ashamed to say that it scared the hell out of me. I couldn't breathe because of the intensity of the love I felt for you in that moment." Malik lifted my head. "Lonnie, please look at me. I know shutting down on you the way I did was cowardly, but I really needed to deal with me. I needed to get clear about what this all means to me. You see, I knew Sunday night, as I do right now, that there's no way I can survive this life without you. Never have I felt this way before, not even with my ex. I married her more because I thought it was the thing to do. With you, I know better." He smiled that Malik smile. "Baby, although it wasn't a test, the way you and Mom interacted and bonded pretty much sealed the deal for me. Yeah, I know my mom is nice to everyone, but the easy vibe between the two of you is not something I've ever seen her share with any other woman I've cared for. You two were like old girlfriends."

He took a breath. "Remember when I went back into the house to get my plate? Well, my mom told me that she thought you were extremely special. She said you have a truly joyful spirit and that she feels we'd be perfect together. And, oh yeah, you have just the right amount of attitude to deal with me."

He laughed, but I couldn't.

"My mom has never expressed anything like that to me about a woman, not even my wife."

I could tell that Ms. Jewel liked me, but it never occurred to me that she would be feeling me like that. *Perfect for her son? Wow!* She apparently saw things in me that I didn't even know were there. This, of course, pleased me, but it still didn't explain Malik's actions.

"Malik, that's all well and good, but I still don't understand why you did what you did."

"Like I said, I've never felt this way before. It took me by total surprise that loving someone could be so all consuming. Yes, I panicked at the enormity of my feelings. Please, Lonnie, try to understand how major it is for a man, for me, to discover that without you, I have no life; to feel that if I ever lost you, I wouldn't be able to breathe, to function."

"So what are you saying? You've spent the last two days trying to get over me? What were you trying to figure out? How not to feel the way you do?"

I could see Malik's frustration with me building. Obviously, I wasn't grasping what he was trying to convey to me.

He tapped me on the leg to indicate I should stand. "Please sit over there, Lonnie." He pointed to the chair I was originally sitting in.

I obliged him, attitude welling inside me.

Malik stood. He stuck his hand in his pants pocket and pulled out a ring box.

I nearly fell out of my chair. My head began spinning. *And where the hell did he get a ring from?* I knew he wasn't doing what I thought he was doing.

Malik actually got down on one knee and took my hand in his.

I started crying immediately. Like that was new. Crying was all I had been doing lately. At least this time they were happy tears.

"Lonnie, I can't express how much you truly mean to me. The one most important thing I've learned in the past few months, especially the last two days, is that you are all I need and want in this life. Will you be my wife?"

All the anger, fear, and despair I'd felt this week fell away in that moment. I did love this man, and, yes, I wanted to be his wife. I started sobbing harder than ever. I had never experienced such joy.

Malik wrapped me in his arms and rocked me until I could get myself composed enough to actually answer his question.

I dried my eyes and looked into his. "Yes, Malik, I'll marry you. Nothing would make me happier."

The look on his face was one of pure joy. This man did indeed love me beyond reason, and that was exactly what I needed in my life. I realized in that moment that all of my doubts about him were totally unfounded. I was it for him, and I could see that now.

In the next moment, Malik's face became serious. I couldn't guess what was going on in his mind. That was, until he took my face in his hands and kissed me like only he could. Just the thought of being Malik's wife made his touch take on new meaning for me. It was pure peace in that moment.

The second Malik released me from his embrace, I slid my body down his until I was on my knees. I unbuttoned his pants and slid his zipper down with my teeth, never taking my eyes off his. I slid my hand inside his boxers and released his huge dick. *Damn!* With reckless abandon I began to lick and suck every lovely inch of him like a starved animal. I couldn't get enough.

I released him from my mouth long enough to blow on his balls.

"Oh, baby, I love the way you do that."

"Yeah?"

"Oh, hell, yes!"

I continued to suck Malik's dick until I felt his body begin to shake. I let him go just before he popped.

Malik reached down and took my hand. He guided me up onto the dining room table. He lifted my nightgown and pulled my panties off. "I want to see you play with the pussy."

I used my fingers to massage my clit and slide in and out of my pussy while he watched.

"Damn, babe! That shit looks so good. That pussy is so wet. I want to see you come." Malik stood there holding his dick as he watched me work myself into a frenzy.

Watching him watch me took me over the edge, and I squirted all over his stomach.

He threw my legs up over his shoulders, entered me, and started pounding and thrusting so hard, that he came within minutes. He lay on top of me without pulling out, panting, trying to catch his breath. "Damn, Lonnie! I never had a woman who squirts. I've only seen it in porn. That shit amazes me every time you do it, and I get to get it for the rest of my life." He laughed.

I'd saved that little trick until we had gotten closer. I'd made the mistake of sharing that skill with a guy too soon and wound up with an obsessive nut. With Malik I was fine. Hell, yeah, I knew how to put it on a nigga, and this one was mine for life.

I punched him on his arm. "Not funny, Malik. That better not be the reason you're marrying me."

"Stop trippin', woman, you know damn well that's not it. Yo, that's the bonus!"

"All right, goofball, get up off me. I can't breathe."

Sleeping in Malik's arms that night was the most restful sleep I'd had in a long time.

Chapter 28

The next morning, I woke up in a state of euphoria. I couldn't remember the last time, if any, that I had felt so at peace. I rolled onto my side and watched Malik sleep. *Finally,* I thought. *This feels exactly right.* I breathed a sigh of relief. Maybe, I, too—like so many other women—had been waiting to exhale.

Almost as soon as I'd finished my thought, that damn alarm clock went off. It was back to the real world. We both had to take our asses to work. I shook him and let him know it was time to get moving, and then I headed into the shower. It dawned on me halfway through that Malik didn't have any work clothes at my house.

When I came out of the bathroom, Malik was dressed in yesterday's clothes. Actually, when I looked a little closer, I realized he was still wearing the outfit he'd had on this past Sunday. *Damn, he was really out of it as I had been.* Well, that was behind us now. We'd both come to our conclusions, and our future was ahead of us, together.

"Good morning, lady."

"Good morning, man."

He stood and kissed me on the forehead as he headed to the bathroom.

I'd spent enough mornings with Malik in the last few months to know that it took him a while to get his senses together in the morning, but for whatever reason, this morning his quietness bothered me. I guess I thought that the morning after you get engaged would be a little more upbeat or something. Maybe it was more of my nonsense kicking in.

I quickly shook it off. Malik was who he was, and I loved him.

I went downstairs to the kitchen to make some coffee, and Malik came into the kitchen just as I was pouring him a cup.

"Hey, babe." He put his arms around my waist and pulled me close.

I loved his affection. "I'd better get going so I can change my clothes. I'm sure I'm already going to be late for work, but let's have lunch together. I guess we should start talking about our future. What do you think?"

"I agree. Big plans mean big decisions," he said.

"Malik, wait. Before you go I want to run something by you."

"OK, shoot. What's on your mind?"

"Well, it occurred to me that I shouldn't wear my ring to work, at least not until we share our news with our families and our special friends. I know it sounds silly, but I'm not up to having all of those people up in my face. Not today."

Malik smiled that smile at me and said it was cool with him. "Just make sure you lock that ring up safely."

"OK, so lunch it is. I love you, and I'll see you whenever I get into the office, OK?"

"Yes. Kiss me and then go on about your business."

Malik kissed me and ran out the front door. As soon as he was gone, I snatched the phone off the counter and called Lena.

"Hello," she answered groggily.

"Good morning, Lele. Guess what?"

"What?"

"I'm getting married!" I screamed.

"Married?! You're shittin' me! When did that happen?"

"Last night! Malik came in here and got down on one fuckin' knee and proposed!"

"Aw, Lonnie, I'm really happy for you."

"Thanks! I'm so excited!"

"I can tell, goofball." She laughed. "But I think this is wonderful news. I also think it's time for me to meet this man of yours.

"I know, right? Have you noticed that we've allowed the men in our lives to monopolize our time? We don't see each other as much as we used to."

"Of course I've noticed that, but we're allowed to live separate lives from one another without it being a problem. We're sisters and nothing will change that. I'll always have your back."

"I have no doubt about that. Anyway, I agree it's about time you met Malik and I should get to know Devon better."

"This is true. Maybe we can start doing things together as couples."

"Damn, Lele, double dating? Who are you?!"

"Not funny, bitch. How was that for bringing out the old Lena?" She laughed.

"More like the sister I know, thank you. Now, can y'all come to dinner tomorrow night."

"We sure can, what time?"

"How about around seven?"

"Perfect, we'll be there, and Lonnie?"

"Yes?

"Congratulations again, girl."

"Thanks, sis."

Just like on Monday morning, I didn't remember anything about my commute to work. Only, this time it was for a totally different reason. This morning I was so happy, all I could think about was my future with the love of my life.

The moment I got into the office, I ran to Asia's desk. I was grateful she was in already. "Hey, Asia."

"Hey, girl. Are you all right? I tried to call and check on you. I got a little worried when I didn't hear back from you."

"Yes, I'm fine. I was just a little out of it. Anyway, I have something to tell you, but you have to promise to keep it to yourself. Now promise."

"I promise, I promise. What is it, bitch? You look like you're about to jump out of your skin."

"OK, well, Malik came by last night and asked me to marry him."

"Call the cops!" Asia screamed. "Did he, really? What did you say?"

Her excitement got me excited all over again. We were both sitting there with these stupid grins spread across our faces.

"I said yes. What do you think I said? And be quiet. You know how these folks around here are. Besides, I haven't even told all of my family yet. This all just happened last night."

"Oh, right, right, I got you. So have you guys made plans, set a date, or anything like that?"

"No, we haven't gotten that far. I suppose the next thing I should do is take him to meet my parents. Not that they'll object or anything. It's just that I want them to know him before we actually have a ceremony."

"Do you think your parents will like that nigga?"

"That nigga? Asia, don't you know how to talk without calling everybody bitches and niggas?"

"Hell, no, bitch. Now answer the question."

All I could do was laugh. Asia was as ghetto as they come and wasn't going to change that, no matter where she was or who she was with. Truth is, I loved her just like that. She was a homegirl through and through, and that made her a joy to be around.

"I'm sure they will. They've both spoken to him over the phone, and they are cool with him in my life. It's odd, but I've never asked my parents' permission or for their approval about who I chose to be with. Fortunately for me, they've never gotten involved in my personal life like that. They've always let me make my own decisions."

"That's cool. I know this may be a stupid question, because the answer is written all over your face. But, how do you feel?"

"It's hard to explain exactly, but I'm happy, excited, ecstatic, scared to death! You name it, I feel it."

Asia then squeezed me tightly and whispered in my ear, "I'm so happy for you, Lonnie. Let me know if there's anything I can do to help when y'all start planning."

"I sure will, girl. Thank you so much for your support." I left Asia and went back to my desk. I had two days worth of work waiting for me, and I needed to get to it.

At ten fifteen I stopped to take a break. I decided to call upstairs to see if Malik had made it to work yet. He answered on the first ring.

"Hi, sweetie, you made it, huh?" I said.

"Yup. I just got here ten seconds ago, and I see there's a bunch of shit piled in my chair. I guess I've missed a lot."

"Yeah, me too. I've knocked some of it out, but if I want to clear it up today, I'd better work nonstop."

"Sounds like a plan," he said. "Why don't we push lunch back to one o'clock? That way I can get the bulk of this out of my way."

"That's fine. I'll see you at one. Oh and one more thing, I invited Lena and Devon to dinner tomorrow night."

"That's great. I can't wait to meet them. I love you, Lonnie."

"I love you too. Bye."

I hung up, determined to tear through my work. If I was lucky, there would be no interruptions.

No such luck today. It seemed as if every time I got on a roll, either my phone would ring, or someone came by to ask a question or to chat about something trivial.

I would have much rather focused on the work at hand, because without that distraction, I was just beaming at anyone who came by. No less than three people asked me what the hell I was so happy about, but I couldn't tell them. I needed these people to stay away, at least until I spoke to Malik about how we were going to handle our change in status. Since being engaged was a much bigger deal than dating, keeping our business to ourselves was going to be much more difficult.

Somewhere around eleven-thirty the interruptions ceased, and I was able to focus on my work. I was grateful to have done as much as I did. Before I knew it, Malik was calling to see if I was ready to go to lunch. I snatched my purse out of my drawer and ran out to meet him.

During lunch Malik and I decided to share our news with a few select friends at work and, of course, our families and friends away from work. The only other thing we wanted to decide right then was when we could take time off to go down to Florida to see my parents and brother.

The remainder of the afternoon was uneventful, thank goodness! I was able to get most of my work off my desk. Had I stayed a little later, I could've finished it all, but I chose to take my ass home. I was glad Malik needed to go home and take care of all that he had neglected during his meltdown, because I needed some free time. I was emotionally drained from all that had transpired over the last few days. Not to mention, I knew that pretty soon my life would change dramatically.

I'd been by myself since John, and I was used to having my time to myself. Malik and I hadn't discussed if we would live together before marriage, or where we would be living in either case. As much as I wanted this man, I wasn't sure if I was ready for any of these major changes. They all seemed to be coming too fast. Possibly having to give up my home and start over elsewhere scared the shit out of me. I wasn't sure if I could let go of my independence.

As soon as I got settled at home, I called my parents and Tank. Not surprising at all, they were happy for me and Malik, and gave us their blessing and best wishes. Tank, on the other hand, threatened to kick his ass if he made me shed one single tear. No surprise there. I ended the conversation promising to visit very soon.

I called Sandy next. She was, after all, the friend I'd had the longest.

"Hi, Sandy, what's up, girl?"

"Not much, *chica*. I'm just cooking some dinner. Where the hell have you been anyway? I called your office three times yesterday, and your house at least four."

"I was in bed. I wasn't feeling well." For reasons I couldn't explain, I didn't feel comfortable telling Sandy all that had been going on this past week. I was a little embarrassed by my mini breakdown, even though she wouldn't have cared.

"So I take it you're feeling better now, *mami*?"

"Yes, I am."

"*Bien.*"

"So, anyway, I have some news to share with you."

"OK, what's the news?"

"Malik and I are engaged."

That fool screamed so loud, I had to move the phone away from my ear.

"When did this happen?" she asked, once the screaming was over.

"Just yesterday. Last night, actually."

"Congratulations, Lonnie. I'm so happy for you. Have you set a date already?"

"No, not yet. There are plenty of things we need to discuss, but there's no rush. We'll sort everything out as we need to. For now we'd simply like to enjoy this new phase."

"That's great, but I have to go. *¡Ay Dios mío!* I'm burning my damn dinner!"

I laughed and let Sandy go. That girl couldn't stay focused on one thing for too long anyway. But I really did have more to say to her. Although I was ecstatic about getting engaged to Malik, I wondered if we were moving too quickly. Sandy was my first friend away from work to meet Malik, and I felt that she might be able to dispel my fears about possibly rushing into this huge commitment.

As a matter of fact, I had invited Sandy out to dinner with us one night. I wanted my oldest girlfriend to meet my new man.

While at dinner Sandy and Malik talked each other's ears off. As it turned out, they had gone to the same high school, Camden High, to be exact. I went to Woodrow Wilson across town. Those fools from "the High" were our rivals, and although Malik and Sandy hung in different circles, they vaguely remembered one another from back then. I thought that she could help me with this minor hesitation because after dinner that evening she called me to tell me that Malik had been one of those quiet guys that she never paid much attention to, and she didn't think he ever did do "the dog thing" in high school, and considering how good he looked even then, he could have. If she had seen him in college, she would have been shocked. She also told me that I really had gotten a good guy this time. I guess I just needed some reassurance from someone who kind of knew Malik.

Tracey was my next call. I filled her in on the events of the last four days. Her reaction was the best. She cried. Her sheer happiness for me touched me more than I could say. What a wonderful friend she'd become so quickly. Tracey expressed love, support, and joy about my good news. Her words had me in tears right along with her.

After I got off the phone I turned on the TV and lay down to watch the evening news.

Without my permission, physical and emotional exhaustion completely took over my body, because the next time I opened my eyes, the sun was up. I had slept through my alarm and was still in yesterday's clothes. That damn clock had been going off for half an hour. I didn't give two shits about waking up late, though. I figured that if I'd slept like that, my body and soul must have really needed it.

I checked my cell once I'd realized I had lost the entire evening. There were three messages from Malik. The man was worried sick. I felt bad for putting him through the worry, but at the same time I thought, *Now he knows how I felt*. Not good of me, but true. Anyway, I called him right away.

Relieved and satisfied with my explanation, he let me go, so I could prepare for my day.

Chapter 29

I was so joyful about the future I envisioned for Malik and me. I knew with everything in me that this man was the one I wanted to share a life and family with. He was for sure my soul mate. I was on top of the world, knowing without a doubt that there was nothing but good things ahead of me.

But every time I started to feel that damn good, something happened to knock my black ass back down. Drama entered my life without fail.

It was a beautiful day, and I couldn't have been happier about my life. That was, until I got to work. The minute I sat down at my desk, there was a note sitting there. I opened it, curious to see what it said. It read as follows:

> Lonnie, just thought you should know that Malik is not who you think he is, and although I'm not yet ready to reveal myself to you, I will tell you that Malik and I have been seeing one another for about two months now.

Needless to say, my world shifted on its axis. It never occurred to me to disregard this note as a hoax. I immediately became lost in thoughts of betrayal. *Not again!* I could not do this again. I couldn't think of a thing to do right then, except to call someone. I chose Tracey because I knew she would be reasonable.

Once I had relayed my story to Tracey, she commenced to convincing me that I worked in a place where there were plenty of haters, and obviously there was someone there who had a major crush on Malik. Whoever she was, this girl wasn't too happy about the fact that Malik had given his attention and his heart to me.

Tracey also convinced me that Malik was a true and faithful man who had chosen me. With my mind a little clearer, and my soul at ease, I thanked Tracey and got off the phone.

I decided not to mention any of this to Malik. It was time I made a sincere effort to trust. After all, I had consented to be this man's wife. If we were going to have a successful marriage, I had to try.

Wanting to relax was one thing, but convincing myself to chill was another thing altogether. I spent the entire day pissed, trying to figure out who had written that note. Of course, Cherie crossed my mind, but even she would not be so stupid as to start this old shit again with me. It didn't matter whether any of it was true; someone was trying to fuck with me, and I didn't appreciate it one bit. The moment I found out who the culprit was, some shit was going down.

I was glad Lena and Devon were coming over to have dinner with us. At least they would keep my mind off the drama with these stupid bitches at work. We spent the evening laughing and talking. They got a chance to bond over me and Lena's stories about our escapades of the past. Not once while they were with us did I think about the nonsense at work that day.

Unfortunately, the next day was worse than the day before. Early in the workday, I began receiving prank phone calls. Some silly ho kept calling and whispering that I'd better stay away from her man. This shit went on for at least an hour. I was heated big time.

I went over to Asia's desk and told her what had been going on. I also showed her the note, and of course, Asia was outraged. She did outrage very well. That girl had a little drama queen inside her. And her theatrics only helped to fuel my anger.

"Ooh, girl, you know I'm going to find out who this bitch is. Shit! It's probably Cherie," she said.

"Do you really think she would be that stupid?"

"Hell, yes! From what you've told me of all the shit she's done, why not?"

"You may be right. One thing's for sure, if I find out it's her, or whoever it is, I'm going to kick that bitch's ass. It's that simple."

"Well, if that's the way you want to handle it, you know I got your back. I'll just say, make sure you don't get into it in the building."

"Don't worry, I got this."

I went back to my desk, still pissed off that some silly chick in this office was trying to start some shit. I put my head down on my desk and did my best to calm down. That didn't really work, so I decided to go up and see Malik for a few minutes.

While walking to his desk, I could hear voices from his area. Just as I turned the corner, I saw Tamika leaning on his desk cheesing at Malik, like Chester Cheetah. And, get this, he was smiling just as hard. That man didn't even realize I was standing there. My mind screamed, *Cheater!*

I cleared my throat to get their attention, and the looks on their faces were ones of guilt. Malik looked as if he'd been busted with his hand in the cookie jar.

Tamika looked me up and down as if I had no right to be there. This bitch had the nerve to suck her teeth and roll her eyes at me. She turned to Malik. "Anyway, Malik, I guess I'll see you later."

I couldn't believe my ears. "What the hell was that about? And what the hell is she talking about, she'll see you later?"

"It's nothing, Lonnie. She was just telling me that some people are meeting up at the bar after work. I told her that we might stop by, that's all. Don't start trippin', Lonnie."

Honestly, Malik appeared to be sincere in his explanation, but I wasn't buying it. Whether he knew or cared, Tamika's ass was up to no good. We hadn't spoken since I'd called her out on her stank behavior. Now this little incident was enough to let me know without a doubt that she was behind the current bullshit. That girl was going to find out real soon that she was messing with the wrong one.

"OK, Malik, that sounds like a good idea. We'll go to happy hour. Just let me go back down and get back to work."

"Cool. I'll meet you at the bar later."

I went down, found Asia, and told her what our plans were. I let her know about my suspicions concerning Tamika, and she agreed without hesitation to go to the bar with me.

Since the bar was right around the corner from work, Asia and I rode over there together in my car. We couldn't have been there for more than ten minutes before the drama began. Neither of us had even ordered a drink when Malik and James walked in the door. Malik came over to the table Asia and I had found. He took our orders, and he and James headed for the bar.

Before Malik even had a chance to take a breath, Tamika slithered up to him like the snake she was. That bitch placed her hand on the small of his back and whispered something in his ear.

Asia looked at me, I looked at Asia, and it was on. We were both at the bar in a flash. I grabbed Tamika by her fake ponytail and dragged her ass outside. We were out the door before anybody else could figure out what the hell had happened.

Asia sure knew how to roll with me, because she was out the door right behind me, making sure none of Tamika's cronies tried to jump in. I had that bitch bent backward over my car, punching her repeatedly in her jacked-up face. She tried to grab my hair, but just before she could get a grip on it, Malik tried to pull me off her. Apparently he didn't know who he was dealing with, because he found out real quickly that it wasn't easy to stop me.

The moment I felt Malik pulling me backward, I grabbed as much of that ponytail as I could, and I kept right on punching the shit out of Tamika. I could hear Malik yelling at James to help him. James must have been close by, because the next thing I knew, my fingers were being pried from Tamika's head.

By then several people were standing outside the bar watching the spectacle. I didn't give a damn. This trick needed to know that I wasn't the one.

Malik pushed me a little way down the street. "Lonnie, what the hell is wrong with you? Why in the hell did you attack that girl like that?"

I stood there huffing and puffing, trying to catch my breath and calm down. I was still hot, and the outrage in Malik's voice didn't help the situation. As far as I was concerned, my behavior was justified. Besides, I never told that man I didn't have a temper. I just said I had it in check. OK, so maybe that wasn't completely accurate. Whatever.

When I finally did catch my breath, I took a minute to fill Malik in on what had been happening at work.

"All right, Lonnie, I understand why you would be angry. But what I don't understand is, why do you think Tamika was the one fucking with you?"

I looked at that fool like he was crazy. He was such a damn man. Malik didn't understand that in a situation like this, I didn't need hard proof. Tamika's actions were plenty. Women had a way of letting the enemy know what they were up to—a look, a smirk, a hard breath. Every move she'd made today told me what I needed to know, and hell no, Malik's stupid-man ass wasn't going to get that on his own.

"Malik, even if I tried to explain, you probably wouldn't get it. Let me just say that I can't have these fools at work creating a bunch of drama in my life."

"Girl, listen. Right about now you're the one with the drama. Lonnie, there's always a better way to handle these things."

Now at this point I thought about putting up a fight against Malik's argument, but, you know, something told me that might not be such a good idea.

"Malik, I truly am sorry for this. I didn't mean to cause you any embarrassment. It's just that I feel like these ridiculous women at work will never allow me to be happy. With them, it's one thing after another."

Malik looked concerned. "Lonnie, has it always been this way for you at work? I thought you were happy there."

"I am happy there, Malik. I'm sure this nonsense with Tamika is a byproduct of Cherie's mess. They've become friends, and we all know that drama breeds drama. You know this is no longer my normal life or way of dealing with things. I've tried to chill with all of this fighting, but enough is enough. How do I continue to deal with this shit without blowing up? I'm human, damn it!"

Yeah, I bet you that man understood where I was coming from then.

Malik pulled me close and rubbed my back. "Lonnie, I get it, but did you have to beat that girl like that?"

"Hell, yeah!"

Malik started laughing. "Your ass is crazy, but it's cool. You're a tough chick, huh?"

"Yup, and don't you forget it."

"I won't. Damn, woman! That shit got my dick jumpin'."

I punched him in the arm. "Malik, stop playing."

"Who's playing? I'm serious, Lonnie. I'm going to tear that ass up when we get home."

"Whatever, man. Anyway, I'm calm now. Let's go back."

We walked back toward my car where Asia was standing, laughing at Tamika, who was still talking shit about what she was going to do to me. I found that shit funny too. She could try whatever she wanted. I had made my point, and I told her so.

Once I shut her shit down, and Asia pointed out how embarrassing it was to get your ass kicked in public, Tamika and her girl stomped off to her car like two-year-olds throwing a tantrum. I anticipated that she might want to keep this shit going, but if she had any sense at all, she'd let it go.

Asia, James, Malik, and I went back into the bar and had a good time, like nothing had happened.

I didn't lay eyes on Tamika again until a week later when her bruises had healed. Apparently she didn't want any more of this, because every time we crossed paths, she averted her gaze. I never saw that bitch talking to Malik again either. Hell, she didn't even press charges against me. Dumb ass.

Chapter 30

Malik and I were both exhausted when we left the bar. We could do no more than go to sleep that night. Neither of us could open our eyes until after ten the next morning. When we finally got up and started moving, he suggested we go have brunch.

"That sounds good to me. Where do you want to go?" I asked.

"There's this new place in Lawnside that I've been wanting to try. How about there?"

"Sure."

We wasted no time getting ready. After a night of drinking and kicking ass, I was starving.

The restaurant we went to had a nice setting, with fresh flowers on all of the tables, and a buffet with all of my favorite breakfast foods. Malik and I chose to sit at one of tables set up on the terrace. It was actually very romantic.

As soon as we started eating, Malik wanted to talk about the previous night's events.

"Lonnie, you know you were a mess yesterday, beating on that girl like that. Why did you go off on her like that?"

"Babe, I thought I explained all of that yesterday. Why are you questioning me again? Besides, I thought you said it turned you on?"

Malik hesitated for a moment. "I know that, but I'm just trying to understand if you feel OK with using violence to solve an issue you have with someone. And 'the hard dick' was more of a joke than anything. I don't need to see you acting like a fool to desire you."

Damn! Did this man think that I would physically attack someone every time I got pissed off? "Let me put your mind at ease. No, I don't feel that violence is always necessary. It was more a matter of me being completely fed up, and sometimes kicking ass is the best way to drive home the point that I'm not to be fucked with."

"You see, that's that shit right there. That was the kind of attitude I had in college, and acting on it almost ruined my future."

I gave Malik a look that said, *Are you kidding me with this?*

At that moment he pulled back from giving me the third degree. "Don't get me wrong, Lonnie. I love that you don't take shit off of people. That's not really a problem for me. Hell, you can handle yourself, and I guess, on some level, that *is* a turn-on for me."

I just laughed at that fool.

"It's just that I don't want to see you get into any trouble. I mean, really, babe, hitting another person *is* a crime."

"All right, man. I get it. Now can you shut up and let me eat?"

"I guess I'd better. Otherwise, you might just come across this table and kick *my* ass."

"That's not funny, Malik. How about I just come across this table and kiss you instead, silly-ass man?"

"Now, that I can handle."

We finished our meals and decided to stop at a flea market we passed on our way to the restaurant.

While we were there, I found an antique lamp that would go perfectly next to my reading chair. And Malik brought some used CDs that he put on as soon as we got back into the car. The first was an old-school mix with Kurtis Blow, Run-D.M.C., and Public Enemy songs. We went off in the car as soon as we heard the first bars of "Fight the Power." We were laughing and singing every song at the top of our lungs on the way home.

It was days like that one which showed me just why I loved that man so much. No matter what his objections to my behavior might have been, Malik accepted me just as I was; faults and all. Not only that, he didn't seem fazed too much by anything I said or did. He just pretty much went with the flow.

We spent the rest of the afternoon laying around and talking about our future. We decided then that we would sell our homes and purchase a house together. Because I had been in my house for so long, I was apprehensive about giving it up. Nevertheless, Malik convinced me that it would be best to have a fresh start to our new life.

That evening we ordered a pizza and relaxed in front of the television.

There was one thing on my mind that I needed to get Malik's feelings about. "Malik, I love you, and I know how much you love me, but do you think we're moving too fast? We're planning a marriage after only six months of dating. Doesn't that seem like a big leap to you?"

Malik lifted my head from his lap and looked me directly in my eyes. "No, I don't think it's too fast. First of all, we're not getting married tomorrow, and secondly, I'm very clear about how I feel about you and what I want with you. Babe, are you having second thoughts about us?"

"No, it's not that. It's just that because this is all happening so quickly, I'm feeling a little unsteady or maybe a little scared. I'm not sure. I guess that because I'm not used to having something so wonderful happen in my life, I don't know how to accept it as it is."

"Well, rest assured that this is the real deal, and there's nothing that will change that. So, precious woman, relax and get used to having me around, because I'm in it for life."

Feeling a little more at peace with our choice to marry so soon, I lay my head back in Malik's lap and fell asleep with him playing in my locks.

Chapter 31

The following Monday morning I ran into James in the elevator. Cherie's dumb ass was in there as well. Not knowing my history with her, he proceeded to ask me how I was enjoying being engaged and planning a wedding. At this point not too many people in the office knew that Malik and I had taken that particular step.

I told James I was very happy and left it at that, trying to pretend it was no big deal.

Cherie stood behind James with this stupid look on her face like she knew some major secret. That bitch! I could only imagine what she was feeling so smug about.

As soon as I reached my desk, I called Malik, but he hadn't gotten in yet, so I set about getting my work done.

Forty-five minutes later, one person after another started coming by my desk to give me their best wishes on my pending nuptials. It wasn't that I had a problem with people knowing, at least not those particular people who came by. It was just that Cherie was the one who took away the pleasure of Malik and I being able to announce our engagement. I could have strangled that chick. She had stolen some of my joy about our announcement. Not to mention, it was up to us who we chose to tell in the first damn place, but of course, she told everyone she knew.

I called Malik and told him what had happened, and he was pissed. I asked him not to be angry with James. It wasn't his fault. He had no idea what an ass Cherie was. I also told Malik I wasn't up for the bullshit, and that I was going to find Cherie. He tried to talk me out of a confrontation, but I was having no part of that. I had some things to say, and damn it, Cherie, was going to hear them.

Now maybe if I were a more secure woman, I would have listened to Malik's protest. However, I wasn't, and I wasn't even aware at that time that I was more than likely overreacting to this latest crap of Cherie's. That woman set things off in me that I had no control over.

Fate must have been on her side, or mine, depending on how one looked at it, because when I didn't find her at her desk, I went to ask Logan if she'd seen her. Logan informed me that Cherie had left early, stating that she wasn't feeling well.

Yeah, right. That bitch ran her mouth then ran her ass home, knowing I was going to be on her. This made me even angrier, and I couldn't shake it.

I went back to my desk and sat there fuming. I was going to get at that girl before the day ended. I sat there until I couldn't take it anymore. I had to find a way to get that ugliness out of me before it consumed me. I promised Malik no more violence, so I had to find another way.

Fortunately for me, Malik was too busy to do lunch with me, so I called Tracey. We decided to do a quick fast-food lunch at a place we could both get to quickly.

After I let Tracey in on what had happened that morning at work, she tried to help me formulate a plan.

"Lonnie, you know who her friends are at work. Just make something up and ask for her number."

"That won't work. I'm sure that anyone she's friends with knows about the animosity between us, especially after what I did to her buddy, Tamika."

"Oh, yeah. Maybe you're right. They wouldn't be so quick to give her number to you."

We both sat there deep in thought, like we were planning some major jewel heist or something.

"I've got it!" I said finally. "People at work leave their cell phones sitting on their desks all the time. If I'm lucky, one of her silly followers does that. I'll just have to search the contacts quickly."

Tracey agreed that was the way to go, and she also understood my need to speak my mind to Cherie that day.

I made it back to work in record time and went straight to Marla's desk. She was Cherie's biggest follower. It seemed as if after her ass-whooping, Tamika had figured out that participating in Cherie's bull was detrimental to her health, so she bowed out of her circle. Marla, on the other hand, was just another drama follower who couldn't think for herself.

Anyway, as I had suspected, her phone was sitting on her desk plugged into a charger. Thank goodness, the office was still pretty deserted. The lunch hour always lasted at least two hours for most folks around that office. I quickly scrolled through the phone and found Cherie's number.

I ran back to my desk and called Cherie immediately. She barely got the word *hello* out of her mouth before I lit into her.

"Listen, bitch, this is the only time I'm going to warn you. I know you ran your mouth this morning, telling mine and Malik's business to anyone who would listen, and I know damn well you're behind the bullshit Tamika tried to pull with Malik. Make no mistake about it, if you start this crap all over again, I will fuck up your entire world! You can think I'm playin' if you want to, but trust and believe, I will make you sorry you even exist!"

I banged on her ass before she could even think of how to respond. It wasn't necessary to go back and forth with her. I said what I had to say, and that was that.

Now I knew the real drama was going to begin again. Cherie didn't have enough sense to back off, and I did in essence call her out. The difference this time was that I wouldn't be participating in the drama. The first thing she did would be the last thing. There was no way I was going to let this nut cause any more harm in my life.

My phone rang a few seconds later. It was none other than Ms. Cherie herself. I didn't even bother to listen to her nonsense. I hung up and continued to do so the next fifty times she called.

Finally, I just took the phone off the hook. She didn't get it. There would be no arguing between us. She had been warned, and there was nothing left to say.

Malik came down to my desk at the end of the day. He looked exhausted. Obviously he wasn't kidding when he said he had a ton of work to do.

"Hi, babe, are you about ready to go?" he asked.

"Just a couple more minutes. Let me wrap up and clear off my desk."

"OK. We should go get something to eat and maybe see a movie. How's that sound?"

"Sounds good to me. So how was your day?" I asked.

"Interesting. In addition to being so busy, I had plenty to keep me hopping today."

"Oh, yeah? Interesting in what way?"

"First of all, at least ten people came to say something about us, all positive, which, of course, was cool. I don't know what I expected, but for whatever reason, I wasn't sure these people would act like mature adults."

I had to laugh at that. "You probably felt that way because there aren't too many mature adults in this office to begin with."

Malik laughed too. Most days it felt like high school there, instead of a place of business.

I grabbed my purse and jacket, ready to go. As I stood, I noticed Malik had a strange expression on his face. "What's on your mind, Malik?"

"I got a phone call from Cherie earlier. What the fuck did you say to that fool, Lonnie?"

I sat back down. I wasn't in the mood to discuss Cherie. I had all but forgotten about that drama. I took a deep breath and decided to spell it all out. "What the hell did she call you for?"

"She was crying, or at least pretending to cry. She said that you were calling and threatening her all day. She also said that you threatened to hurt her son."

Now, I didn't give two shits about her calling Malik, because I knew he wouldn't fall for her bull, but to say I threatened to harm a child was low.

Malik could see the explosion I was about to have written all over my face. He pulled me back with a quickness. "Lonnie, don't even think about it. I know, just like everyone else who knows you, that you didn't say anything about her son. I remember you telling me about how you came to care so much for the kid when you were with that nigga. I also know how wrong she is, but please don't let that girl upset you any more today."

I agreed with him. It was the weekend, and it was time to go home. There was no way I was taking Cherie into my free time with me.

Malik walked me to my car, and we agreed to meet at my house in an hour. He needed to go home and pack a weekend bag.

As I started the car, Malik asked, "You know what's so funny about that simple-ass girl?"

"No. What's that?"

"It's that she's so damn stupid. I mean, think about it. It's obvious she called me in an attempt to have me get mad at you about your behavior, but couldn't she come up with a better lie? She doesn't have enough sense to think things through, because if she had, she'd have realized that if we've gone so far as to get engaged, we would know one another's character and what the other would or would not do."

I just smiled. "Well, sweetie, now you know not to give that girl credit for having the ability to think. She doesn't."

Malik laughed, kissed my cheek, and walked to his car.

Yeah, maybe Cherie wasn't too bright, but she was definitely slimy as hell, and she was good at that sometimes. I wasn't quite sure if Malik fully understood the level of Cherie's drama. She took the term *ghetto* to a new high. She simply didn't know how to behave in any area of life, yet she thought she did. Cherie truly believed that she was on the ball.

I didn't think her dumb ass realized that most folks saw through every move she made. I'd always be baffled about John's inability to see who she really was. Maybe I gave him too much credit for being able to think. Nevertheless, I felt I'd better let Malik know that Cherie was about to start acting a fool because of my warning to her. I knew things with her were far from finished.

Chapter 32

Malik and I had a beautiful weekend together. We shut the rest of the world out and began planning our future. Mostly, we laughed and played like children, enjoying one another's company without distraction. We did, however, iron out some definite plans for our wedding, and since neither of us was interested in a big spectacle, we decided to keep it small and simple. We also agreed that Christmas, our favorite time of year, would make a beautiful setting for a wedding.

I was both surprised and pleased to learn that Malik was willing to help me decide on a color scheme, and if that wasn't enough, he had ideas about the flowers as well as the ceremony itself. I never would have thought that the man would want to do any more than just show up. But I guess it would be different with him considering his mom was an event coordinator and she made him work with her on all of her jobs. I really did get a good guy this time around.

"Malik, I still can't believe we're actually getting married. After all, we've only been together for a little over six months. Honey, are you sure this is what you want? That it's me you want?"

Malik gave me a look of confusion. "Why would you ask me a

question like that? Of course, I'm sure it's you I want."

"I don't know. I guess I'm just making sure you won't want to change your mind."

He grabbed my hands and looked me in the eyes. "LonnieStop trippin'. I've never been happier, and that's because of your crazy ass. Hell, no, I won't be changing my mind. Besides, who else will laugh at my silly jokes?"

I couldn't express to Malik why I felt the need to question his sincerity. There were always moments when I was alone with him in which my love would overwhelm me. And in those moments I would wonder what I would do without him. Or how I would survive if he found someone he liked better. The closer I got to fulfilling my dream life with him, the more insecure I felt.

Unfortunately, our weekend had to come to an end. It was Monday morning, and time for us to leave our cocoon and face the grown-up world. I knew I was going to have to deal with some shit from Cherie, but I wasn't all that concerned. I had Malik's support, and I knew exactly how to deal with Cherie.

The shit started in the parking lot. I had one foot out of Malik's car when I saw Cherie approaching. I said, "Babe, here comes the drama."

Malik saw what I was talking about and exhaled deeply. "I am not in the mood for this bullshit first thing in the morning. Lonnie, please just ignore her and let's go to work."

"I'll try, but let's get real here. Cherie is not one to be ignored when she wants trouble."

"I'm well aware of that, but just remember you're a lady."

"Yeah, funny, Malik. Like I said, I'll try."

By the time I closed my door, Cherie was there with her finger in my face. "Hey, bitch, don't you ever call my phone and threaten me again!"

I promptly slapped her finger out of my face with my left hand and wrapped my right hand around that bitch's throat. Just before I could bash her face into the hood of Malik's car, he interceded. I allowed him to pull me away and usher me into the building.

"You sure do have a strange way of ignoring people," he whispered in my ear.

I don't know why he bothered to whisper, because enough people had witnessed that brief altercation that it damn sure didn't matter what they might hear him say.

"How are you going to make it through the day without getting an assault charge?" he asked.

"So you got jokes, huh? I'll be fine. Outside is one thing, but in the building I know how to act."

"Just promise me I won't have to bail your ass out of jail today."

"OK, I promise. I'll keep it hands-off today."

I didn't tell Malik I was going to deal with Cherie in the only manner she would understand. As soon as I set my things at my desk, I went to speak to my supervisor. It was time to play the role.

"Good morning, Logan," I said.

"Good morning. What's the matter? You look upset."

"I am. I just had an altercation with Cherie in the parking lot, and she got physical."

Logan jumped out of her chair. "What? Did she hit you?"

"No. She approached me and started talking shit, and then poked me in my forehead." I couldn't care less about stretching the truth at this point.

"She did what? Why was she in your face at all?"

"Well, you know our history."

"Yes, but I thought that was over. You haven't mentioned any issues between you two lately."

"That's because I was trying to ignore her little nonsense, but lately it's been escalating again. That's why I was looking for her on Friday. I was trying to make an attempt to clear the air and put an end to this crap. Anyway, I only succeeded in pissing her off."

"OK, Lonnie. I'll talk to her and see if I can't get a resolution."

"I'm not here for a resolution. I've had enough of the drama. I'm here to find out if you have the forms I need to file a grievance. Cherie has harassed me one time too many. From the first day she came to work here, she's made every attempt to make my work life a living hell. Well, I've had enough! She's done more than create a hostile work environment. She assaulted me, and I'm done! So do you have the forms?"

Logan was shocked by my outburst, but she didn't say anything about it. She pulled out the forms and explained the process to me.

Before I left Logan's office, she asked again if I wanted her to speak to Cherie about the situation.

I managed to squeeze out a couple of tears. "No, Logan. It's too late for that now. I need to handle this my way. I can't go on dealing with this craziness, and if something doesn't change soon, I'll have to seek employment elsewhere."

Again I could tell Logan was shocked. I knew she would be. Never had I played the victim before in any situation, so for me to come at her in this way was the perfect way to convince her that I was innocent of any wrongdoing, if Cherie should come running to her. And of course she would. Also, throwing in that remark about quitting my job really drove home my point.

I knew Cherie would try to pull a similar stunt with Logan, but I beat her to the punch. And, true to form, the moment I opened Logan's door to leave, Cherie was fast approaching. Her eyes shot daggers at me when she saw me come out of that office. I threw that bitch the sweetest smile and wink as I walked by. It was all I could do not to burst out laughing.

Whatever she had in mind to say to Logan was of no consequence to me. I was a true believer of good always prevailing over evil. It didn't matter if I had to play evil for a while. I didn't deserve this, and I was going to win this war.

I went up to see Malik and let him know what I had done and how I wanted to handle it. He didn't really agree with me being dishonest or underhanded, but he loved me enough to support me nonetheless.

I have no idea what Logan said to Cherie, but I saw her several times that day, and she wouldn't even make eye contact with me. Curiosity got the better of me, so I went to Asia and put her on the case. I told her everything that had happened the other day and this morning, and I asked her to go pump Logan for information.

Although Logan wasn't supposed to discuss these things with other coworkers, we both knew she would. That chick couldn't keep her mouth shut, especially with those of us who had been working here as long as she had. At the job there were some insiders and some outsiders. Asia and I were definitely insiders. Cherie? Not!

Maybe about ten minutes later, Asia came to my desk. "Come on, let's go outside," she said.

We walked out to the lot and sat in Asia's car, so she could smoke a cigarette while she filled me in.

"OK, what happened?" I asked.

Asia took a long drag on her cigarette and exhaled deeply. "That damn Logan ain't got no sense. Her ass knows she has no business telling me y'all's business, and she told me everything she knew."

I started laughing. "Girl, please, you know she has diarrhea of the mouth with us. I bet she didn't even wait for you to ask her anything before she started spilling her guts."

Asia cracked up and hit me on my arm. "You know that's right. So, anyway, first of all, she really believes you're upset, instead of just pissed and bent on revenge."

"I'm not bent on revenge. I'm just fed up."

"Yeah, whatever, bitch. Listen, Logan never really gave Cherie a chance to speak. She told Cherie she wasn't going to stand for any drama or harassment of any member of her staff, her exact words. She then told that bitch that you had explained to her what went down, and that she had no choice but to write her up."

"Get the hell out of here! She wrote her up?"

"She sure did. You know she don't like that bitch anyway because of her smart-ass mouth. Shit, Logan's been looking for an excuse to discipline that one, and you just gave it to her."

I had been so busy living in my own world these last few months, I had completely forgotten that Cherie had been rubbing Logan the wrong way on a regular basis. She half-ass did her work, and when she turned any of it in, it was usually late. This all worked out perfectly for me.

Asia finished her cigarette, and we strolled back into the building. I parked myself at my desk, determined to complete the grievance forms. There weren't many questions, but I had to write a detailed account of everything that had precipitated the grievance. Thankfully, this was relatively easy for me, because from the moment Cherie came to work there, I had been keeping a notebook to write down everything she had done, both serious and minor.

Once this chore was done, I put the forms in an interoffice envelope and sent them up to the human resources office. Although I was happy that I had formally accused Cherie of harassment, I soon came to the conclusion that this wasn't enough to get my point across. By attempting to turn the tables on Cherie, I believed that I might have to play a little dirtier. The only issue I had with this was that such behavior would take me away from my true nature. The level of immaturity it would take for me to sink to her level wasn't something I felt comfortable with. But by now it no longer mattered. I was done with the bull, and I was ready to end things in any way possible.

Although I had shared everything with Malik, I didn't feel that these thoughts were something I could share with him, because I knew he would not appreciate or support me acting like a high-schooler or doing anything malicious. I thought that kind of behavior would turn him off and I would lose him for sure. I also didn't think he could fully understand my need to remove this psycho bitch from my life. My rage against her was building to the point where I might do something that I couldn't take back.

I called Lena first then Tracey and Sandy, and invited them all to dinner at my house. I needed opinions other than my own about how I should proceed with Cherie. Besides, it was time Tracey, Lena, and Sandy got together. Since I wanted all of them in my wedding, they needed to develop a relationship. Hopefully, they would hit it off, as well as be able to help me with my situation at work.

Chapter 33

Wednesday night was the evening of my dinner with my girls. I decided to invite Asia as well, since she, Lena, and Sandy hadn't seen each other in a while. I also figured that if the others and Tracey didn't click, Asia would be the perfect buffer. She could keep a room light and full of laughter with her silliness. The only thing that would have made the evening better was to have Reggie's silly ass there. Unfortunately he was back on tour with his shows.

We chose Wednesday because we all thought it would be a good way to break up the workweek. Dinner with the girls was as good a way as any to accomplish this.

All four women arrived at my house by seven. I kept dinner light and made a quick stir-fry meal. No fuss, no muss. I wanted to get down to the main reason for this little gathering, and lingering over a heavy meal wasn't part of the plan.

Sandy came rushing through the door first, yelling, "I have to pee." She pushed me aside. "Make way, *chica!*"

I cracked up. I said to the other ladies, "That girl is nuts!" I then took Asia and Lena by the arm. "Anyway, Asia meet Tracey, Tracey meet Asia and my sister, Lena"

"Ahh, we met outside, Lonnie," Asia said, a look of *Duh* on her face.

"Oh, whatever. Shut up!"

Then to my surprise, instead of shaking hands, Tracey did that mom-like thing she does and pulled Asia, then Lena into a hug. There was a brief moment of awkwardness, but Asia, being Asia, went with the flow, like she always did. My sister, however, was just a little put off by the physical contact.

"It's very nice to finally meet you both. Lonnie has spoken highly of you guys."

Lena just smiled and nodded, which was odd. She'd never been at a loss for words.

"It's nice to meet you too, girl," Asia said, taking a seat on the sofa. "But let me ask you something. Do you always talk like that? You know, Lonnie *has spoken* of me."

I couldn't believe Asia. She didn't censor herself for anyone.

Right at that moment, Sandy came marching out of the downstairs powder room. "So, *mami*," she said, talking loud, "when do we eat? I'm starving!"

"We'll eat in a few minutes. Will you just sit your ass down first? Oh, and meet Tracey. Tracey, this little loudmouth is Sandy."

"*Hola*, Tracey. It's nice to see you finally. My friend here sure took her time getting everyone together."

Tracey didn't get a chance to say a word before Sandy turned to Asia and said, "So, *chica*, how the hell have you been? I haven't seen you in a minute."

"Yeah, whatever, bitch. Would you shut up for two seconds, so Tracey can answer my question?"

"¡*Ay Dios mío*! Tracey, whatever the question is, don't answer it. This one is a psycho." Sandy plucked Asia in the head, on her way to taking a seat.

"Owwww, bitch! That hurt. And what the hell is *Ay Dios mío* anyway? Every time I see your ass, you yelling that shit."

By this time Tracey had taken a seat in the recliner, all the while amused by Asia and Sandy's antics. "Sandy, I really don't mind answering Asia's question. After all, I am here to get to know you guys and to let you know me."

"OK, chica, but I better warn you. Don't tell this one anything personal. She can't hold water."

We all laughed at that one, even Asia because she knew that was the truth. She couldn't deny it.

"In answer to your question, Asia, I grew up in the suburbs. There weren't many people of color around, so, of course, my vernacular was influenced by my surroundings. It's just that simple."

"That makes sense, girl," Asia said. "And before you other two bitches say anything, yes, I know what *vernacular* means."

We all fell out laughing again. Well, everyone except Lena. She was unusually quiet, all the while watching Tracey with an eagle eye.

"Aw! Little ghetto Barbie," I said. "We know that you know stuff."

"Not funny, Lonnie."

"Yes, it is, *chica*. When are you going to stop wearing that long-ass ponytail from the nineties anyway?"

By now, I was laughing tears at those two and their nonsense. Once we pulled ourselves together, I escorted the ladies into the dining room.

Before we sat down to eat, I realized I needn't have worried about the women getting along. Tracey and Sandy took to one another instantly, which put me at ease. I took it as a sign that my wedding was going to be a wonderful day, with these women by my side.

"OK, ladies, listen," I said. "You all know what I've been through with Cherie, and she's starting her shit again. This time around I want to put an end to the drama as quickly and as painlessly as possible. The problem this time around is, I have to deal with her daily. The last time it was a little easier to get rid of her. All I had to do was get rid of the man."

I tried to laugh that statement off like it was no big deal, but the truth was, every now and then, the destruction Cherie had caused in my personal life with John still played in my mind. I hadn't completely forgotten that pain. I don't think I ever hated someone until Cherie. What I didn't realize then was that my hatred was beginning to take over who I was.

"What did you have in mind?" Tracey asked.

"The complete and total destruction of her life."

All three giggled a little, and Lena just raised an eyebrow, but when they noticed the seriousness on my face, their giggles took on a nervous tone before they got completely quiet.

"What the hell's wrong with y'all?" Lena asked. "My sister has every right to be done with that bitch Cherie, and if she wants her out of her life then that's what's going to happen."

Sandy took some time before voicing her opinion. "Look, *mami*, as you know, I'm always down to cause problems for someone who's pissed me off, but complete and total destruction, as you say, that sounds a little *loca* to me."

"OK, then I guess you won't be much help," I said.

None of the ladies missed the sarcasm in my statement.

I turned to Asia and asked what she was thinking.

"I think you should explain what you mean," Asia said. "Like, what kind of destruction are you talking about?"

I sensed hesitation in Asia as well. Which was a little odd, because she was always ride-or-die with these sort of things. The air in the room had changed, setting off all kinds of warning bells in my head. I didn't think my means to an end were all that bad, because I hadn't actually come up with a plan, but apparently I must have been putting something ugly out there.

It hit me that my girls weren't really interested in what I wanted, and I no longer wanted to involve them. This was my fight, and if I was going to get dirty, it wouldn't be fair of me to cause problems for anyone other than Cherie.

I looked into each of these women's eyes and realized that there was no way I could ask them to participate in any drama. I was, as Asia had said, bent on revenge, but I still had enough sense to know it was a bad idea to take anyone else along for the ride.

"You know what? Maybe this isn't such a good idea. I lost my head for a moment. I've already filed the grievance, so maybe that will be enough to put an end to all this shit."

The relief in the room was tangible after I'd said that.

The evening didn't last much longer, because some awkwardness lingered until I couldn't take it anymore. By eight-thirty my company was ready to leave. It was for the best.

Lena started clearing the dishes and Tracey lingered for a few minutes after the others had gone. She put it to me straight. "Lonnie, the others may not have noticed, but I sure did. You have no intention of backing off, do you?"

"I can't answer that. I'll just say that whatever I do, no one else has to be concerned."

Tracey gave me an odd look, like maybe she saw something in me that wasn't quite right.

"OK, let me just say that you should be careful. If you go too far, there may be some fallout that you can't foresee. You're finally living happily. You might not want to chance ruining that." With that, Tracey said good night.

Lena was standing in the kitchen doorway listening. She waited for Tracey to leave before she spoke. "Lon, how well do you know that girl?"

"I don't know, why? I think she's a good person."

"Maybe, but I have to say that, something's not quite right with your friend."

"What are you talking about?"

"I can't put my finger on it, but I don't like the look in her eyes. It's like there's something lingering behind them. I'm telling you Lon, she may very well be a good person, but she definitely has something to hide, or is afraid of."

I didn't know where Lena was coming from with that assessment of Tracey. I could only guess that she might be a little jealous of the bond we'd formed. Nevertheless, I wasn't going to try and change her mind. I simply didn't want to deal with any of it at that point.

"All right, sis. Maybe I'll talk to her and see I can sense anything, but for right now, I just want to get some rest."

Lena let it go and headed on home. *Damn, that hussy left me to wash them dishes by myself too,* I thought.

No matter what anyone else said, I wanted Cherie out of my life by any means necessary, and I didn't have time to fuck around with a bunch of punks. My justice needed to be swift and final.

I quickly cleaned the kitchen and sat down to call Malik. He asked if he could come over and spend the night with me, but I wasn't in the mood.

Somewhere in the last few days something had shifted in me. I was losing focus on what was important in my life. I noticed the shift, but I couldn't pull myself back from it.

After I finished talking to Malik, I settled in to watch some television, but I couldn't concentrate on anything. My mind was racing. I don't know how long I sat there before it came to me that I should try to find John's number and do some fishing. I needed a plan. His dumb ass wouldn't know the difference anyway. If he knew anything about Cherie that I could use against her, I would.

I ran upstairs to the second bedroom. I used this as a small office, and I kept some of my old yearly planners there in the bottom desk drawer. I remembered the last time John had reached out, I'd written down his number in one of those books.

Luckily for me there wasn't much of a search to do. I found the number in the second book I picked up. All I had to do now was think of a good excuse for calling.

I couldn't really come up with anything, but I figured, what the hell? I sat down at the desk and dialed the number. I only hoped that he hadn't changed it. I couldn't recall how long it had been since he'd called.

I hesitated for a brief moment when I heard his voice, but then I forged ahead. "Hello, John. This is Lonnie."

"Lonnie? How the hell are you?"

"I'm good. And you?"

"I'm doing well, actually. I'm also really surprised to hear from you."

"I know you are. I was cleaning out this office, and I found your number, so I took a chance. It's OK that I called, isn't it?"

"Sure. I'm glad you did. It's great to hear your voice again. I've been thinking about you and wondering how you're doing."

"Really? Why is that?

"Oh, I don't know. Every now and then you cross my mind, and I begin to remember us together. It wasn't always bad. We did have a good relationship for a while."

"This is true. I could never say our relationship was horrible. Due to certain circumstances, though, it had to end. I had no choice."

John became quiet then. The few times we'd spoken since our breakup, Cherie was still very much a sore subject, so we never mentioned her or what had happened. This time, however, she was my only reason for calling him.

"So, anyway, how's John Jr. doing? I bet he's gotten to be a big boy now. He's in kindergarten, right?"

I could hear the smile in John's voice when he answered, "Yeah, he's five now and getting so tall. Hey, maybe I have a future baller on my hands. I wish I could see him more often, though. Cherie creates a bunch of bullshit at every turn. What a pain in the ass that girl is!"

"You don't have to tell me that. I'm sure by now that you know we work together. Trust me when I tell you it hasn't been easy, but I've become very good at ignoring her. So what's going on? Why don't you see your son?" I asked as if I didn't already have a clue.

Cherie was messing with some thug, and John wasn't the type to associate himself with that lifestyle. Unfortunately for his son, he also wasn't the type to take a stand and remove his child from harm's way. What a coward! The man simply had no backbone at all.

"Let's see, where do I begin? If I don't call before I go to pick him up, drama. If I do call before I go pick him up, drama. If that dude Rasheed is there, drama. Sometimes I swear that girl is getting high, because she's so erratic. I don't know what's going on in that house. There's always people going in and out of there, and J.J. barely makes it to preschool five days a week. Let me ask you, does Cherie go to work every day?"

"Actually she does, but she's been looking tore up for a while. There were some rumors that she was getting high, but then I heard she was dealing with some guy that ain't shit and he's putting her through it. Cheating on her, knocking her around, that sort of thing. I guess that must be this Rasheed you spoke about?"

"Yes, he's the only one I've seen there. I think she's been with him for a while."

At this point I felt comfortable digging a little deeper. "Tell me, John, what's this guy's deal? Is he doing anything positive for her or your son?"

"Hell no! Personally, I think that nigga is a crackhead. I know he used to sell that shit, but I believe he got twisted in the game and started getting high on his own supply. That's mainly why I think she's doing it too."

To me it was a stretch to think that Cherie was getting high too. Nevertheless, I knew exactly how I was going to use this information. Better still, I decided then that I could use him to do my dirty work.

"John, if you believe that's what's going on, why would you leave your son in a home like that? Don't you think he deserves better? Don't you think you could give him better?"

"Lonnie, I'm still trying to get my business off the ground. I'm not stable enough to give him the things he needs. I couldn't possibly take care of him now."

"John, I cannot believe you just said that shit! It doesn't matter what your circumstances are. He's your son. Not to mention, you're on this phone telling me that you think your son is being raised by crackheads. What the hell are you thinking?"

That punk-ass bitch got to stuttering and twisting his words, but said absolutely nothing. I was too through! I got off that phone in five seconds flat.

"What an ass he is!" I said out loud.

I couldn't use John, but I could use his information. Cherie's ass was going down. I was single-minded in my desire to get rid of her once and for all. Lucky for her, murder never crossed my mind. Then again, who the hell knew? In my current state of mind, anything was possible.

I left the office and walked down the hall to my bedroom. A long hot bath was at the forefront of my mind by then, so I went into the bathroom and turned on the hot water full blast. I added some bath salts and went into my room to undress.

Not until I sank down into the tub did I notice how much tension my body held. I recognized this feeling. It wasn't only physical, but it also consumed my soul. The last time I experienced this was when I was with John and I desperately needed the drama to end.

I felt a little better after my bath, but I still wasn't at ease emotionally. I was in a battle with myself. As much as I wanted to get back at Cherie for existing, some intuition deep inside me was trying to warn me that I was about to go too far.

I had a happy future to look forward to, and that did not include her drama. I would find peace in my life. I would not continue to live with Cherie in the same space as me. She'd already shown me that she wasn't going to stop fucking with me unless I made her, so that was what I was going to do.

Chapter 34

Although dinner with my girls hadn't gone as I had anticipated, I decided to forget about the awkwardness and focus on the fact that Asia and Sandy hit it off with Tracey. I was sure that Lena would eventually come around. I felt that it was time for Tracey to meet Malik as well.

When I arrived at work the next morning I bypassed my floor and road up to the sixth, hoping that Malik had already gotten in. The more I thought about it the more excited I became. Once I'd gotten rid of Cherie, I felt for sure I could live a peaceful and happy life.

"Good morning, honey," I said as I approached Malik's desk. "I'm glad you're here."

"I'm glad I'm here too, precious. So what's up with you? You have that goofy grin on your face like you have some great idea forming in that twisted mind of yours." He laughed.

"I am not twisted!" I laughed and punched him in the arm. "Anyway, you're right, I do have a great idea."

"OK then, let's hear it."

"All right so, I was thinking that it would be a good idea for you and Tracey to meet. I mean, she's going to be in our wedding after all, and of my few friends, you two have never laid eyes on one another," I explained.

"OK, precious, I agree. It is about time I get to meet this new friend that you think so highly of. What did you have in mind?"

"How about drinks this weekend? Maybe even tomorrow if she can make it. That way we can keep it casual—a simple meet and greet."

"That's fine, Lonnie. Anything you want. Just let me know when and where. Now, it's well after nine, don't you think it's time for you to get downstairs and get to work?"

"Maybe, but so what? You're not my supervisor so don't be clocking my time, Malik."

"Uh, whateverrrr! Isn't that what you say all the time?" He laughed.

"No! I don't talk like that."

"Yeah, you do."

"Whatever, Malik." I stomped my foot and said, "Damn it!" as I realized that I had just proven him right. He laughed and stood to give me a kiss and send me on my way.

"You are a nut, precious, but that's what I love about you. Now seriously, I have work to do and you need to go down and show your face.

"True enough. Now kiss me again and I'll go."

I called Tracey immediately after I sat down and was happy that the strain from the night before hadn't carried over. Tracey readily accepted my invitation to have drinks with Malik and me.

We had already ordered our first drinks by the time Tracey arrived at the restaurant we chose. When I spotted her coming through the door, I sat my drink down and turned toward Malik. "Here she is now."

He was taking a sip of his drink just as Tracey approached and at the very moment Malik turned and looked up, their eyes met and he began choking on what was left of the alcohol going down his throat. "Oh my goodness, are you OK, honey?" I asked as I patted him on the back.

"Uh, yes. I'm fine."

When I finished attending to him, I turned around and noticed that Tracey was standing statue-still and stunned into silence. Her eyes were glued to Malik's face. The pleasant expression she wore when she entered had turned to one of shock and disbelief. Actually it was more like sheer terror in her eyes. I then looked back at Malik and noticed that his face wore almost the same expression as Tracey's. Without knowing what the hell was going on, I felt a chill run down my spine.

I continued to look back and forth between the two, and although I wanted to shake that dreadful feeling, I knew that my eyes had not deceived me and that something was seriously amiss in that moment.

I addressed Malik first. "Babe, what's wrong? You look as if you've seen a ghost." I tried to calm the tremor in voice, but I failed. Malik could not look me in my eyes, nor could he speak, and I was becoming more fearful by the moment.

I looked at Tracey and asked her the same question. "What's wrong?"

She began shaking her head from side to side, also unable to speak. Her eyes welled up with tears that quickly began to run down her cheeks. I grabbed Tracey by her shoulders and asked again, "What the hell is wrong with you?"

"I, I, I can't," Tracey stammered. She pried herself from my grip, and, in a flash, ran out of the restaurant. I just stood there staring after her. *What the hell was that?* I turned back around again and reclaimed my seat at the bar.

"Malik, I'm really not feeling whatever the hell this is so, babe please, tell me what the fuck that was about before I lose it."

Malik still looked to be a little surprised but he had gathered himself to speak.

"You're not going to believe this but, remember the college girlfriend I told you about?"

"Which one?"

"The one I said lied about being pregnant. Well, that was Tracey."

I jumped up out of my seat involuntarily. My body physically reacted to the words my ears had just received.

"OK, Lonnie now, don't go getting crazy on me. Please sit back down."

I did as I was asked.

"You and Tracey? You and my friend Tracey? Are you kidding me, Malik?!" I simply could not believe the absurdity of the situation.

"Come on now, Lonnie. It's not that serious."

"Oh no? Then why in the hell did you start choking when you saw her?" I demanded.

"I don't know. I guess it was because it was so unexpected. Think about it, I was expecting to meet a friend of yours and it turns out to be one of my exes. How would you have reacted? It just threw me, that's all."

I considered Malik's explanation for a moment and realized that he did make a great deal of sense. Nevertheless, I still didn't understand Tracey's reaction to Malik.

"That's all well and good, Malik, but I'm not stupid. If she's just an old girlfriend, why the fuck did she start crying and run out of here like she ain't got no damned sense?"

"Lonnie, you can't seriously think I have the answer to that."

"Oh yes the fuck I do, and you'd better start explaining that shit right now."

"OK first of all, you better stop speaking to me like that. And second, I don't have the answers you're looking for. Only Tracey can tell you what that was all about. And third, it wasn't even that serious between us. We were together for a few months then it fizzled and I was ready to move on. She told me that bullshit lie about being pregnant and when that didn't change my feelings about the situation, she confessed that it had all been a lie.

"This was around the time when I was still running around, and after that nonsense I decided that it was time to do some growing up. I don't even remember seeing her around campus after that."

"All right. Whatever, Malik. Why didn't you tell me about this before now?"

"Lonnie, stop trippin'. How could I know that your Tracey is the same Tracey I dated a million years ago? You never even told me her last name."

That was true. In fact, I don't even remember if I ever mentioned his last name to her. I'm sure if I had, she would've reacted. Nevertheless, Malik was really becoming agitated by the situation. I knew it was because he wasn't sure what I might do and whatever it was going to be, he couldn't control me.

Bottom line? He may not have gotten it, but Tracey had a secret, and whatever it was, I was going to find out.

Chapter 35

Malik tried to keep me busy the next day. Hell no! He was not going to keep me from getting to the bottom of the bullshit. Around lunchtime he tried to coax me back into bed with him. Not! He knew I was determined to get at Tracey, and he wasn't trying to let that happen. Malik couldn't understand why the events of the previous night bothered me so much.

I wasn't surprised that he thought it was no big deal, but at the same time, I wondered how he could not see the obvious. Or maybe he did and just refused to admit that something was up with her.

That man was watching me like a hawk, and I needed to get out of there if I was going to get some answers. This conversation was going to take place in person. I got my opening when Malik went to use the bathroom. I grabbed my cell phone and texted Lena to call me. She rang my phone at the very moment Malik came back downstairs. I pretended to react to something serious and told him that my sister really needed me and I had to go.

Just like a man, it never occurred to him that I was faking. Good for me. I was on a mission. I got dressed, bolted out of that house, and jumped on the Ben Franklin.

I was at Tracey's house, ringing her doorbell within thirty minutes. When she came to the door, I couldn't believe my eyes. It was obvious that she had been crying. A lot.

"Oh, Lonnie," she cried, "Why did you come here?"

"Why would you think that I wouldn't? Can I come in?"

She hesitated briefly before reluctantly stepping aside.

I entered and took a seat without being offered one. I didn't have the patience to beat around the bush, so I jumped right in.

"All right, Tracey, I'm not here to cause you problems or to fight about anything, but no bullshittin'. You've got a major issue with my man, and I want to know what it is."

Tracey slowly walked to the chair across from me and sat down. "Lonnie, I understand how you feel but, I don't owe you anything."

"Are you for real? Check this out, I've grown to care a lot about you. You've been a really good friend, and because of that, I'm not here to accuse you of anything. If you could just put yourself in my shoes for a minute, how would you feel if you watched your friend have an emotional meltdown at the sight of your man? I mean come on now, you have to know that Malik told me about your past relationship, so yeah, you do owe me."

"What exactly did he tell you?"

"He told me everything, not that there was much to tell. But if what you really want to know is if he told me about the pregnancy lie, then yes. He told me that as well."

She began sobbing all over again. I'd never seen her so upset and to see that degree of distress had me shook. *What the hell is the secret?* I wondered.

I knelt down in front of her and took her hands. "Damn. Tracey. Whatever it is, it can't be that bad."

"Yes, it really is."

Shit! I didn't want to hear that.

"OK, maybe it is, but as your friend, I'm saying that we can get through it, whatever *it* is."

"What I've done is much bigger than our friendship."

"What did you do?" I asked, not so sure anymore that I actually wanted to hear the answer.

"I have to face this," she whispered to herself. "I can't keep it any longer," she continued to whisper.

For a moment I thought that she'd forgotten that I was there. I tried again. "Tracey, just tell me. If you talk about it you'll feel better."

She looked at me strangely, like she wasn't sure of who I was for a moment. Then, she closed her eyes, took a deep breath, and without preamble said, "I gave birth to a baby girl twelve years ago and put her up for adoption."

I blinked several times, trying to quiet the alarms that were going off in my head. No, I didn't need to stop and figure this one out. It hit me instantly that Malik was that child's father.

"You did what?" I screamed and jumped up.

She started sobbing all over again.

"Answer me, damn it! How could you?"

Through her tears Tracey said, "Lonnie, please try to calm down."

"Calm down! Are you out of your mind? How in the hell am I supposed to calm down?! You're sitting here telling me you had a baby with Malik! Why didn't he tell . . . oh my God! He doesn't know, does he? You lied!" I screamed and kept screaming.

The magnitude of Tracey's confession was not lost on me. My head began spinning and I felt nauseous. I began screaming again, *No, no, noooooo!* I had to get the hell out of there.

"I've got to get out of here!"

Tracey grabbed my wrist, "Don't leave. Let me explain."

"No, no, I can't deal with this," I said as I snatched away from her. I ran out of there and jumped into my car. I had to get to Malik.

Chapter 36

I drove home with a million questions running through my mind. *What will Malik say? What will he do? What does this shit mean for us as a couple? How could this crap happen in my life? And why am I being punished?* At that time, I didn't see the selfishness in my concerns about how Tracey's revelation would affect my life.

By the time I made it home, I was crying uncontrollably. I burst through my front door, screaming Malik's name hysterically. He came running from the kitchen.

"Lonnie, what's wrong? What happened?'

"That damn Tracey!" I cried.

"Tracey? I thought you went to see Lena," he said with confusion.

I could only shake my head no.

"Lonnie what the hell is going on? What about Tracey?" he asked as he guided me to the sofa. He sat me down and picked up the tissue box from the coffee table. "Here, take this. Try to pull yourself together, and please tell me what's happening."

I wiped my tears, which were determined to continue flowing. I blew my nose and cried even harder. Malik wrapped his arm around me and rocked me until my tears dried. He didn't say another word until I finally came around. When he was sure I was over my crying jag, he asked again, "What happened with Tracey?"

I looked him in the eyes. "Tracey lied about not being pregnant all those years ago. She had a baby—your baby—and put her up for adoption." I exhaled.

He could only stare at me, and that reaction scared me. I thought for sure Malik would be outraged.

"Malik, what are you thinking?" I asked.

He remained silent, but his face reflected all of the thoughts running through his mind. I could see confusion. I could literally see him replaying the events of that time in his mind, then the realization hitting him that he could actually have a child he never knew existed.

"Lonnie, are you absolutely sure about this?"

"That's what she said. Why would she make it up? You saw her behavior last night."

Malik stood up and began pacing the room. I couldn't say anything. After all, there was no way in hell I could understand what he was feeling. I wanted to help ease his anxiety or whatever it was, but I was struggling with this news as well. More than anything I felt a strong sense of foreboding. My rational mind knew that this development was nothing like the situation with John and Cherie, but my emotional self was terrified about how this might play out. Would he choose Tracey? Would he find the child and make a family with them? My insecurities kicked into overdrive. I had no sense of safety in that situation.

I immediately went to a negative place within myself. I could only see more devastation barreling toward my personal life.

Malik finally stopped pacing. "Lonnie, give me your cell phone."

"What? Why?"

"Just give me the damn phone, Lonnie!"

I did as I was told. Considering the state he was in, putting up a fight about his tone wasn't a good idea. I handed him my phone, knowing full well that he intended to call Tracey. But what he did next confused the shit out of me. He took my phone and went outside. This action served to intensify the emotional rollercoaster I was on; however, I had to remind myself that this all had to be a million times worse for him.

I sat there rocking back and forth, trying to wait patiently—if that was at possible—for Malik to return. All the while, I could hear him out on the porch yelling, although I couldn't quite make out what he was saying.

After a few more moments he came back in.

"Well, what did she say?" I asked as soon as he entered, but I need not have bothered. His turmoil was evident.

"It's all true," he said as he took a seat. "How could she do such a thing? I have a fucking twelve-year-old daughter! Damn her!" he yelled and pounded on the coffee table.

I reached for him in an attempt to give comfort, but, Malik snatched away and said, "No, don't touch me! Just leave me alone!"

Now OK, yes the man was going through something serious, and like I said before, beyond my comprehension, but taking that shit out on me? Not cool. Y'all already know I don't do understanding all that well, so at that point that brotha was skating on very thin ice.

Malik got up and went upstairs without a word. At that point I decided that he wasn't the only one who could walk away. I got back in my car and headed for my sister's house. I was halfway there when I remembered that I had interrupted her and Devon on their weekend away when I'd texted her earlier. Shit! I turned around and went to Sandy's. I was so grateful she was home.

At the sight of me Sandy exclaimed, "*Chica*, you look *muy loca!*

What happened to you?" Apparently my anger and confusion showed all over my face.

"*Bente mami*, come sit down."

"I'm so sorry to bother you, Sandy, but some shit has gone down that I don't even know how to deal with."

"*Ay mami*, you're freakin' me out here. *¿Que paso?*"

"Long story short, Tracey and Malik dated back in college. She had a baby, gave it away, and never told him."

Sandy leaped from her seat and began fluttering around. "*¡Ay Dios mío!*"

"Really Sandy, you have to stop. I can't handle the hysterics right now."

"Oh OK sorry, *mami*, but what does Malik say?"

"He didn't say anything. He's angry for sure, but he walked away without saying a word to me about it."

"OK, then how do you feel, *chica*? This must be a terrible shock for you. She's your friend."

"I don't know. It's fuckin' me up, but I don't know what to think. I'm not even sure of how I should feel. I'm upset for Malik, I'm upset for myself, although I'm not sure why, and I'm a little upset for Tracey. I hate that she lied to him and that he has to go through this, but the truth is, I didn't know either of them back then, and I didn't stay around long enough for Tracey to explain why she made the choice she made."

"Damn, Lonnie. This is huge. Does she even know where the child is?"

"I don't think so. Like I said, I didn't ask. I just don't know what to do."

"I understand you're upset, but right now, your man is going through something bigger than you, *chica*."

I started crying all over again. Sandy was right; this issue didn't really have anything to do with me, but Malik was my man and Tracey was my friend. The hell if I wasn't smack dead in the middle of it.

Chapter 37

After an hour I left Sandy's to go home and face my reality, only to find an empty house. There was no Malik, nor was there a note or any other indication of where he had gone. I called his cell phone and his house phone and got no answer. I thought about letting it go—leaving him to himself for a while—but I couldn't. I wasn't going to sit around and wait, and I for damned sure wasn't going to let him shut down on me again.

I got back in that damn car again. When I arrived at Malik's house, his car wasn't there, so I kept on going and headed straight for Ms. Jewel's house.

The second she opened the door, I could tell that Malik had been there and filled her in.

"Hi sweetheart, come on in," she said. She offered me a seat and a drink. A real drink was exactly what I needed by then.

"Ms. Jewel, do you know where your son is? I've been to his house and there's no sign of him."

"No, I don't. He really didn't say too much. I've never seen my son so distraught. He told me that you were the one found who out about all of this."

"Yes, ma'am. Tracey and I recently became friends, very good friends actually. Anyway, I wanted her and Malik to meet. When we got together last night, she lost it and ran off when she saw him. Therefore, I went to her earlier to find out what was up. That's when she confessed her secret to me."

"Dear Lord! I can't understand any of this. Tell me, what kind of woman is she?"

As much as I wanted to bash Tracey, I couldn't.

"Well, to tell you the truth, she seems to be a really good person. I know she's had some difficulties in her life, but she seems to have come out of it with grace and forgiveness." At that moment I remembered what Lena had said about Tracey. "You know, Ms. Jewel, my sister told me that she thought Tracey had something she was hiding or was afraid of, and I ignored her. Apparently, she was right. But I think the reason Tracey told me was because of our friendship. I'm sure she never thought she'd see Malik again. But, at the same time, I kind of think she really wanted to get that secret out of her."

"Maybe, but I still don't understand how she could do something like this to my son." She appeared to be just as agitated as I was.

"Ms. Jewel, what do you think Malik will do?" I asked.

She saw my worry, clearly. "Oh sweetheart, try not to worry yourself. He'll be fine. My son has this way of going inside himself when there's something this hard for him to deal with. He first did that when his father left; it's just his way. He shuts down and won't deal with any outside distractions until he works through the problem."

She said those words like it was OK. Like shutting me, of all people, out was cool. I was his fiancé, not some fuckin' outside distraction. I finished my drink, thanked her for her time. and got the hell out of there. All I wanted to do was take a bath and go to bed.

Over the next several days, I tried to keep myself from suffering as I had when Malik disappeared on me before. At least this time I understood his ways a little better. However, with every day that passed, I got more pissed off. Just because I sort of understood it didn't mean that it was all right. I don't know, maybe I lacked compassion or something, but I was no longer concerned with what Malik was going through. I was concerned with my man walking out on me without a word. He kept his cell phone off and did not reach out to me once, and, I had left several messages. He had completely disappeared, and I was beyond fed up.

In the middle of me being fed up, I experienced another one of those shifts in my rational thinking. Although I tried to remain objective about Tracey, I was beginning to get angry at her. Resentment was beginning to set in. After all, her actions were the reason my man was gone. I decided that I should call her. Not that I knew what I would say, because by the time I'd made that decision, I was going back and forth from understanding to anger.

I took a chance and to my surprise she answered.

"Hi, Tracey."

"Hello, Lonnie. I'm glad you called. I was afraid I wouldn't hear from you again."

"Well, honestly, you almost didn't. In fact, I'm not sure why I'm calling you now."

"I understand. You do know that I had no idea who your Malik was?"

"Yes, I know. That's the reason I'm trying to deal with this in the right manner. Not that I know what that is."

"I'm not sure if there is proper protocol for a situation like this. I do know that I need to thank you."

"Thank me for what?" I was thoroughly confused by that statement.

"Well for getting me to release. I've held on to that secret for so long. If I had run into Malik under any other circumstances, or if I'd never known you, I would not have told him about our daughter."

"Our daughter." That fucked me up. Nevertheless, I allowed her to continue.

"Lonnie, your appearance at my house and your unwillingness to let go when you knew there was something up, is what forced me to come clean. Now I feel relieved that I had no choice but to face my past. Malik, however, wasn't as understanding as you're being. I certainly can't blame him, though."

"Wait, what did you say? When did you speak to Malik?"

"He tracked me down and showed up here a couple of days ago. I explained to him what led to my decision and all that I was going through at the time. He didn't care to hear it; he just wanted to know where the child is now. Of course I couldn't tell him because I don't know myself. It was a closed adoption. Didn't he tell you this?"

"Tracey, I haven't seen Malik since the day I last saw you."

"Oh my, I had no idea."

"Oh my, my ass, Tracey. I'm trying not to take this shit out on you because I wasn't there back then, but your actions have my man running away and suffering in ways that I can't even imagine. Now you tell me he's been over there yet I haven't heard a word? This shit ain't working for me. I have to go." I hung up.

I couldn't talk to that girl another minute. The realization that Malik had been to see her did some fucked up things to my already fragile state of mind. I had been trying to hold on to the anger because I knew that if I allowed my heart to take over, I would surely begin to lose myself. If that happened, life was going to get difficult to say the least.

Chapter 38

I went into to work Thursday morning with the weight of the world on my shoulders. I still hadn't heard from Malik, and I was beginning to lose my resolve, my understanding, and my damned sympathy. Fuck that! He was getting on my damned nerves acting like a big-ass baby.

I dialed Asia's line as soon as I sat down at my desk. "Can you come over here for a few?"

She was at my desk in five seconds flat.

"What's up? Where your ass been?"

"I've been at home trippin'."

"About what now?" she asked.

I proceeded to fill Asia in on everything that had happened.

"Call the fuckin' cops! Are you for real?"

"Do you honestly think I would make this shit up?" I asked just as I noticed a peculiar sound coming from the wall that divided my workspace from Bridgette's. I pointed to the wall and Asia got up and peeked around the corner.

"You nosy bitch! What are you doing at this desk?" I heard Asia say.

I got up to see who it was, and of course, who else would it be but

Cherie?

As soon as she saw me she said, "So damn, Lonnie, that's fucked up, huh? You always got a man who got a baby with someone else. That's make me wonder, what do they really want with you? Can't be much if he ain't even been home all week."

Before she could fix her mouth to say another word, I snatched a discarded cup of coffee off the desk and threw it in her face.

Asia jumped in between us and Cherie yelled, "That's the last time you going to assault me and get away with it!"

"Or what? You not going to do shit."

"Oh, no? You just wait and see what I do to you this time."

"Bitch, go 'head with that bullshit before I go find Bridgette and tell her you over here fuckin' with her shit," Asia said.

"Fuck both of y'all bitches!" Cherie said as she stomped off, dripping coffee.

"Damn, Asia. That girl will have all my business around this entire office before the day is over."

"I hate to say it, but you're right. Look, Lonnie, it is what it is, and there's nothing to be embarrassed about."

"I'm not embarrassed; it's just that it's my business. Period."

"I know, girl, but for now there's nothing we can do to stop her short of putting a bullet in her head."

"Don't tempt me. Anyway, you're right. I'm just going to try and do some work."

I hardly got anything done before the first person came by to grill me about Malik and his mysterious offspring. If I had a gun Cherie definitely would've caught a bullet that day.

I did the only thing I could do and got the hell out of there. Damn, it seemed like I was doing a lot of getting the hell out of places lately. I went on home and by day's end I was back to feeling as messed up as I did when Malik took off before. I wanted to call my sister but I just couldn't. Not only would she say "I told you so," she would also be on the warpath. I didn't want that. My siblings and I had worked very hard to change our behaviors in stressful situations, and because we found life to be a little easier that way, I didn't want to involve them in anything I thought might start an all-out war. Besides, I still wasn't sure of how things would play out with Malik, so I didn't want to make him their enemy. I was trying to hold on to what we had. Maybe we could salvage our relationship.

I was lying down for a while when Cherie's words began to haunt me. Given my existing insecurities, I found it difficult to dismiss her words about the men in my life. The fact that I had to deal with two baby momma issues—although very different in nature—only served to make me wonder about why I kept running up against the same shit. Maybe it was me. Maybe it was something I had done in the past and I was now being punished for it. Whatever it was, I was starting to believe that I had brought this craziness on myself.

I had fallen asleep only to be awakened by a foul odor that I could not indentify. I forced myself to sit up and follow the scent. My senses became clear when I realized it was smoke. I got up and looked out my bedroom window and, to my horror, I saw there were flames all over my front porch. I screamed, grabbed the phone, and dialed 911. I didn't normally panic, but I didn't know what to do next. All I could think was, *I can't get out the front door. I'm going to burn to death!*

Thankfully, within minutes, the fire truck rolled up and quickly doused the flames. I got dressed and went down to speak with them. The fire wasn't nearly as bad as it first seemed. They informed me that someone had set a bag of trash on fire. They assumed it was a prank by some neighborhood kids. Idiots! That kind of shit is not a prank. My whole damned house could have burned to the ground with me in it.

The moment the truck pulled off, I looked up, and who did I see standing across the street in the crowd with that sinister smile on her face but Cherie. I couldn't say a thing. What could I have said? Should I have gone over there and kicked her ass again? No, that would not have stopped her. The only thing I was sure about was that she had gone too far this time. It was over for her dumb ass.

Chapter 39

I'd had enough of the drama in my life. It was time to start removing every remnant of bullshit I could find. The first was Cherie. That bitch tried to kill me. There was no other way to call it. And fuck calling the police; I had no proof. It was time I used John's information against her and got rid of that demon bitch.

I sat down, turned on the lamp, and picked up the phone. I started to dial the number then stopped. I hadn't changed my mind about calling in an anonymous tip on Cherie to the abuse and neglect hotline. I just wanted to make sure my story was together before I made the call. I knew the best way to get that bitch fired and out of my life for good was to have her investigated for substance abuse and neglect. With the minimal information John had given me, I knew it was enough to get the investigators over there.

Since referrals could be made anonymously, there was no chance anyone would know I had made the call. I could be a concerned neighbor, teacher, whatever. It didn't matter. Someone like Cherie had plenty of people who couldn't stand her, so it wasn't a stretch to think that a neighbor would be one of those.

I dialed the toll free number, cleared my throat, and waited for an answer.

"Good evening. Abuse and Neglect Hotline. How may I help you?"

The voice on the other end of the phone sounded tired and not too pleased to be working on the night shift.

"Hello, I'd like to report a possible case of neglect," I said, disguising my voice, even though I knew the person on the phone had no idea who the hell I was.

"OK," she said. "Please explain the situation."

"First of all, I wish to remain anonymous. I'm simply a concerned party."

"That's fine, ma'am. It's not necessary for you to reveal your identity."

The operator remained professional, but I could tell this chick was already losing patience. I could hear it in her tone.

"Well, there's a child in my neighborhood who's living in what I believe is a drug house."

"Do you have any information to support that allegation, ma'am?"

If this bitch calls me ma'am *one more time...* "Yes, I do. The man who's staying there with the mom is a known drug dealer named Rasheed. There are people in and out of the house at all hours of the day and night, and the mom appears to be using that stuff."

"Can you please tell me about the child or children? By the way, which is it?"

"It's one child, a five-year-old boy named J.J. who rarely goes to school."

"May I ask how you know so much about the goings-on in the home?"

This bitch was starting to get on my nerves. "I'm retired, bored, and nosy. I spend my time watching and minding everybody else's business. Is that good enough for you?"

I half-expected this girl to hang up on me at that point. Instead, I could hear the laughter in her voice when she spoke again.

"OK, ma'am. Would you happen to know the mom's name and the address?"

"I sure do." I proceeded to give the screener Cherie's information and further explained that there was also domestic violence going on in the home.

By the time I hung up the phone, I was sweating bullets. That was the most nerve-racking thing I had ever done. I was relatively sure that any investigator who went out there would find enough evidence to at least open a case. There was no way Cherie could hold on to her job if that happened.

It may have been better to wait for a weekend night to do this, because that was when most people did their biggest partying, and if Cherie's house garnered as much traffic as John had said it did, that would have been perfect but, fuck that, I had no time to play.

I drank several glasses of the wine Malik kept at my house then went to bed.

Friday morning I woke up with a major hangover. I spent most of the day throwing up. I suppose that was punishment for what I had done the night before. Although I felt deathly ill, I felt no remorse whatsoever. The reality that another human being's life could be torn apart was not completely lost on me. I simply didn't give a damn.

I spent the rest of the weekend avoiding people. Lena wanted to go shopping, Asia called to check on me, and Sandy even called and invited me to a movie. When I informed her that I still hadn't heard a word from Malik, she wanted to come over and sit with me. I didn't need girlfriend comfort at that time; I needed answers from Malik. I had started calling his cell and house phones as soon as I opened my eyes. Still no answer. I had been leaving voicemails all week and now his box was full. Obviously since that was the case, he hadn't even bothered to listen to them. I could only wonder where he was or what he was doing.

By now, I was losing all hope of working things out. If he had bothered to let me go through this with him, that would have been different, but he had completely lost himself and shut me out. An entire week had passed since we learned about the child. How was I supposed to accept this? I couldn't make excuses for him when he wouldn't show his face or call to say what his deal was. All of it was wearing me out.

Chapter 40

Monday morning was both stressful and painful for me. One more day had passed without a word from Malik. I had to get out of that house and out of my head. Everything and every space in my house reminded me of him. I couldn't get him or the fears that Cherie had planted off my mind.

As much as I wanted to hide from the world, especially since Cherie had spread my business, I couldn't. I had to go into the office to find out first hand if my anonymous phone call had done the trick. I needed desperately to control something in my life, and finally removing Cherie and her crap would have to be it.

The moment I sat down at my desk, Asia came over to check on me.

"What's up, Lonnie?" she asked.

"Not much. What's up with you?"

"Same old, same old. How was your weekend?"

I filled her in on everything and swore her to secrecy. Of course she agreed to keep her mouth shut, which wasn't easy for Asia, but I really didn't care all that much either.

"I hope it worked. I can't believe that bitch tried to burn your fuckin' house down! She deserves whatever her stank ass gets."

I was glad she understood. Asia may not have been all that comfortable with getting her own hands dirty, but she would still have my back nonetheless.

While Asia went to grab a pen and a pad, I spent the next ten minutes sitting at my desk, wringing my hands, waiting for our monthly unit meeting to begin. As soon as the clock hit ten, I grabbed a pen and pad and made a beeline for the conference room. I parked myself right next to Asia. Our only concern was finding out whether Cherie was in the building.

It took less than five minutes for me to discover that she hadn't come to work. Now I needed to know why.

Logan satisfied my curiosity immediately. "Good morning, everyone. Before we get started, I must tell you all that Cherie won't be coming back to work here."

"Call the fucking cops!"

Everyone just laughed and laughed. Asia was Asia—wherever, whenever.

Just like that? I wondered. Logan didn't say another word about it other than to inform us that Cherie's duties would be divided among us. She gave no clue as to what had happened. I needed to hear more, damn it.

Before Logan could continue with her agenda, my coworkers began asking questions. Logan fielded the questions diplomatically.

"I don't have much information myself," she said. "All Sheila told me was that she'd received a call yesterday, and that Cherie would not be coming back."

I didn't hear another word Logan said after that. I sat at the table lost in thought, trying to imagine just what had occurred at Cherie's house. The realization that Cherie was gone hit me hard. I felt so free in that moment, I couldn't have been happier. Maybe I could finally be free of her. Now I just needed to wait for the gossip to begin. I knew somewhere in the midst of all the different rumors that would be flying around, the truth would be in there, and I'd know exactly what that bitch was facing.

Asia broke me out of my reverie. "Lonnie, Lonnie, what the hell is on your mind? I called your name three times."

"Oh, sorry. I was wondering what the hell happened with Cherie. I need more details," I whispered.

"I know. Me too. You know it has to be serious if Sheila, the damn office director, got a call on a Sunday. Don't worry, we'll find out soon enough. I bet your ass is relieved you won't have to deal with her shit anymore."

"Hell yeah. I only hope that whatever happened, that shit sticks."

"I know it. Damn, I wish Logan would shut the hell up so we can go get the details about that bitch."

I laughed just a little. This was the first time in a week that I had even come close to a damned smile. I was so glad when that meeting finally ended.

The lunch hour came quickly. I barely noticed the time. My black ass was on cloud nine about Cherie's exit from my life until thoughts of Malik and his absence took over.

By early afternoon the rumors about Cherie started flying. It wasn't long before the truth about what was going down surfaced. As it turned out, everything I'd reported was actually happening in Cherie's home. When the emergency investigators had gone out there, they found evidence of drug use and sales. There was no food for John Jr., and the house itself was a pigsty. Rasheed and Cherie were both arrested on the spot.

For the first time I began to wonder if Cherie was actually smoking crack. Not that I gave a damn, but still I wondered. It never really occurred to me that everything I reported might actually have been true. When I first spoke to him, I thought that maybe John had exaggerated some of the facts because I didn't want to believe he would leave his son to live that way. I guess I shouldn't have given him the benefit of the doubt.

Sometime during late afternoon, I learned that John Jr. had been removed and placed in a foster home. This development had me shook. I thought for sure that John or one of Cherie's family members would step in and take responsibility for the child. I couldn't understand why no one had stepped up. The agency always sought out family members in situations like this. Placement was a last resort. I verbalized this concern to Asia, who was sitting with me at my desk when we heard this detail.

"Lonnie, you shouldn't be surprised that no one in that trifling family would step in and do the right thing. It's all about self with those fools. What I don't understand is what is up with that nigga John? How could he allow his son to go into placement? I know damn well he was called."

I too wondered what John was thinking. I knew he said he wasn't stable, but not to make an attempt to take responsibility for his own son was ludicrous. I was beside myself with worry about J.J., but he was still better off in my opinion.

"All right, Asia, it's four-thirty, and I've had enough of this place today. I'm going to call it a day," I said.

"Do you want me to come and keep you company?"

"No, I'm OK. Anyway, I think it's time to speak with my sister."

"All right, girl, have a good one."

"You too. Good night."

I drove home feeling a little guilty. This scenario hadn't played out the way I had envisioned it. True, I wanted to tear down Cherie, but having her child caught up in it wasn't my intention. I didn't know what to do. How could I fix this? Maybe I could call John and convince him to do the right thing. Weak or not, coward or not, I refused to believe that this man wouldn't do what was best for his son.

Chapter 41

Before I entered my house, I called Lena and asked her to come over. I didn't want to talk to her with Devon around. I didn't know him well enough to let him in on what I had done. Not that I had actually done anything wrong. I mean, anybody could make a referral. It was just that I had done so for malicious, personal reasons. The truth was, I didn't know that the child actually needed intervention on his behalf when I picked up that phone.

Lena wasted no time getting to my house. I couldn't have been home more than fifteen minutes when she came knocking.

"Hey, sister girl. Where the hell have you been? I haven't heard from you all week."

"I haven't heard from you either."

"Yeah, yeah, I know. Oh wait, I called you when you texted me last week. What was that about?"

"Sit down Lele, so much has happened since then."

"Oh, damn. This must be serious."

"Yes it is," I said and proceeded to share every detail of the last nine days with my sister. When I finished and took a breath Lena sat there stunned.

"Oh my God! Why didn't you call me sooner?"

"It was just so much to deal with all at once, and I was afraid of what you might do. Sometimes I think you'll easily go back to your old ways. You've worked pretty hard to rein that drama in."

"Afraid of what I might do?" Lena asked indignantly.

"Look at you getting all huffy like you acting a fool is something so unheard of. Shit, I never know when your ass might have us both sitting up in the jailhouse."

"Well maybe, but\ seriously, Lon, you really have been through it. That Tracey and Malik shit has to have your head spinning. And that nigga done disappeared on you? Wow! Oh and, don't get me started about Cherie's ass. Girl, I think you're right; if I had known about that shit, at least one of us would have ended up in the county."

"Yeah, well I'm just glad it's Cherie sitting up in there and not one of us. It fucks me up though. What if she was really trying to burn my house down? With me in it at that!"

"Man, that bitch is so lucky I didn't know about that shit, but let's forget about that nut job for now. I want to know what you're going to do about Malik."

"That's the million-dollar question. I have no idea. I mean, what can I do when I can't even find him?"

"Well, I guess the first thing to do is to find him."

"Oh, yeah? How?"

"Let's see, does he have a key to your house?"

"Yes, why?"

"Uh, I'm guessing that you probably have a key to his as well."

"Of course I do, but so what?"

"Damn, Lonnie, is your brain working? Let's go over there and see if we can find a clue."

"Oh."

"Oh?! Girl, what would you do without me?"

"I can think for myself, smart ass. I've been in distress, damn it."

"Whatever you say, baby. Let's go."

My stomach was doing flip-flops the entire ride to Malik's. When we pulled up to the house, despair returned. I didn't want to get out of the car. It was obvious that Malik wasn't there, but I didn't want to go in and I couldn't figure out why.

Lena sensed my hesitation and said, "Stop sitting there, Lonnie, and get out of the car. I know this is hard for you, but you have to take action."

We walked up to the house and I unlocked the front door with shaky hands. We entered and found the house dark and stuffy. I left the front door open to let some air in.

Lena began looking around for who knows what. It seemed like a huge invasion of privacy to me. After a minute she walked over to Malik's desk.

"Come here, Lonnie, and stop acting like a damn chicken. Look at this."

Once I stood beside her I noticed she was looking at what appeared to be the name of an adoption agency.

"I don't recognize this area code," she said. "Oh, I know; I'll just hit the redial and hope this was the last number he called."

"Why, Lele? The number's right there in your face, just dial it."

"No, I think that if he called them, maybe that's where he went."

"OK fine, you do that and I'm going upstairs right quick."

While Lena was on the phone I was rummaging through the closet. I found Malik's travel bag was missing along with some of his clothes. When I got back downstairs, Lena informed me that he had called the adoption agency and he had more than likely gone there.

"So it's obvious that he went searching for the child. Where's that place located anyway?"

"Silver Spring, Maryland."

"Damn, that's where Tracey's from."

"Maybe we should call her. You said she talked to him."

"Yes, but it was a closed adoption. Besides, she wouldn't know anything, especially since Malik has to be completely pissed with her. I can't see him sharing his plans with her. You know what? I really can't stand the way I'm feeling about either one of them right now. I'm having a hard time not blaming her for all of this."

"Why wouldn't you put some blame on her? Her secret is the reason Malik is gone right now. I blame her too."

"Yeah, but you blame her because I'm upset, not because she did anything to me personally."

"Lon, this shit is personal. Your man is gone because of her. And I don't want to hear you defending her. Check this out, little sis: if the woman who had caused this bullshit in your life was a stranger, you'd be ready to kick her ass right about now so, why is it different because it's someone you know?"

"That's your answer right there, Lele. She *is* someone I know. She's my friend for real. That was never fake, not to mention, we all have secrets. Certainly none as ironic as this one, but shit happens. I'm trying to hold it together and see this situation with Tracey rationally. If I allow all of the different feelings I have to take over me, then I'm likely to do some dumb shit. That girl is already suffering; she doesn't need any crap from me."

"Whoa, girl. That's very mature of you."

"And this surprises you why?"

"Mainly because you're emotional about everything, and at a time like this, I would expect you to be going off the deep end by now."

Lena was correct in her assessment of me most of the time, and in the not so distant past, I would have been reacting instead of thinking first. I wanted to grow up and be better. In the past it had been either fight or run from it, and although that behavior still lingered and won out sometimes, I wanted to get beyond that kind of immature, reactionary shit.

"You're right about that, but I can't live a happy life if I don't get myself together and stop acting so simple. This is the biggest thing that's happened in my personal life, and I want to handle it in the right way for real. Not like that stupid move I made when I took John back. This shit with Malik is different and possibly worth fighting for. Although I'm still debating about that."

"That's sounds good, Lonnie, but it's OK if you don't get this one right."

"That's that big sister thing. Don't allow or encourage me to do wrong just because you think things should be easy for me. You've done that my whole life. Time for a change."

"OK, girl. I get it, and I'm going to let you do you however you see fit. Now, let's deal with the fact that Malik probably went searching for his kid, which is understandable, but he took off without a word. How do you feel about that?"

I had to take a seat and think about that for a moment.

"It's a little difficult to explain. I've been struggling with my feelings. I'm trying to be that understanding and supportive woman, and realistically I have no idea what this must be like for him. But then I'm angry as well, because we're engaged and he's gone. With that, understanding goes out the window every time I think about the fact that he's done this before."

"He's done what before?"

Damn I forgot I'd never shared Malik's first disappearance with my sister.

"Right before we got engaged he had some . . . I don't know . . . emotional conflict, I suppose. And he disappeared for two or three days then."

"No the fuck he didn't! What's with that guy?"

"I can't say. I really don't get it myself. I mean, I wouldn't characterize Malik as a weak man, you know? He's always presented himself with strength and determination to me. But this Houdini shit of his is contradictory to that and it's getting old."

"So what are you going to do when he gets back? You do think he'll come back, don't you?"

"Sure he will. According to his mom, this is how he works things through. Evidently he's trying to fix this by finding his daughter and the shutting everyone out is how he copes."

"Well, if you ask me, he's selfish. Now don't get me wrong, I like Malik. I like the way he makes you feel any other time of course, but no matter what he's going through, he shouldn't run off and leave the people who care about him to suffer."

I had to admit that Lena was right about that. It was a selfish act, and the more I sat there and thought about it, the more rage began to take over. I could feel it coming over me and I couldn't pull it back.

"You know what, Lele? You're right, and, at this very moment, I don't give two shits about his fuckin' struggle. Let's get the hell out of here!"

I stood to leave and heard a strong intake of breath from Lena. She whispered, "Lonnie."

I looked at her, then in the direction of her gaze. There he was, in the flesh, without warning, standing in the doorway. Malik.

Chapter 42

I couldn't move. Malik looked haggard and run-down, drained and exhausted, but in that moment I couldn't muster up an ounce of sympathy for him. This made me question my love for him or my capacity to truly love a man. After all, how true could it be if, even knowing he was suffering, my own feelings were all that mattered?

"Lonnie," he said as he walked toward me and pulled me into his arms. To my amazement, I wasn't comfortable in those arms.

"Let me go, Malik."

"What?" He backed up and looked at me with so much pain and confusion. Yet, I didn't care. I *couldn't* care. Every bit of the pain, longing, and not knowing that I had suffered at this man's actions, both the first time and this time, engulfed me. There were so many different feelings rushing through me at that moment, I couldn't breathe.

"Precious, what's wrong with you?"

"What's wrong with me? Are you kidding?"

He took a step back and stared for a moment before understanding crossed his face. "Oh, Lonnie, I'm so sorry for leaving you, but you have to understand, I had to do this."

"I don't have to understand anything. This isn't the first time you've done this, and no matter what the reason was, it's unacceptable!"

He tried to stop me from getting past him. I had to get out of there.

"Please don't leave, Lonnie."

"She's not going anywhere," Lena said. I had forgotten she was still in the room.

"Oh, no? And why is that? I'm not staying here to listen to the bullshit."

"Come here, damn it." Lena pulled me away from Malik and closer to her.

"Lonnelle, I'm not usually the one to cut a nigga a break when they're wrong, but I really think that this situation is different. These are special circumstances. Look at him; he's defeated. You're his fiancé, not just his girl or some piece of ass."

"So what, Lena?!"

"So, you just got finished saying how you want to grow and mature and get shit right. Well, this is the perfect time for you to prove that. Do you love that man?"

"I believe I do. So?"

"Well, if that's true or even if you're not quite sure, you should at least talk with him so you can figure it out. You have things you need to say to him about this past week, and you can't make another move unless you listen to him. Now give me your keys. I'll go wait in the car."

She snatched my keys out of my hand and ran out the door before I could even begin to protest. I knew I was stuck because once Lena decided what was going down, it was a wrap. That hussy probably would've locked me out of the car anyway.

I returned to my seat, but I swear I wanted to bolt. I tried to keep Lena's words in my mind while I waited for Malik to speak. I had to do the work basically.

"Lonnie, there's so much I have to tell you about what's been happening."

"I'm listening. Get on with it." There goes that funky-ass attitude again.

Malik was not at all put off by my mouth. He continued to speak.

"Let me start with when I left your house. I went straight to my mom's and told her what I'd just learned. I was so pissed that I couldn't calm down. I was hoping my mom could bring me down 'cause I really wanted to go find Tracey and wring her fuckin' neck. Right now, I want to fuck her up. Yo, I've never had the desire to harm a woman before, and that shit is taking over me."

"Malik, Tracey told me you spoke to her a few days ago."

"Yes, I did. I needed to know the details of why she gave my child away."

"What did she tell you?"

"She said that after we broke up and she told me that she was pregnant, my reaction messed her up."

"Why? what did you do?"

"I told her that I didn't want a kid and if she was lying to hold on to me, she was wasting her time. I told her that because I honestly didn't believe her anyway. That was that arrogance I was still stuck in back then. I thought she really was just trying to hold on to me."

"Yeah, arrogant all right."

He just smirked and kept talking.

"Anyway, she decided that she wanted the baby and that she didn't need me so she left school and went back home. I hate you say it, but I barely noticed her absence. The one thing that happened was that that was when I decided to get my act together. After what I thought was her lie I figured that if I acted like a man and stayed with one woman, I wouldn't have to deal with that kind of shit anymore." He took a breath and moved to a seat closer to me.

"OK, so if she wanted the baby, why did she give it up?" I asked, beyond curious now.

"Her parents. They wanted her to complete her education and refused to take care of her and a child. Not that they couldn't afford it, but that was it. Either get her degree or be disowned."

"Damn, that's fucked up. My brother and sister have always driven my mom and dad nuts with their nonsense—me too I guess—but they've never even so much as threatened to leave us hanging. Shit, they're helping Tank raise his daughter right now. That must be the worst feeling."

"How do you figure that?"

"Imagine being all alone in this world without the emotional support of your own parents. You may have only had your mom, but you had her."

"Lonnie, you sound like you're feeling sympathy for that girl."

"Maybe, and I've been going back and forth on that, but you want me to feel sympathetic toward you. How can I give you that and not give it to her as well? I get that you're hurting, but I'm sure she is too. Probably has been all along."

"All right, precious. I get that. Anyway, her parents pretty much forced her to put the child up for adoption."

"OK, that's Tracey story, but what I want to know is where you've been."

"I got the name of the adoption agency from her and I went down to Maryland to look for my daughter."

Hearing those words had me twisted inside. It's not that I hadn't just figured out what he was doing, but something about hearing it out loud knocked the wind out of me.

I was afraid to ask the question, but I had to.

"Did you find her?"

"Yes, I did."

"What? You found her? Where is she?"

"Well, she lives in Baltimore with her adoptive parents."

This was the first time Malik even showed a glimmer of a smile since that last day we'd spent together.

"Hold up,. Tracey said it was a closed adoption. How did you find her?"

"Working in CPS, even in Jersey helps. I know some people, precious." This time he smiled full out.

"I won't bore you with the details of what kind of strings I pulled. Oh, and yo, I owe mad favors now, but it was worth it."

"Well, did you get to meet the child?"

"No, but, as it turns out, her parents have been sending pictures and updates on her to the agency since they got her."

"Huh, is that normal practice?"

"Not necessarily, but it's obviously is allowed. Apparently, they knew the child came from a young, single mother and although the child was theirs legally, they wanted the birth mother to have access to the child's progress, and they didn't want to make it hard if she ever came looking. And of course, none of their personal information was included."

"Oh, so that's how they protect themselves."

"Yes. It's not that the agency would have given that information out before the child turned eighteen, which is when both sides can start looking. So anyway, a friend of a friend of another friend shared the file with me. I kept one of the pictures—the most recent one."

He pulled that picture out of his duffle bag like only a proud parent would and handed it to me. OK, y'all, I still wanted to be disinterested, but let's be real. Curiosity was kicking my ass. I took the picture from him and looked into the eyes a female version of Malik. Damn, that girl looked just like him, only cuter. I told him so.

"She's beautiful. Will you ever get to meet her?"

"I hope so, but I can't really attempt to find her until she turns eighteen."

"Wow, six more years."

"Yes, but now that I know she exists and that I can hopefully have a relationship with her, I can be patient."

"That's great, Malik."

I meant that, but now that I had heard his story, I had some shit to get off my chest.

"All right, Malik. I've listened and I'm actually happy that you found what you needed and apparently have made peace with it but, how fuckin' dare you take off on me again!"

He looked at me like I had two heads.

"But, Lonnie, I was going through something."

"I don't give a damn! Shit, because of you, I was going through something too. Oh, and in case you were wondering about me at all, Cherie started her dumb shit again. She spread my business—your business—all over the office then that bitch tried to burn my house down with me in it!"

Malik jumped up, "What the hell are you talking about?!"

"You see? That's my point right there. You're all upset about it, but where were you? You certainly weren't here for me."

"I get that, Lonnie, but don't you get that I needed to do this? Try to put yourself in my shoes for a minute. Imagine how you'd feel if someone lied to you and kept your very own child away from you. You're coming off really selfish right now."

"Why you weak ass son of a bitch! I have tried to put myself in your shoes. I have tried to understand and get this. I'm not bothered by you doing what you had to do. What pisses me off is that you take off and don't say a word. You stay gone and don't say a word. Fuck that dumb shit, pick up a goddamned phone and say something! Turn your goddamned phone on! Not once did you turn that phone on, so what was I to think? You didn't give a damn about what might be going on in my life. You want to be in a two-sided, caring relationship, correction, *marriage* but, when shit gets hard you forget I exist! What kind of shit is that?"

He stayed quiet for what seemed like forever before he found words to say.

"Precious, you're right. You really are right. I guess I do that because I am used to being alone when there's something I have to deal with. For my entire life this is how I've handled difficulties, but this is the first time I've gone through really hard shit at the same time I've been in a serious relationship. Damn, my marriage wasn't even this serious, and I don't really remember going through anything then. Well, except the divorce, but she was gone by the time I needed to work through those issues."

"Damn, Malik, you know what? You disappeared then too. You were out of work for a couple of weeks. I just didn't know you too well back then."

"Wow, I sure was. So I guess it's time for me to learn how to go through these things as a twosome huh?"

"No. I don't want your black ass no more." I had that man shittin' in his pants right then, my face was so serious. Honestly, I did want Malik even with all of my own confusion about real life shit. Being in his presence for those few minutes allowed me the opportunity to see just how affected I was by him and that I did really want this life with him.

"What, are you for real? You're going to leave me now? Maybe I deserve it but, don't you think what we have is worth working at?"

"I don't know, Malik," I said as I looked into those damn Malik eyes. That punk winked at me and my simple ass melted completely.

"Aw, come on, precious. Be mad at me, I can deal with that but, you have to forgive me and marry me." He smiled.

"Oh, really, and why is that?"

"Because you love me."

"Oh, right. Did I forget to mention that I'm over that?"

"Not funny, Lonnie!

"Yes, it was. You should see your face."

"OK, all jokes aside. I do get how I've handled things wrong and now that I see it, it damn sure won't happen again. I promise you that. I think maybe we should get some couple's counseling or something. We both have to learn how to do the important things as a couple."

"That might help. I know I have some things to work on, like my willingness to run away when I can't deal with something."

He smirked. "Oh, you mean just like I do?"

"Damn! I never saw it as the same thing. Well, actually it's not, because when I can't take anymore, I'm usually gone for good. Anyway, I also used to use my temper to ignore my true feelings about something. It was easier to fight."

I considered Malik's proposal about getting professional help for us.

"I guess this could work, it certainly can't hurt. We could both be better, stronger people if we work at it."

"Good, then. No more running for either of us, and we promise to never shut down on one another again."

"Deal. Now kiss me."

"Not until you tell me what happened with Cherie."

"No you didn't just bring her into our peacemaking moment."

"I sure did, damn it. I need to know if you'll be facing murder charges in the near future."

"OK, good one, and no, I won't. I got that bitch arrested for something entirely different. I'll tell you about it later. I think I should get Lena's ass out of the car. That nut is probably sitting there with the doors locked and windows rolled up, suffocating herself just so I can't get in."

"Oh, damn. I forgot she was out there." He laughed. Then he took me and kissed me in that Malik way I loved so much.

Epilogue

It had been a year since Malik and I found out about his daughter. So many things have changed in that time. Through couple's counseling we've both learned how to lean on one another as opposed to keeping the tough things inside. It's OK for your partner to have the answers when you don't. Running is never the answer.

I've learned that I possessed only two ways of coping. Fight or flight. Malik, on the other hand, only took flight. We both now understand that our future together is worth nothing if we can't change those behaviors.

I've done a lot of self reflection this past year. I've come to understand that most of my reactions and behaviors were a direct result of me not being clear about who I am as a woman. I didn't know Lonnie very well. Therefore, I couldn't find the balance between Lonnie with the temper and good Lonnie. I get *me* now. I know that I am a strong, independent, determined woman who is capable of so much more if I focus on what's really important in life. I no longer react without thinking first.

I was controlled by my emotions, which always clouded my understanding about a lot of real-life situations. I would say that the maturity that I claimed to possess then is in full effect now. And it's a good thing, because Malik and I are expecting our first child in a few weeks. I've had to admit that a lot of my anger and resentment about those other women having children was more about my desire to share that experience and life with the man I love. I guess I was a bit jealous.

It has taken this entire year for Malik and Tracey to resolve their issues. There are still days when he's openly affected by her choices, but he shares instead of running. They will never be friends, and because of that my friendship with Tracey has suffered. I see her occasionally, but because of my husband, I can't be completely comfortable with her. Maybe someday we'll be able to rebuild what was beginning to be a wonderful friendship. That would be nice, especially since Lena and Devon have just gotten married and have been talking about relocating before they start a family. My sister has grown into the woman she wants to be. Happy and peaceful with a little bit of 'kick ass' thrown in for good measure. She'll never be completely domesticated. Personally, I hope she stays right here in Camden with me. I still need her protective force sometimes.

Now Cherie's dumb ass was sentenced to five years probation as a first time offender on her possession charges. She hasn't come near me since. I don't know what her deal is, but I let it be known to her face that I was the one who set those wheels in motion. And to my surprise, she didn't start any shit with me. Something was different about her. I'm guessing that actually spending a few weeks in jail really shook her up.

By the time she'd been sentenced, her son was living with John's sister, who'd come down from Newark and applied for custody on John's behalf. From what I've heard the boy is thriving there. My vindictive actions may have actually been the best thing for him. So far, so good.

The biggest and most dramatic change of all was with my brother. He started his own cleaning company. He has one employee, another ex-offender, and they clean office buildings at night. He actually has several contracts and is making a decent living.

Tank has fallen so completely in love with his daughter that she has mellowed his ass a lot. He's even brought her up a couple of times to see Deja who, despite our differences because of Cherie of course, is not nearly as bad as I once believed. Apparently she has hopes and dreams for a better life for herself and her children. She and I have managed to have a few civil conversations, while Tank mediated of course, where she expressed that she did not want to continue to perpetuate the stereotypical hood mentality. Ghetto maybe. Stupid, not so much.

My brother's love for his daughter has brought some semblance of peace between the Devlins and at least one member of the Johnson family, which is the best thing for my niece.

I can see clearly how we've all handled our lives improperly. What a mess! The transition from our childish ways to becoming emotionally grown-up was a crazy, hectic, dramatic ride, but I believe that somehow, we're well on our way to getting it right, by any means necessary.

Discussion Questions

1. Considering the troubles that followed her decision, should Lonnie have taken John back after initially discovering his affair with Cherie?

2. Although Cherie was full of drama, did Lonnie do enough to make the situation work? What could she have done differently?

3. Lonnie's siblings were always willing to use violence to deal with problems. Did their influence dictate her behavior? Without them would she have been mature enough on her own to deal with Cherie in a peaceful manner?

4. Were Lonnie's fears and reservations about Malik a direct result of her experiences with John or do you think there may have been some other underlying issues? If so, what might those issues have been?

5. Lonnie was depicted as a strong and fiercely independent woman. However, she had a complete meltdown during Malik's first disappearance. Why? Was her outward toughness simply a façade? Or could there it been her lack of experience with serious relationships? Does true love tear you up like that?

6. Malik proposed six months into the relationship. Had Lonnie taken the proper time after John to recover and mature enough to take such a major step in her life?

7. Was Malik's reaction to finding out about the baby Tracey's fault in any way? How should he have handled the news?

8. When Malik finally returned, did Lonnie give in too easily? Would you have made him sweat and why? Is punishment the answer when we lack understanding? Or do we continue to fight for the end result?

Melodrama Publishing Order Form
WWW.MELODRAMAPUBLISHING.COM

Title	ISBN	Qty	Price	Total
Drama with a Capital D by Denise Coleman	1-934157-32-5		$14.99	$
Cariter Cartel (Mass Market) by Nisa Santiago	1-934157-34-1		$ 6.99	$
You Showed Me by Nahisha McCoy	1-934157-33-3		$14.99	$
Return of the Cartier Cartel by Nisa Santiago	1-934157-30-9		$14.99	$
Who's Notorious Now? by Kiki Swinson	1-934157-31-7		$14.99	$
Wifey by Kiki Swinson (Pt 1)	0-971702-18-7		$15.00	$
I'm Still Wifey by Kiki Swinson (Pt 2)	0-971702-15-2		$15.00	$
Life After Wifey by Kiki Swinson (Pt 3)	1-934157-04-X		$15.00	$
Still Wifey Material by Kiki Swinson (Pt 4)	1-934157-10-4		$15.00	$
Wifey 4 Life by Kiki Swinson (Pt 5)	1-934157-61-9		$14.99	$
A Sticky Situation by Kiki Swinson	1-934157-09-0		$15.00	$
Tale of a Train Wreck Lifestyle by Crystal Lacey Winslow	1-934157-15-5		$15.00	$
Sex, Sin & Brooklyn by Crystal Lacey Winslow	0-971702-16-0		$15.00	$
Histress by Crystal Lacey Winslow	1-934157-03-1		$15.00	$
Life, Love & Lonliness by Crystal Lacey Winslow	0-971702-10-1		$15.00	$
The Criss Cross by Crystal Lacey Winslow	0-971702-12-8		$15.00	$
In My Hood by Endy (Mass Market)	1-934157-57-0		$ 6.99	$
In My Hood 2 by Endy (Mass Market)	1-934157-58-9		$ 6.99	$
In My Hood 3 by Endy (Mass Market)	1-934157-59-7		$ 6.99	$
In My Hood by Endy (Trade Paperback)	0-971702-19-5		$15.00	$
In My Hood 2 by Endy (Trade Paperback)	1-934157-06-6		$15.00	$
In My Hood 3 by Endy (Trade Paperback)	1-934157-62-7		$14.99	$
A Deal With Death by Endy	1-934157-12-0		$15.00	$
Dirty Little Angel by Erica Hilton	1-934157-19-8		$15.00	$
10 Crack Commandments by Erica Hilton	1-934157-10-X		$15.00	$
The Diamond Syndicate by Erica Hilton	1-934157-60-0		$14.99	$
Den of Sin by Storm	1-934157-08-2		$15.00	$
Eva: First Lady of Sin by Storm	1-934157-01-5		$15.00	$

MELODRAMA PUBLISHING ORDER FORM
(CONTINUED)

Shot Glass Diva by Jacki Simmons	1-934157-14-7		$15.00	$
Stripped by Jacki Simmons	1-934157-00-7		$15.00	$
Cartier Cartel by Nisa Santiago	1-934157-18-X		$15.00	$
Jealousy the Complete Saga by Linda Brickhouse	1-934157-13-9		$15.00	$
Menace by Crystal Lacey Winslow, et. al.	1-934157-13-9		$15.00	$
Myra by Amaleka McCall	1-934157-20-1		$15.00	$

Instructions:

*NY residents please add $1.79 Tax per book.

**Shipping costs: $3.00 first book, any additional books please add $1.00 per book.

Incarcerated readers receive a 25% discount. Please pay $11.25 per book and apply the same shipping terms as stated above.

Mail to:

MELODRAMA PUBLISHING

P.O. BOX 522

BELLPORT, NY 11713

Please provide your shipping address and phone number:

Name:_____

Address: _____

Apt. No: _____ Inmate No: _____

City: _____ State: _____ Zip: _____

Phone: (____) _____-_____

Allow 2 - 4 weeks for delivery

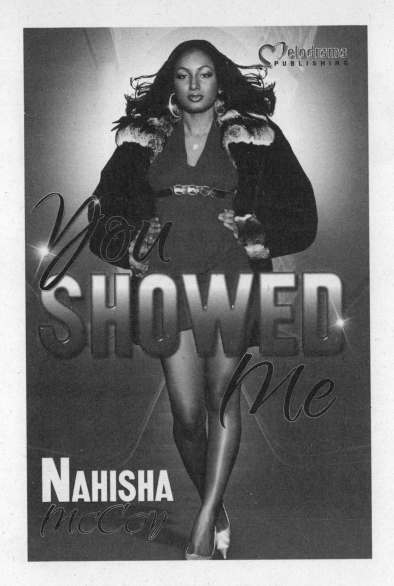

You Showed Me by Nahisha McCoy
Available Now!

Dating a hustler was never on Naheema's to-do list. But after the charming yet deceptive Mike sweeps her off her feet, dating a hustler is the least of her worries. Mike's charming sweetness toward Naheema turns sour when the abuse, cheating, and his street mentality kicks in. The life of a hustler's woman takes its toll on Naheema physically, mentally, and emotionally, taking her from a fairy tale to a horror flick.

The Saga Continues...

Book 2 Coming in October 2010

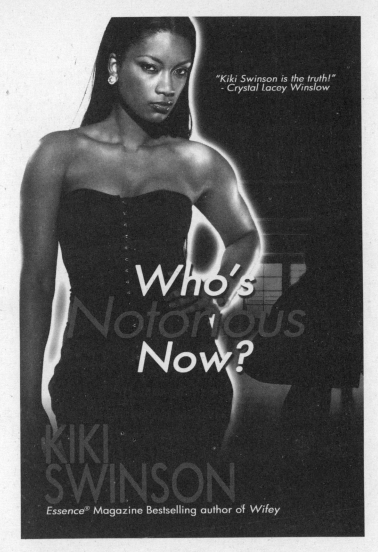

"Kiki Swinson is the truth!"
- Crystal Lacey Winslow

Who's Notorious Now?

Essence® Magazine Bestselling author of *Wifey*

KIKI SWINSON

Who's Notorious Now? by Kiki Swinson
November 2010!

Criminal defense attorney Yoshi Lomax finds herself on the other side of the bars in the third book of the riveting Notorious series. While Yoshi tries to prepare herself to face the music once she's extradited back to Miami, the ordeal she encounters en route is more than she could have anticipated. Knowing deep down in her heart that she isn't equipped to handle all of this strife, she has no other alternative but to play the game to save herself.

Visit us online
for excerpts, videos, discounts,
photos, and author information.

MelodramaPublishing.com

Also visit us on:

MySpace, Twitter, YouTube,
and Facebook